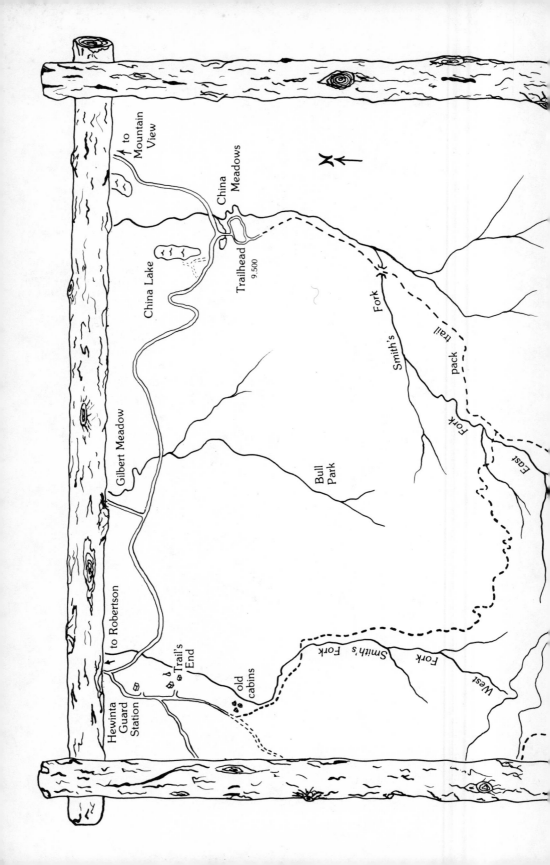

Return to Red Castle

Return to Red Castle

Dorothy M. Keddington

SKYBIRD PUBLISHERS

9025 Chablis Circle • Sandy, Utah 84092 • (801) 571-4599 • (801) 572-0028

TO MY MOTHER

**who loved the mountains
and shared my dreams . . .**

Acknowledgements

The following have contributed their time, knowledge and skills for the benefit of this novel. To them, and to all those who have expressed interest in this work, I offer my heartfelt thanks and warmest appreciation.

. . . Fred and Sylvia Butterfield—our dear friends who first introduced us to the wonders of Red Castle. Their knowledge and experience of the wilderness have been invaluable to the writing of this book.

. . . To my husband Mike—for tramping over seventy miles with me, giving constant support and encouragement, and for taking a beautiful photographic record of our journeys.

. . . To Bethany Chaffin—for providing a "cabin retreat" where much of the actual writing took place, and for her friendship.

. . . To Ron Griffin—a modern "mountain man" who graciously shared his knowledge of tipis, black powder and wilderness skills.

. . . To Ronald Parr—for patiently instructing me in balistics and police procedures.

. . . To Don Stoner, JoAnne Bloomfield and Jo Ann Ray for greatly contributing to my knowledge of the Uintas.

Author's Note

In researching and preparing this book I have made every effort to give a true representation of the Red Castle area and other locations mentioned in the novel. With one or two minor exceptions, I have taken no literary license with actual locations. Trail's End and its occupants, however, are entirely imaginary.

It is my hope that anyone desiring to visit and experience this unique wilderness area will do so with respect for the land and a desire to preserve and protect its fragile beauty.

NOTE: All characters in this book are fictional and any resemblance to persons living or dead is purely coincidental.

Foreword

The ground crew was waiting at dawn. Two vans and a camper pickup truck sat on the crusty ground of a western Utah desert. Inside one of the vans, a man was carefully monitoring highway patrol frequencies on a high-powered police scanner. Another was double checking large amounts of currency in a leather briefcase. The others were watching the pale sky and growing restless.

Some yards distant was a small aircraft, a shiny red and white Cessna Skylane. On the outside, the plane was equipped with extra fuel tanks and a special pumping system to enable it to cover greater distances without refueling. Except for the pilot's seat, the plane's interior was stripped and naked. Here, a thin young man sat smoking and staring at the sky.

Ron Snyder shoved a stringy lock of straw-colored hair away from his face and drew deeply on his cigarette. Dressed in a cotton shirt and cut-off jeans, he looked much younger than his twenty-seven years. The only item jarring his youthful appearance was the solid presence of a .357 magnum revolver in a black leather shoulder holster.

The winds of dawn rustled through dry sage and parched rabbit brush, then moved without a whisper over dry lake beds where the alkali-bitten ground was harder than cement. Over the southern hills, a silver gleam appeared in the brightening sky and Snyder straightened up with alert satisfaction.

Soon the desert was rumbling with the sound of a vintage DC-3's engines. The vans and pickup truck moved out to meet her even before the big plane taxied to a stop. The desert sun lifted its face over the harsh horizon as the ground crew swiftly transferred the 4200-pound load of marijuana into the waiting vehicles and small plane. The cavity of the Cessna's fuselage was nearly filled with bales of marijuana when the head man

ix

walked over to Snyder and lifted up an unobtrusive cardboard box.

"Here's a little bonus for the man in Rock Springs. The ground units have been notified and they'll be waiting for you at the assigned place."

Snyder took the box and glanced inside briefly before placing it on the floor of the plane. To the inexperienced eye, the contents resembled ordinary baking powder in plastic sandwich bags.

"How much?" Snyder asked.

"Around two million. There'll be a bonus for you, too, once you get there."

Snyder nodded and excitement coursed through his veins. Moments later, the small plane's single engine roared into life and the Cessna moved smoothly along the crude desert runway. Snyder's spirits lifted with the aircraft as it headed northeast, away from the arid deserts and plateaus of the Great Basin.

*   *   *

Some miles outside Manila, near the Utah-Wyoming border, Karl Moser had his ground unit on the road, traveling to the previously arranged pickup site. Swirls of dust boiled up behind his dark blue van and the brown pickup truck following, but there was no one to see it. The few roads traversing this wild landscape were hardly worthy of the name. They were used primarily by local ranchers, and infrequently at that. The drug market had made good use of the wild, almost inaccessible lands of northeastern Utah and western Wyoming. Areas around Flaming Gorge, Browns Park and Manila were ideal sites for illegal shipments and pickups. There were numerous places where a small aircraft could set down while her costly cargo was loaded into waiting vans and four-wheel drive vehicles. From the landing site, the vehicles could move along seldom-traveled dirt roads and then onto highways leading north to Rock Springs, west into Salt Lake City, or east toward Cheyenne.

Moser's pale blue eyes assessed the surrounding country as

he drove. Yellow-white cliffs mottled with dark green junipers, rolled against the horizon. Stretching away from the cliffs were flatlands where some grasses and the ever-present sagebrush managed to survive. A hot, dry wind blew Moser's long blond mane around his face. He swiped at the unruly strands then glanced at the watch encased in a thick leather bracelet on his wrist. Eight-fifty a.m. Pickup time was scheduled around nine-thirty. It wouldn't be long now.

*   *   *

Ron Snyder had had a pleasant two-hour flight from the pickup point in southern Utah to his present location over the western Uintas. The weather, always unpredictable over the mountains, was calm and clear. There were a few clouds moving his way from the northeast, but he would be down and gone from the area long before they arrived with the promise of rain.

He was nearing the crestline of the range when he heard a sudden sputtering and felt a loss in the plane's power. Snyder tensed and immediately checked the instruments and fuel gauge. No trouble there. The sputtering stopped and Snyder relaxed. In the six weeks he'd been flying this particular plane, he'd had no mechanical difficulties to speak of, but he had no way of knowing how long she'd last. It might not hurt to ditch her after this trip and steal another.

Suddenly, another series of sputters shook the plane's engine and she began losing altitude. Fear clutched at Snyder's innards and left his hands clammy as they tightened on the yoke. The crestline was rushing toward him with jagged peaks of 13,000 feet and more. Straight ahead loomed a fortress of wine-red rock, standing apart from the surrounding ridges like a lonely citadel.

Snyder grabbed the radio and signaled the ground crew. The lack of saliva in his mouth left his voice sounding strangled and dry.

"I've got engine trouble! Losing altitude fast. I'm going to try and set her down!"

xi

The voice on the other end demanded: "Where? What's your location? Dammit, Snyder, where are you?"

The red fortress loomed ever nearer and Snyder fought to maneuver the crippled plane to the left, away from the treacherous rock walls.

"Red Castle," he said through gritted teeth. "I'm over Red Castle!"

The Cessna skirted over a backbone of solid rock with a scant few feet to spare, then fell like a wounded bird, plunging past a high mountain lake where sunlight caught the ripples of blue-green water, toward another ledge of rock.

Snyder looked beyond the rocky ledge to a forest far below and a small patch of open meadow beyond that. He kept his eyes rivited on the meadow and cursed the airplane. His mind and body were beyond fear. Cold anger was shaking him now. If he could just make that ledge . . .

The plane's belly scraped rock then plummeted over the ledge. Snyder watched the forest rush forward in a blurry haze of brown and green. He pointed the fuselage directly between two massive pines and heard the shriek of metal as the wings sheared off. He was scarcely aware of the pain that flooded his abdomen with the impact of the crash. He only knew he must get out of the plane before it exploded or caught fire. He wrenched the door open and tumbled to the ground, managing to crawl several yards before blackness blotted out the sunlight and he lay still on the forest floor.

*   *   *

Chapter 1

*"Ink cannot tell the glow that lights me
at this moment in turning to the mountains."*
John Muir

The mountains were rising up to meet me. I was coming back to a world I hadn't seen for three long years and everything was just the same as I remembered. I felt halfway tempted to shout a welcome out the car window, but with my brother Doug behind the wheel of our family's big Chevy Blazer and his friend Travis Young settling down in the back seat for a nap, I decided against it. Besides, I was no longer "little Missy," the child who used to amuse her parents and two older brothers by saying hello and good-by to things like bushes and trees—and mountains. Twenty-year old Melissa Heydon had taken her place. Still, I couldn't resist leaning my head out the window and smiling a greeting to the misty crestline of peaks and ridges some forty miles to the south. The High Uintas. Even the name carried with it a kind of magic and spirit of adventure.

A voice from summers past came to me like a sigh on the breeze. "I'll be here waiting for you—just like the mountains . . ."

Loneliness that was more akin to pain blotted out the welcome. I turned my head away and rolled up the car window, as if that could somehow block out the voice. But it couldn't stop me from remembering. Years of bittersweet memories

1

came rushing back. I shoved them away, focusing all my attention on the long gray ribbon of asphalt stretching out before us. The mountains might be the same as I remembered, but nothing else was. This summer vacation could never be like all the others, but that didn't matter any more. I couldn't let it matter!

"It won't be long now," my brother said, a smile of anticipation lighting his features.

I nodded and gave him an answering smile before he could detect anything else in my face. Doug is just two years my senior and we are enough alike in personality and disposition that we've always been able to read each other's moods. We're alike in looks as well, from the light brown hair brightened with streaks of sun-gold, to the gray-green eyes and freckles. On Doug, the combination is super, but there are times when I wish I had a little more allure. I know I'm not unattractive, but it's difficult to exude gobs of feminine mystique when you look so wholesomely healthy—like a corn flakes commerical, or something.

Doug's expression suddenly shifted to a scrutinizing glance. "Are you nervous, Missy?"

His observation was too close to the truth to be comfortable, so I laughed and said, "Nervous? No, just excited, like I was nine years old again. It's so wonderful to be coming back. I don't think I realized until now, just how much I've missed the mountains."

"You call these mountains?" Travis Young sat up in the back seat and flicked a bored glance out the side window. "Man, the Canadian Rockies make these look like foothills!"

Nothing could make me ignore a remark like that! (Not even the fact that my main goal for the summer was to get Travis to fall madly in love with me.) I twisted around on the front seat, ready to do battle, but he only laughed.

"I thought that'd get a rise out of you," Travis said with a grin. "If you ever look at a man the way you were looking at those mountains, heaven help him!"

My brother glanced over his shoulder and said, "Hey, ol' buddy, I think I'd better warn you right now—no one insults

2

the Uintas around my sister! The Forest Service might not be aware of the fact, but Melissa Heydon is the official 'guardian spirit' of these mountains."

"No kidding? Sort of like Mother Nature's little helper?"

"Exactly."

"You two go right ahead and laugh," I said airily, "but don't expect to catch any fish tonight."

"Don't tell me your special powers include talking to the fish," Travis said.

"Missy talks to anything and everything," Doug supplied before I could answer. "She always goes a little crazy in the mountains. Ignore her, Travis."

My brother's friend flashed me a meaningful smile and said, "Now that's one thing I could never do!"

I faced the front once more, feeling slightly breathless. Teasing I could handle, but the expression in those hazel eyes was something else again. Actually, hazel is far too ordinary a word to describe them. To me, they're "jungle eyes"—earthy brown with flecks of gold and green—that do positively primitive things to my backbone. Travis himself could easily be compared to a jungle cat with his lean, bronze body and tawny hair. Even his movements have a certain lazy, feline grace.

"How much longer before we get to the Chisholm's cabin?" Travis was asking Doug. "What was it you called the place?"

"Trail's End," Doug told him. "I figure we've got a good hour and a half drive ahead of us."

"Just time enough for me to take a nap," Travis said and stretched out across the back seat. "Wake me up when we get there, Missy."

When we get there . . . Trail's End was only an hour and a half away. Trail's End and Jesse Chisholm . . .

I gave myself a hard mental shaking and stared out the front window.

We were traveling due south, across the wide, windy plateaus of southwestern Wyoming. Few crops grow well in this region because the elevation reaches 6800 feet and more, and the growing season is too short. But where the land is fed by mountain streams, the grass grows long and lush, supporting

3

both cattle and sheep. Fences of wire and wood define the various properties, but the immense, open feeling of the land itself can never be contained. Rising up to the south, beyond the plateaus and foothills, are the Uinta Mountains of northern Utah. I watched the crestline growing ever nearer and excitement swelled within me. I loved these mountains! Doug could tease me all he liked about being "guardian spirit," but I really did feel a strange sort of kinship with the Uintas. A *belonging* that was sometimes greater than the feelings I had for my own home in Scottsdale, Arizona.

If only Jesse weren't—I felt the sudden sting of tears pricking my eyelids and angrily blinked them back. Melissa Heydon, you're a fool! Forget the past. Think of now! You're going to have Travis Young all to yourself for two whole weeks—miles away from the nearest competition. Think of that!

Glancing over my shoulder, I saw that Travis' jungle eyes were closed, and took the opportunity to study his face relaxed in sleep—the expressive mouth, the clean line of his jaw, the smooth forehead where the breeze was teasing a bit of tawny hair. Strange, how sleep had a way of softening some of the tough independence that was always a part of his expression. During the two years or so that he and Doug have known one another, I have never seen Travis anything but cool, controlled and confident.

"Stop drooling," my brother said.

"I'm not drooling!" I whispered. "I was just checking to see if Travis was asleep or not."

"Sure you were!"

"Well, I was, and would you please keep your voice down!"

Doug lowered his volume to one shade above a whisper and said, "Do you mind if I give you a little brotherly advice?"

"Yes, but I know you'll give it to me anyway. You always do."

Doug's jaw tightened and his mouth got that stubborn set to it that I know so well.

I sighed and said, "O.K., I'm sorry. What's the advice?"

"Don't get any ideas about Travis. He's not your type."

"Not my type!" I exploded, then glanced quickly behind me

4

to make sure Travis was still asleep. "I'm perfectly capable of deciding who's *my type* and who isn't!" I finished in a whisper.

"Missy, don't be a stubborn dope! Travis is a lot of fun, but you know what kind of a guy he is."

"Meaning?"

Doug's cheeks reddened slightly and he cleared his throat. "Well, uh—Travis has been around a lot. I don't want you to get hurt," he added gruffly.

"Look, I didn't invite him along—you did! If you're so worried about me, why did you ask Travis to come with us?"

"Well, I—" My brother's cheeks went a shade darker and he said almost sheepishly, "I guess I didn't think you'd turn him on."

"Thanks a lot! It's nice to know what you think of me!"

"Hey, Missy, don't get all uptight. You know what I mean—"

I folded my arms and stared out the window.

Doug sighed and gave the steering wheel a thump with his fist. "Mountain View is just ahead. Maybe we ought to stop at the ranger station and check on the condition of the roads."

I answered him with stony silence as he slowed the car and we entered the confines of the little town.

Mountain View is a homely place with the minimum of services and no frills. There is a gas station or two, a few small stores and very little else. Doug left the main road and turned onto a narrow lane where grassy fields lined one side, and a few trailer homes plus the guard station were situated on the other. It would have been a natural mistake to assume the two white-frame buildings with their tidy lawns and flower gardens were private residences, had it not been for the flag pole on the front lawn and an official sign hanging over a doorway. A large gravel parking area separated the two buildings and here, I saw a late-model, brown pickup truck and a dark blue van parked side by side. Both vehicles were pulling horse trailers and two broad rumps and two swishing tails protruded from the back of each trailer.

"Looks like someone else has the same idea we do," Doug commented.

5

"I hope they're not going up the West Fork," I said.

"I really think these mountains are big enough to accommodate more than three people," Doug said dryly and parked next to the van. "Want to come in with me?"

"No, thanks. I'll wait here."

Doug frowned and glanced toward the back seat. "Be back in a minute."

As he approached the ranger station, the screen door opened ahead of him and four men came out. The first was well into his forties with thinning brown hair, a florid complexion and a stomach that bulged over his wide western belt. The second man was much taller and younger, with a long blond mane that hung well past his shoulders and sideburns that grew low on his jawline. A tuft of pale hair curled beneath his full lower lip. I suppose he would have to be considered good-looking in a surly sort of way, but there was something about him that made me want to shudder. Next, came a thin young Chicano with lank hair and an unkempt mustache that straggled down the sides of his mouth. He had bright black eyes and the nervous, darting look of a weasel. The last to exit was a big, burly ox of a man with small, puffy eyes and beard that bristled around his heavy face like a fuzzy brown bush. The middle-aged man was dressed in a short-sleeved shirt and slacks, but it didn't take a second glance to realize the clothes were expensive and well-made. The other three looked like rejects from a hard-rock festival. Their Levis were dirty and stained, and the bearded man was wearing a muddy gray t-shirt with a large hole that exposed his navel.

Doug gave all four his usual warm hello to which the first man responded with a nondescript grunt. The rest walked on by. The ox and the weasel climbed into the pickup truck, while the older man and the blond giant came my way toward the van. As the blond approached, his pale blue eyes turned in my direction. It was too late to pretend I hadn't been watching them. I struggled to keep my expression as blank as possible, then bent forward to get a map out of the glove compartment. I gave it my wholehearted attention, all the while feeling those pale eyes moving over me like a pair of dirty hands. He didn't speak, but

6

it seemed an eternity before he was behind the wheel and backing the van out of the parking lot. I didn't look up again until both van and truck were gone.

Doug came out a moment later with the news that all the roads on the north slope were open and in good condition.

"There's still some construction going on below Bridger Lake, but the ranger didn't seem to think it would hold us up any," he told me.

"What sort of construction?"

"They're building a dam. I thought you knew. They've been working on it for a couple of years now."

"I haven't been here for more than a couple of years," I reminded him. "Why are they building a dam up here? That's terrible!"

"The wheels of progress, sister dear."

"Progress my foot! Why can't they leave the mountains alone?"

Doug laughed and started the engine. "You're beginning to sound like John Denver."

"Doug! How can you joke about something like this?"

"Look, Missy, I know how you feel, but things change— even up here. You can't stop it."

I carefully refolded the map, fighting to keep back the painful emotions and memories his words evoked. As we left the parking area and headed for the main highway, I was no longer thinking about the dam, but Doug gave me a sympathetic glance and said, "Hey, if it'll make you feel any better, we don't need to take the Bridger Lake route. There's always the Gilbert Creek road or—" His mouth widened into a grin. "—the Chisholm Trail!"

Just hearing the name again released the flood of memories I had been damming up inside me for so long. They came bursting forth as fresh and vivid as the present. I gave Doug an answering smile and said softly, "Let's take the Chisholm Trail."

Chapter 2

"Oh, come along boys an' listen to my tale,
I'll tell you of my troubles on the old Chisholm Trail . . ."
American Cowboy Song

To most people, the dusty red track which leaves the tiny Wyoming community of Robertson and heads south through miles of sagebrush and open rangeland toward the high meadows and forests of the Uinta Mountains, might not have a name. To local ranchers it's simply the Smith's Fork Road. But to the Heydon family it will always be known as the "Chisholm Trail." Years ago I christened the last few miles of dirt road leading to the Chisholm's cabins after the famed cattle trail, and not only because the name is the same. Once, my father decided to save time and take what he thought was a more direct route to the cabins. We ended up getting stuck behind some 300 head of bawling, stubborn Herefords on their way to the summer range. By the time we got through the herd, an hour and half later, the cattle weren't the only ones bawling. After that, the "Chisholm Trail" became a rather infamous Heydon family tradition.

I was a scrawny, freckle-faced tomboy of eight when we first received an invitation to spend our summer vacation with the Chisholm family at "Trail's End." The name may sound like a vintage John Wayne movie, or maybe a Western novel by Zane Grey, but actually, Trail's End is a beautiful five-acre parcel of land, complete with two cabins and a barn for horses.

8

Up until that first summer, I knew very little about Charles Chisholm and his family; only that he and my father had been close friends during World War II, and every year we received a Christmas card from them, plus a calendar for the new year, courtesy of Chisholm's Sporting Goods in Logan, Utah. When the invitation came, it didn't take long for Mom and Dad to agree with the Chisholms that it was high time for our two families to get together. Plans for the 780-mile journey from our home in Scottsdale, Arizona, to Trail's End began immediately.

My two older brothers, Mark and Doug, went wild with excitement, but I remember feeling quite disappointed, even angry, because I wanted to go to Disneyland or the ocean. What did they expect me to do in some dumb old mountains for two whole weeks, anyway? Chase squirrels or something? I made up my mind that I was going to be totally bored the whole time. I was always an intense child, either excruciatingly happy or in the depths of despair. Acting nonchalant was really beyond me, but I tried. For two entire days I fought against loving Trail's End, the Chisholms, and the Uinta Mountains. I stayed behind when everyone else went fishing and made a ritual of reading the few comic books I found in our guest cabin. There wasn't anyone my age to talk or play with. The Chisholms had a fourteen-year old daughter, Barbara, but all she did was comb her hair and follow my brothers around. Their nineteen-year old son was the most aggravating one of all. He never talked to anyone, except to be polite, and he never smiled. He seemed to spend most of his time horseback riding or hiking by himself. What the adults neglected to tell me (or purposely did not tell me at that time), was that Jesse Chisholm's young wife had been killed exactly a year before while they were on their honeymoon in the mountains. To this day, I don't know the details of her death.

On the third morning of our stay, Jesse left the cabin area for another of his solitary walks. When lunchtime came, he had not returned. By mid-afternoon, Mildred Chisholm abandoned her forced cheerfulness, and before I was sent firmly outside to play, I saw her weeping in the bedroom. Even Mr. Chisholm and my father were looking tense and strained. Fishing for the afternoon was canceled and a search party was organized instead. If

9

Jesse didn't return by five o'clock, the Chisholms would notify the nearest ranger station.

No one cared about me. It was worse than being ignored. I might just as well have been invisible. Feeling thoroughly sorry for myself and thoroughly disgusted with Jesse Chisholm, I wandered away from the cabins and headed for the rushing waters of Smith's Fork Creek. I followed the course of the stream until I happened upon a rough bridge formed by some fallen lodgepole pines. I climbed nimbly onto the bridge and proceeded to throw the handful of stones I had stashed away in my jeans pocket into the water, one by one.

A voice somewhere nearby said, "You'll scare the fish," and my head jerked up. Jesse Chisholm was walking toward me from the opposite side of the stream, and as far as I could see, he looked perfectly healthy. The very least he could have done was come staggering back all bloody from an encounter with a bear or mountain lion.

He stepped onto the bridge and I noticed that his face looked kind of funny. Now, I would hardly use the word 'funny' to describe his expression. Drained, haggard, washed with grief, but certainly not funny. Eight-year old Melissa was not sensitive to grief, however. Up until that moment, I had never encountered it. The most tragic event in my young life was the time my pet kitten ran away.

I stood up and my nose barely reached his belt buckle. I lifted my chin even higher and glared up at him.

"Just where do you think you've been all day?" I demanded.

He blinked, then lifted his shoulders in a half shrug. "It doesn't matter."

"Doesn't matter! Boy, are you going to get it when you get back!"

Jesse's mouth twitched slightly as he looked down at me.

"It's not funny!" I told him. "Don't you know you're not supposed to go somewhere without telling your Mom or Dad? Your Mom's been crying all afternoon and my dumb brothers didn't get to go fishing 'cause everyone's been so worried about you. Boy, are you going to get it!" I said again in dire tones.

10

Jesse squatted down so we were eye to eye, then he said, "I'm sorry, Tidbit. I guess I wasn't thinking about the others."

"Mothers get awful worried if they don't know where their kids are," I said, but not angrily now. He had the bluest eyes, even if they were all red around the edges. And somehow, I didn't mind him calling me "Tidbit." I hated my usual nickname, "little Missy," but "Tidbit"—that was different.

"From now on, I won't leave unless I tell my folks where I'm going and when I'll be back," he said gravely.

His words made me feel terribly important. I smiled and asked shyly, "Do you think—well, the next time you go for a walk—could I come, too?"

"You bet you can!" Jesse said and smiled for the first time since our arrival. His smile was like the sun coming out. I felt warm all over. "You can come with me anytime you want," he added and we walked back to the cabin hand in hand.

For the rest of our vacation, Jesse and I were inseparable. We explored the forest trails and he taught me the names of trees and wildflowers. We spent hours patiently watching for and observing the wildlife. I'll never forget one evening, just after sunset, when we glimpsed a cow moose and her calf leaving the forest to eat and drink in the lower meadows. I was ecstatic. Other times, we saw porcupines and deer, marmots and chipmunks. The surprises and discoveries were endless. In the evenings, Jesse played his guitar and we all sat around the fireplace and sang old songs. We toasted marshmallows, popped popcorn and told stories. And sometimes, it was more than enough just to sit within the encircling warmth of his arms.

If our families were surprised at this sudden friendship, they said not a word. Jesse was smiling and laughing again and as I seemed to have had something to do with that, I could do no wrong. When our two weeks were over, I clung to Jesse's neck, soaking his shirt with my tears. "Don't cry, Tidbit," he told me gently. "There'll always be another summer. And I'll be here waiting for you, just like the mountains."

During the endless year which followed, I would look at the heat waves shimmering around the palms and eucalyptus trees

11

that surrounded our desert home and try to remember how cool it was in the mountains. Was there really a place called "Trail's End," or did it exist only in my childish imagination? When summer reigned the year round in Scottsdale, it was hard to believe that somewhere up north, the mountains were slumbering under several feet of snow. Sleeping and dreaming in white silence until summer and I would come again.

There was no act of boredom on my part during our second journey to Trail's End. In fact, Dad threatened to lock me in the trunk or tie me to the luggage rack if I didn't stop asking how much longer until we were there. When the Uintas came into view I breathed an audible sigh of relief. If the mountains were still there, Jesse must be, too. And he was. The moment our car pulled up, he came out of the cabin to meet us. I knew Trail's End wasn't a dream when he wrapped his strong arms and wide smile around me and asked, "How's my little Tidbit?"

In the years which followed, vacation at Trail's End became a Heydon family tradition. No matter what else was planned, no summer was complete without a week or two spent at the cabin. Charles and Mildred Chisholm became Uncle Chuck and Aunt Milly to us, just as my parents were Uncle Will and Aunt Beth to Jesse and Barbara.

Every year, I saw a different mood, discovered a new facet of the Uintas' unique personality. Some years it was June when we came. In June, the snow still lingered in dingy heaps under the pine trees and wild iris bloomed in the meadows. Other years it might be August, when the mountains trembled with daily thunderstorms. But most often, we came in July, that glorious season of summer in the mountains when forest trails are ablaze with Indian paintbrush and a thousand other flowers living out their brief, beautiful existence.

Seasons came and seasons passed, and one day I realized the season of my childhood was over and gone, and the bewildering season of adolescence was upon me. Inside, I felt the change, the new awareness, but for the most part, I still looked and acted like a tomboy. Nature was very slow and very stingy in supplying me with the equipment other girls had in such generous supply. Mom was forever feeding me a steady diet of "late bloomer" stories, but I was sure I was doomed to remain "little Missy" forever. During this time, I was vaguely aware that Jesse was attending some university, eventually earning a master's degree in geology. I was fifteen when he was hired by the Forest Service as a geologist.

Finally, I was sixteen and proud to the point of being smug because Mom had no further cause to feed me "late bloomer" stories. It happened so suddenly, my brothers had a hard time believing their sister—the toughest little tomboy in the neighborhood—was wearing makeup and filling out dresses in all the right places. Mark and Doug still called me "little Missy" on occasion, but somehow, I didn't feel like slugging them in the stomach anymore.

I could hardly wait to go to Trail's End that summer. I was sure Jesse would be just as excited about my finally growing up as I was. There were so many things I wanted to tell him. And there were a few things I suddenly realized I couldn't share with Jesse. My first kiss, for example. It was all right, as far as kisses go, but it certainly wasn't anything to get worked up about. Kissing, as far as I was concerned, was highly overrated.

From the very start, everything went wrong that summer. Instead of my usual bear hug and "How's my little Tidbit?", I was greeted by a stunned sort of stare, followed by a casual arm draped around my shoulders. My mother got a bigger hug than I did! Jesse listened politely when I told him all about the various happenings in my life since we had last seen each other, but he didn't seem at all interested. Something was wrong and I didn't know what it was. We went on fewer walks, had fewer talks, and when we were together I felt horribly self-conscious and uncomfortable. For the first time, I was actually glad when our two weeks at Trail's End were over. Jesse gave me a brief good-by hug, but even that wasn't the same as other years. Always before, I had felt the strong reassurance in his arms of another time together, another summer to come. This time, it felt like good-by.

Mom had a long talk with me on the drive home. In her own original fashion she tried to explain that "nothing stays the same"—that "growing up is often painful" and that "sooner or later, we all have to learn to let go." This was ten times worse than her "late bloomer" stories! Mom had tried to tell me before that the ties would lessen between Jesse and me as we grew older, especially with an eleven-year span between our ages. But I flatly refused to believe her. I was Jesse's friend and he was mine. Age never entered into it. Now, suddenly, I wasn't so sure.

Autumn finally came and brought with it the excitement of my senior year in high school. My days were full and rich but sometimes at night, I would remember the summer before and struggle with my thoughts and feelings. Maybe Jesse had acted differently because I had embarrassed him, chattering away about clothes and boys. Maybe I was overreacting to the whole thing. Maybe, next summer when we went back to Trail's End, Jesse and I would be just the same as we always were. But just in case, I would make polite, intelligent conversation, omitting any mention of fellows I had dated during the year—and even try listening for a change.

As it happened, I never had the opportunity for intelligent conversation or listening because, for the first time, Jesse wasn't there. At first, I couldn't believe it when Aunt Milly explained that he had spent a few days at the cabin earlier in the summer and right now he was in the Northwest, meeting some people. I didn't understand. Why would Jesse go to the Northwest when he knew we were coming? Then Aunt Milly sighed and confided with shining eyes that Jesse had met a girl at last. Her name was Sheila. Things must be serious, she told Mom and me, because Jesse had gone to Portland to meet the girl's family. "What a blessing it would be if Jesse got married again," my mother said as I stood frozen beside them. "He's been alone too long."

I felt stunned, then shattered, then thoroughly ashamed of myself. Why hadn't I realized before? It was the most natural thing in the world for Jesse to want to get married again. I should be happy for him. I was happy for him. So happy, I ran out of the cabin and down to the creek where our bridge still spanned the sparkling waters and sobbed for an hour and a half.

I learned a lot that vacation—about loneliness, myself, and

14

growing up. It hurt to admit that I had been childishly possessive where Jesse was concerned. I should have realized he had needs and a life of his own away from Trail's End. Ten years had gone by since the summer his wife died. Aunt Milly and Mom were right. He had been alone too long. How could I have been so blind, so stupid, to believe that we would go on all through our lives spending a magical two weeks in the mountains? No matter how painful the process might be, I had to learn to let go. When we left Trail's End, I would put Jesse Chisholm out of my life the same way one puts away old clothes that no longer fit.

I spent the remainder of our vacation saying good-by—to trails we had wandered along, to lakes we had fished, to the marmots who lived down the road in a rocky culvert—to a thousand and one things that made up the miracle of Trail's End. When our family drove away, I was dry-eyed and silent, having already shed more tears during the previous two weeks than the rest of my life put together. I told myself I was ready to accept Jesse's imminent marriage as (to quote my mother): "One of the changes life brings"—but nothing, *nothing* would ever bring me back to Trail's End again.

So here I was, three years later, breaking that solemn vow. The mountains were growing ever nearer and so was Trail's End. This afternoon I would meet Mr. and Mrs. Jesse Chisholm. We would all be smiling and polite. Jesse would probably be fat and losing his hair, and Sheila-What's-Her-Face was bound to be matronly and dull. Just seeing Jesse again would put to rest the ghosts of summers past, and then—maybe the pain would go away.

For the past three years I have struggled to put Jesse Chisholm out of my mind with about the same effectiveness as when someone asks you to close your eyes and not think of an elephant. Oh, I've been busy and happy enough—hardly what you'd call pining away—with a full schedule of classes at Arizona State, plus an active social life. But whenever I thought I was cured of "mountain fever," all it took was a card or letter from the Chisholms to make me realize the pain was still there, just below the surface.

15

I was in Tucson, spending a week with some girlfriends from school when the wedding announcement arrived, so Mom mailed it on to me. I remember, the temperature was well over a hundred that day, but when I saw the return address on the envelope I felt cold all over. I knew what it was, and somehow I just couldn't face seeing the fact of Jesse's marriage in black and white—so I threw it away, unopened.

I grew very skillful at changing the subject whenever Jesse's name was mentioned and it wasn't difficult at all to come up with legitimate excuses to stay home while the rest of the family made their annual pilgrimage to the Uintas. One year I took summer classes and got a new job. The next, my oldest brother Mark surprised us all by getting married, so none of the family was able to go. But this summer, I ran out of excuses. I was helping Dad part-time in his photography studio, so I couldn't use work as a reason to stay home. There weren't any classes I was interested in taking at the university, and I was too blatantly healthy to fake an illness. Then the letter came.

Doug and I were relaxing by our pool after a late afternoon swim when Mom came outside with a tall pitcher of fresh orange juice in one hand and a white envelope in the other. As we helped ourselves to the juice she said, "Here's a letter from the Chisholms! Milly's so excited—listen to this: 'Chuck and I became the proud grandparents of an 8 lb. 7 oz. boy on April 20th. Little David looks just like his father, but he's got Chuck's forehead and I'm sure his hair (what there is of it) will be curly. You and Will are going to love being grandparents, Beth! There's all the fun of cuddling and loving a baby without missing your sleep at night. Let us know when Mark and Julie's baby arrives so we can all brag together. We'd love to have you come visit us the second week in July if you're able to get away. Trail's End wasn't the same without you last year. Jesse and Barbara both send their love.'"

I finished my glass of orange juice and said in a choked voice, "That's super news, Mom. I'm really happy for them." Then I stumbled over to the pool and made a clumsy dive, letting the chlorinated water mingle with the salty tears in my eyes. Jesse's son! I couldn't begin to picture the infant's face, but I could see Jesse's all too clearly as he held the baby in his strong brown hands . . .

Babies became the main topic of conversation around our house for the next few weeks. I had no idea how silly perfectly sensible adults can be at the prospect of becoming grand-parents. I thought everyone was making entirely too much fuss over something that just cried and wet a lot once it got here. My sister-in-law was positively waddling, but Mark seemed to think she was even more beautiful now than the svelte blonde creature he had married only a year before.

Their baby was due around July 3rd and our family was scheduled to leave for Trail's End, July 10th. On the evening of the 8th, Julie was still waddling around and my mother announced that she simply would not go to the cabin until after the baby came. Dad agreed. Doug had a fit. He was scheduled to go back to work on the 17th of July and he didn't want to miss a single day of his vacation. I stayed strictly in the background, thinking perhaps I wouldn't have to face Jesse after all. Then Doug suggested an alternative plan. Why couldn't he and I drive up to the Uintas as planned, and Mom and Dad come later, after the late new arrival finally made its debut? He could ask Travis Young to come along and share the driving and that way everyone would be happy.

Suddenly, the pain of seeing Jesse again was tempered with thoughts of spending two weeks in the mountains with my brother's good-looking friend. My love-life was non-existent at the moment, but having Travis Young around might change all that. And maybe, if I faced up to my feelings instead of running away from them, I would discover that seeing Jesse and his wife didn't hurt at all.

A voice beside me said, "Say good-by to Wyoming," and I straightened up with a start.

"Hmmm? What?"

"I said, say good-by to Wyoming. We're in Utah now. At least, some of us are," my brother said. "For the past half hour or so, you've been a million miles away."

I straightened my shoulders and stretched. "I was just resting."

17

"Well, unless you want to miss all this gorgeous scenery, you'd better start resting with your eyes open," Doug advised.

"I'd sure like to know where all this gorgeous scenery is you keep talking about," Travis said from the back seat. "One clump of sagebrush looks pretty much like another as far as I'm concerned, and there sure is a lot of it out here!"

I sighed, but said nothing. I would never understand how anyone, including Travis, could find this country dull and uninteresting. We were climbing higher now. Forests of pine and aspen lay directly ahead, but sage still dominated the landscape, the result of years of grazing. The road had narrowed into little more than a dusty trail which was badly pitted and furrowed. Keeping the Blazer out of chuckholes required most of Doug's attention. Then we were into the trees, with cool green arms of pine shading the road on both sides and hills of aspen trembling in the sunlight.

The Blazer surged around a tight little bend banked with a dense wall of aspen on the right and a steep drop-off to the left. I used to curl my toes as a child when Dad drove around that bend, more than half afraid our car would fall over the edge. Trail's End was only a few miles away. I pressed a hand to my stomach, as if that could still the excited churning inside me.

The next moment Doug was applying the brakes and muttering, "I don't believe it! The 'Chisholm Trail' strikes again!"

Some fifty yards ahead, the road climbed through a narrow gap in the pines and that gap was positively gorged with cattle. There were Herefords everywhere. Some were milling around in the trees, others were attempting to navigate their own course downhill against traffic. But the bulk of the herd was in the road, red sides rubbing together and white faces lifted high in vigorous protest. The noise was tremendous!

A lanky cowboy in a sky-blue shirt and dusty leather chaps was attempting to urge the cattle uphill with very little success. The cows and steers at the head of the herd were taking their own sweet time, and with the road so choked with bawling animals, plus thick trees on either side, the cowboy couldn't get through. Three teen-age girls in Levis and short-sleeved blouses

18

were also riding herd, but it looked to me as if all they were doing was confusing the poor beasts.

Doug groaned and rested his chin on the steering wheel. "Looks like we're gonna be here a while."

"Why don't you honk your horn," Travis said. "That ought to get them moving!"

"That poor guy's got enough trouble without us stampeding his herd. We'll just have to follow along behind until the road widens enough for us to get through."

I gave my brother a shame-faced grin. "I'm sorry, Doug. I guess we should have taken the other road."

"Don't worry about it, Sis. We'll get there when we get there."

Forty-five minutes later we had moved perhaps 300 yards along the road. The area was still heavily wooded, which made it all but impossible for the cowboy and his three young riders to keep track of the cattle. Several times, he had to dismount and physically carry a stubborn calf back to the rest of the herd. And whenever he rode off after one little rebel, three or four others took off in the opposite direction. Travis was looking a bit put out as well as bored, and Doug's temper was rising along with the temperature of the car's engine. I wished there were a convenient hole somewhere nearby I could crawl into.

Then Doug glanced in the rearview mirror and said, "Well, well! Here comes company. We might as well have a party. There's nothing else to do!"

I turned around and my heart gave a queer little jerk as the dark blue van and brown pickup truck pulled up directly behind us.

Chapter 3

"What shall I do with this absurdity—
O heart, O troubled heart . . ."
William Butler Yeats

The driver of the van gave his horn an angry blast which immediately sent several steers plunging through the aspens in a panic. The cowboy turned his horse and galloped after them, yelling over his shoulder to one of the girls: "Tell that fool to cut the honking or we'll lose them all!"

Doug was out of the car and heading toward the van before the girl had a chance to ride in our direction. She gave him a grateful smile and urged her horse after one of the frightened animals instead.

I called out, "Doug, be careful!" without thinking why, and leaned over the back seat to watch him.

Travis grinned and shook his tawny head. "Hey, relax, Missy! He's not going out to meet a car full of hardened criminals! You can't blame them for being impatient."

I didn't answer. Maybe my reaction was slightly melodramatic, but it was very real, nonetheless.

Doug approached the van and spoke to the driver for a few moments, but I couldn't hear his voice above the strident chorus of bawling cattle. I watched as the tall blond got out of the van, pushed his long mane away from his face and tossed a disgruntled glance in the direction of the herd. The blond was

20

soon joined by the big bearded man and the Chicano, whose stringy black hair was now tied back with a piece of red cloth. The blond took a package of cigarettes from his shirt pocket and passed it around. I winced as a match was tossed carelessly into the grass alongside the road. Doug refused a cigarette and headed back to our car.

As he climbed into the Blazer, Travis asked, "Have any trouble with our friends back there?"

"No. Why should I?"

"I think Missy was afraid you were going to get eaten alive!"

Doug gave me a knowing grin. "My little sister has her prejudices when it comes to judging a book by its cover."

"I can't help it if I've never liked a mustache and a ponytail on the same person," I retorted, still watching the grassy area where the match had landed. "Where are they headed, anyway?"

"Over to China Meadows and the Trailhead campground."

"But this road is miles out of their way!"

"They know that. Apparently, there was an accident with a logging truck just before they got to the Bridger Lake and Gilbert Creek turnoffs. A big truck rolled over and the entire road is blocked. The ranger turned them back and advised them to take the Chisholm Trail—I mean, Smith's Fork Road," Doug said with a sheepish grin. "No wonder those guys are so ticked off. First, they run into a mess of logs, now they drive right into 300 head of cattle."

"I wish there were something we could do to get moving," I said irritably as the Chicano flicked a cigarette butt into the brush.

"Like what?" Doug asked. "Sprout wings, maybe?"

I raised my eyes heavenward and remained silent, then faced the front to stare at the cattle-clogged road. "It looks to me like the trees thin out not too far ahead," I said. "Maybe I could walk in front of the car and clear a path for us."

Travis stared at me. "You've got to be kidding!"

"If those steers won't move out of the way for a Chevy

21

Blazer, what makes you think they'll skedaddle for a 100-pound girl," Doug said.

"I couldn't possibly do any worse than those girls on horseback," I told him. "I think it's worth a try."

Doug sighed. "O.K., but don't take any chances. If one of those animals even looks at you cross-eyed, you head back for the car!"

"Don't worry, I will!" I slipped quickly out the door before he could change his mind, and for the second time this afternoon, my eyes met those of the tall blond. A lazy, interested smile turned the corners of his mouth and I couldn't have felt more self-conscious if I had been wearing transparent Levis. My first instincts were to climb back into the Blazer and lock the door, but my conscience couldn't forget that smoldering cigarette a few yards away.

I cleared my throat and said over the raucous din of the cattle, "Excuse me—would you please take care of those cigarettes?"

All three men stared at me, then the blond stepped forward and offered me his pack.

"You wanna smoke?"

"No! No, thank you, but I'd appreciate it if you'd crush that cigarette in the grass behind you. Fires can start so easily up here—"

Amusement curled his thick lower lip and warmed the pale blue of his eyes. Two columns of smoke blew out his nostrils and he said lazily, "You're right. They sure can!"

My heart was choking me but I refused to look away from his eyes. Finally, he gave a nod and addressed the other two men.

"Clyde—Tony! The little lady here would like you to put out your cigarettes."

The bearded man glared at me with his puffy eyes. "You can tell the little lady she can cram it.—"

"Now Clyde, what would Smokey the Bear say? You don't want to cause a nasty forest fire, do you? Be a good boy and put out the cigarettes. Tony, there's a butt behind you in the grass." His tone was light and mocking, but the two men moved immediately to do his bidding.

After his orders had been obeyed, the blond turned back to me and there was no mistaking the look in his heavy-lidded eyes. "Anything else I can do for you, little lady?"

"No! Nothing! Thank you very much!"

I walked quickly away from him and moved in front of the Blazer. I was still being eyed suspiciously, only now it was by several nervous Herefords. Frankly, I much preferred their rolling brown eyes to those of the men behind me. I blew out a shaky breath and began talking to the cattle in what I hoped was an authoritative voice. Surprisingly, it took very little urging before the cows and steers were clambering out of my way on either side. I led the way on the dusty red trail, feeling terribly pleased with myself. Melissa Heydon—trail blazer for the Chevy Blazer. I laughed and jumped over a fly-covered mound of fresh cow dung.

It wasn't long before we were completely out of the thick cover of aspens and into a broad clearing. There were still a few scattered Herefords lolling in the warm afternoon sun or grazing in the rich, grassy meadows, but the road ahead was clear! I ran back to the Blazer and hopped inside, saying to my brother, "Head 'em up, and move 'em out!"

Doug laughed and the Blazer leaped forward with an eager roar. I glanced over my shoulder to see if the van and truck were still following close behind and met Travis Young's stimulating gaze.

"You really take your job seriously, don't you?"

"My job—?"

He smiled. "You know, 'guardian spirit' of the mountains."

I looked at the vehicles following behind us and said, "These mountains'll need more than one guardian spirit if there are any more men like those up here!"

My brother gave me an amused glance. "Come on, Sis. I know they're not exactly your type, but the blond guy thought you were really something else!"

I pulled a face. "I thought he was something else, too, but I'm not sure just what!"

23

Travis laughed and his jungle eyes were as warm and sensual as a caress.

Out of all the miles of scenic beauty on the way to Trail's End, the last few are my very favorite. The steep grades and twisting turns are gone, so is all of the sagebrush and most of the dust. Even the aspen aren't quite so prevalent. The road itself subtly changes in form and color. Gone is the thick, reddish-brown color and in its place is a path of wine-red with deep tire grooves making two furrows down the center. On either side, forests of lodgepole pine and Douglas fir fringe radiant meadows where dandelions drink the sunshine and clusters of tiny knotweed sway on slender stems like tufts of cotton in the breeze.

It is impossible to describe the feeling of peace and beauty that permeates this high mountain land. I only know I feel a sense of wonder every time I am here that I have never felt anywhere else.

Because of the heavy winter snows and frequent rainfall in the summer, the Forest Service has had to dig culverts and ditches in some places along the road to permit proper drainage. But even this has been done with care in an effort to protect, not destroy the fragile ecosystems of the forest. In one of these rocky culverts, a family of golden marmots have made their home. I know with the passage of time, several generations of marmots must have come and gone, but in all the years I have come to Trail's End, the marmots have been there to greet me.

"Doug, slow down a little when we get to the marmot's home, O.K.?"

He smiled indulgently and slowed the Blazer to a crawl as we neared the culvert. I scooted over beside him and looked out the window for any movement among the rocks. Sure enough, two inquisitive, brown rodent faces popped up from behind the boulders to see who was passing by their residence.

"I'm so glad they're still here," I said and leaned back against the seat with a happy sigh.

"You're the first girl I've ever known who got excited about seeing a couple of overgrown rats," Travis remarked.

"They're not like rats at all!" I protested. "Rats are so evil

24

and slinky-looking, but marmots are—well, so adorable!"

"Adorable or not, those guys behind us won't understand why we're stopping again, so you'll have to visit your marmot friends some other time," Doug said, then added over his shoulder to Travis, "I told you she goes a little crazy in the mountains!"

Another mile down the road, I spotted the large wooden sign post with its white painted letters and arrows, indicating that Hewinta Guard Station and the Gilbert Creek Road were on the left fork, and Black's Fork Creek and the Mirror Lake Highway were some miles distant to the right. Doug turned the Blazer onto the small side road leading to the guard station, and behind us, the van and pickup truck rushed on by. I scarcely noticed. Trail's End was only a mile beyond the guard station and my heart acknowledged its nearness with a sudden acceleration in tempo.

Doug pointed out the ranger station to Travis and I gave the three log buildings a fleeting glance. The main cabin, barn and storage building hugged the edge of the forest, while a broad expanse of meadow sloped down to the rushing waters of Smith's Fork Creek.

"This is all national forest land, isn't it?" Travis commented as the guard station was left behind.

"That's right," Doug said.

Travis took in the surrounding land with an envious glance. "I'd sure like to know how the Chisholm's managed to buy acreage right in the middle of Uncle Sam's mountains!"

"They didn't," Doug informed him. "Trail's End belonged to the Chisholm family years before there were any national forests. Uncle Chuck had an old bachelor uncle named Amos who used to be a trapper of sorts. Old-timers in these parts still tell some wild stories about him. He must have been quite a character. Uncle Chuck claims that old Amos was a distant cousin to the original Jesse Chisholm who started the Chisholm Trail."

"Just claims?" Travis asked with a smile.

"Well, the strength of the relationship depends on who you're talking to," Doug explained. "Uncle Chuck insists the two were related, but Aunt Milly says she won't believe it until she sees the fact in black and white. Maybe not even then. But that's mainly because it irks her to have a son named after a halfbreed Indian trader. She thought Uncle Chuck liked the name Jesse because of its Biblical connotations," he said with a laugh. "But that's another story—right, Sis?"

I snatched a little breath and nodded, wishing I could do something about the swarm of butterflies that had suddenly taken up residence in my stomach.

"Anyway, to get back to the property," Doug continued, "old Amos was the original owner and he left it to Uncle Chuck in his will."

"Some people have all the luck," Travis said. "Now why couldn't I have had an uncle like that?"

"If you had, we would have been driving through condominiums right now instead of pine trees," Doug said, giving Travis a smile.

Travis laughed. "You know me too well!"

We were totally surrounded by giant lodgepoles. The road picked its own narrow way among them and I caught green glimpses of meadow through the trees on my left. As we drove, I found myself leaning forward on the seat, straining for the first sight of the Chisholm's cabins through the maze of brown trunks, just as I had done so many times as a child. Almost the very moment I spied the presence of a sturdy log cabin, my gaze was dramatically diverted to an adjacent meadow where a massive, white conical structure reflected the brilliance of the afternoon sun.

"Good grief, it's a tipi!" Travis exclaimed. "You didn't tell me there were Indians living up here, too."

"There aren't," Doug answered with a puzzled glance at the tipi. "I wonder if it's Jesse's?"

We drove past the meadow and there in the deep shade of the pines was Trail's End. The Chisholm's cabin was built in the old style with massive, whole logs chinked with mortar. The roof is covered with hand-split shingles and extends beyond the front wall to shelter a long porch. Sturdy support beams, also made of whole logs, hold up the roof on either side and frame the front steps leading to the porch. There are no carved shutters, no brightly-painted window boxes to give Trail's End the appearance of a Swiss chalet that so many modern cabins copy. Its only ornaments are wildflowers—the pink of wild geranium, yellow arnica and blue lupine—blooming on every side. To the right of the main cabin, a worn path leads through the trees to the guest cabin. This, too, is built of logs, but on a smaller scale, without the large front porch.

Doug pulled up beside the Chisholm's cabin and turned off the ignition. Soft mountain silence settled round us. In my mind, I saw the child Melissa darting out of the car ahead of her two older brothers. The screen door opened and a tall man with thick brown hair and eyes the color of a deep mountain lake, hurried out to receive her into his waiting arms. I could almost feel the softness of his flannel shirt against my cheek and the hardness of his arms wrapping my childish body close to his brawny strength.

My throat tightened and it took a moment for me to realize that Travis had climbed out of the Blazer and was holding the door open for me.

"Wonder where everybody is?" Doug was saying. "Some welcoming committee, huh, Missy?"

I swallowed and managed a thin smile.

With a sudden squeak, the screen door opened and my heart flew up to my throat. But it was only Mildred Chisholm who came forward to greet us.

The passage of years and her new title of grandmother had very little effect on Aunt Milly. A few fine lines in the corners of brown eyes that still sparkled as gaily as a girl's, and a slight sag in the skin around chin and jaw, but that was all. Her hair was still the same glossy, nut-brown; her figure trim and youthful in Levis and a crisp gingham blouse, and her welcoming smile just as eager.

"Missy! Doug! I'm so glad you made it this year! It's been too long since we've seen you! Much too long!"

She gave us each a hard hug then stepped back to stare at me with surprise and pleasure lighting her face.

"Missy Heydon, you're all grown up! I don't know whether

27

to cry or praise the Lord! I never thought I'd see the day when that rascally tomboy would turn into such a beauty! And that's just what you are—beautiful!" She folded me into her arms once more and a few tears sneaked out the corners of my eyes before I could blink them back.

"Oh, Aunt Milly, I've missed you so much!"

We looked at each other and laughed through our tears.

Doug said, "Aunt Milly, I'd like you to meet my friend, Travis Young."

"I'm Missy's friend, too, I hope," Travis said with a melting smile and took Aunt Milly's hand in his. "I hope my coming along won't be too much trouble for you."

"No trouble at all! We're happy to have you! But I can see right now I'm going to have to revamp the sleeping arrangements. I don't think Will and Beth would approve of you three all sleeping in the guest cabin," she said, giving me a broad grin. "Where are your folks? Are they all right?"

"Mom and Dad are fine," I assured her, "but Mark and Julie's baby is taking its time getting here and Mom refuses to leave home until after the baby's born."

"I don't blame her," Milly said. "I'd feel exactly the same. Will they come up later, do you think?"

"They're going to try," Doug told her. "Missy and I came now because I have to be back on the job by the 17th."

"Well, it's just wonderful having you here again," Milly said, giving Doug and me another huge hug. "Just wonderful!" she said again, then turned and gave Travis an equally affectionate embrace. "I hope you have a wonderful time at Trail's End."

"I'm sure I will," Travis answered with a warm glance in my direction.

"Why don't you boys put your things in the guest cabin," Milly instructed. "Then you can hunt up Chuck and Jesse. They're both down at the creek somewhere catching fish. At least, I hope they are," she added with a chuckle, "or we'll be having plain old hash-browns for supper."

"I've never known Jesse to come back empty-handed," Doug said. "Missy, where do you want all your stuff? One week in the mountains and she packs three suitcases!" he groaned.

"But only two are for my clothes! The other case is my camera equipment. There are so many things I want to photograph, I don't know where to begin!"

"Your father told me you were getting to be quite the professional," Aunt Milly said.

"I'm glad Dad's pleased with my work. Since his two sons decided not to follow in his photographic footsteps, I figured it was up to me to carry on the family tradition," I said with a teasing glance at Doug.

"Doug, just set Missy's luggage on the porch for now," Milly told him, then took me by the arm. "Come on inside, dear. The baby just woke up and I want you to see my grandson!"

Even my joints seemed to freeze at her words and I moved like an automaton across the porch and inside.

The big living room was exactly the same as I remembered. Thick, braided rugs warmed the floor. Sofas and chairs were covered with the same worn throws, and there were deep hollows in the cushions, attesting to the comfort to be found there. One wall had three shelves brimming over with books many-times read. A few paintings and photographs of the family were tacked to the other walls, but there were no stuffed or mounted trophies at Trail's End. "My husband can hunt all he likes," Mildred Chisholm was fond of saying, "and I'll be happy to cook the meat. But I will not have some poor animal staring down at me on the walls of my home!"

I followed Jesse's mother through the living room and into an adjacent bedroom. Here, curtains had been drawn and the sunlight filtering across a big iron bed with its patchwork quilt, was dim and muted.

Barbara Chisholm had just finished diapering an energetic infant of some two or three months. Now she picked him up for us to see.

"Missy! Hi! Come see this precious little bundle!"

I glanced around briefly, wondering where Jesse's wife was and realized there was no one else in the room. I fixed a plastic

smile on my face and approached Barbara. The baby was sucking one fist and starting to whimper. I was trying to think of
some appropriate comment when she offered him to me.

"Would you like to hold him?"

She placed the baby in my arms before I could reply and all
I could think was, this is Jesse's son! His son!

I swallowed an uncomfortable lump in my throat and
looked down at the squirming infant. He did have a beautiful
little head, with soft, dark hair curling around his ears and neck.

"David, son of Jesse," I murmured. "Just like in the Bible."

Barbara and Milly were staring at me as if I had just
spoken to them in Hebrew.

The baby began to wail and I quickly gave him back to Barbara, saying, "I'm not very good with babies. I don't think he
likes me."

"Don't be silly, he's just hungry," Barbara said. "Sit down
over there, Missy, and talk to me while I feed him. It's been
years since we had a good talk. You're so grownup I can hardly
believe it, but I bet you get sick of people saying that."

I had moved to a soft, wing-backed chair in the corner of the
room, wishing I could make some excuse to leave. There was a
hard, dull pain in my chest that was beginning to make me feel
slightly sick. When I sat down and looked at Barbara again, she
had unbuttoned her blouse and was placing the infant to her left
breast where he eagerly latched on and began sucking fiercely.

My mouth fell open and a flood of heat and emotion swept
over me.

"Ouch! This little man nurses like a mountain lion
sometimes," she said with a painful smile.

"Barbara—he's *your* baby?" I said stupidly.

"Well, of course, he's my baby!"

I put both hands to my face and felt the fire burning in my
cheeks.

"Missy, dear, did you think this baby was Jesse's?" Aunt
Milly said gently.

I wanted to make some flippant remark about my mistake,
but no words came. There was so much rushing and swirling inside me, I could hardly think.

30

"Missy, are you all right?" Barbara asked with a look of genuine concern.

I drew a shaky breath and stood up, grateful that my legs were still functioning. "Excuse me—I've got to get my things. Please, excuse me," I repeated in a rush and fled the room.

Chapter 4

*"For thou art with me here upon the banks
Of this fair river, thou my dearest Friend . . ."*
William Wordsworth

Conscious thought played no part in my flight from the cabin. I only knew I must be alone. Doug and Travis must have been resting or unpacking inside the guest cabin and for that I was grateful. I couldn't bear to give them explanations for my behavior or the state of my emotions at this moment.

I ran through the warm silence of the forest. Bird call and the drone of insects seemed muffled and dim with my heart pounding so loudly in my ears. I reached the stream and my steps slowed to a restless walk. I wandered along the rocky bank, carelessly trodding on wildflowers I would have zealously protected any other time.

'David, son of Jesse,' I thought with utter humiliation. If only I had opened that wedding announcement two years ago, I wouldn't be feeling like the world's biggest fool right now. And why hadn't I noticed the way Barbara looked? I had never seen her looking so lovely—or maternal. She positively glowed! Barbara had always been a plain, quiet girl. She hated fishing and hiking, and nothing in this world could get her on a horse. During our visits over the years, I remember her either curled up in a corner reading a book or helping Milly in the kitchen. Strange, that I never once considered the possibility of Barbara getting

32

married, but then we were never very close. Probably, because I was always with Jesse and when I was with Jesse, no one else existed . . .

I stopped short as the old pine bridge came into view. I wiped my eyes with the back of one hand and walked slowly toward it.

Nothing had changed and everything had changed since that long ago time when Jesse and I had first met here.

I knelt on the bank and dipped both wrists in the clear, cold water. The icy current brought first a shock of pain, then welcome relief to my heated body. I closed my eyes and let the sting of cold creek water rush over my skin. When my wrists began to ache, I removed them from the water, shook both hands vigorously, and rubbed them against the sides of my Levis. After a deep breath, I lifted my head and met the steady blue gaze of a tall bearded man standing directly across the creek from me. The voice of the river muffled my startled gasp, but he must have seen the sudden, surprised jerk of my body. Still, he made no move, either to cross the bridge or walk away. As we stared at one another, I found myself taking in every detail of his extraordinary appearance, almost in an effort to convince myself that he was actual flesh and blood and not the apparition of some mountain man come back to haunt the streams he had trapped long ago.

Long legs were encased in dark leather breeches with fringe hanging down the outside seams, and a hunting knife dangled from his wide belt. A fawn-colored shirt was rolled up over muscular forearms to the elbow, and open at the throat where a rawhide necklace strung with bear claws circled his neck. He wore a full beard and mustache and thick brown hair brushed against his shirt collar. In one hand he carried a fishing rod, while the other grasped a fat catch of some eight or nine cutthroat trout hanging from a metal chain.

I got to my feet and said with some doubt, "Jesse?"

The firm line of his mouth deepened into a smile and my heart began a heavy, hard pounding as he stepped onto the bridge and crossed to my side of the stream. He rested his pole against a tree trunk and let the fish drop on the bank in a slippery heap.

My chin was a good deal higher now than his belt buckle, but I still had to tilt my head back to look into his eyes. I suddenly realized it might be a good idea if one of us said something and opened my mouth to comment on the fine catch of trout now lying in the dirt and rocks at his feet. Instead, I found myself staring into those blue eyes and saying in a voice that was barely audible, "I like your beard."

Without thinking, I reached up a hand to touch it. The next moment I was lifted up and held tightly in his arms. All the lonely years melted away and I thought my heart would burst with pure joy. It was the most natural thing in the world to wrap my arms around his neck and feel his soft brown beard against my cheek. We clung, wordless, and I waited to hear his traditional welcome: "How's my little Tidbit?"

It didn't come. Instead, he said, "Melissa!" in a voice that was low and unsteady. Then, with his lips against my neck, "Lord, I've missed you!"

Something in his voice and the fact that he had called me by my name for the first time, shocked me into the present. This wasn't the way things used to be at all! I never remembered his chest being so hard against me, his hair so soft in my fingers. Had his heart always pounded this loud, or was it mine? I loosened my hold around his neck and pulled back a little to look into his eyes for help in understanding this flood of new feelings. He refused to meet my glance and I realized with a queer weakness in my mid-section that his eyes were focused solely on my mouth. His head bent closer.

"Hey, Missy! What's the big idea taking off on us?"

My head jerked away from Jesse's and I saw Doug and Travis walking toward us through the trees. They both looked surprisingly angry. Jesse lowered me gently to the ground and I faced my brother's frown with a giddy smile.

"Oh, for heaven's sake, Doug! I'm not ten years old any more. I didn't think a little walk down to the creek would worry anybody."

"When Aunt Milly asked if we'd seen you, she seemed to

34

think you were pretty upset about something," Doug said.

"I'm not upset. I'm just fine."

The steady, cool look in his eyes said quite plainly he didn't believe a word I was saying, but I didn't give him the chance to ask more questions.

"Travis, you haven't met Jesse yet," I said quickly. "Jesse, this is Doug's friend, Travis Young."

Jesse extended a hand of welcome and as blue eyes met brown, Travis said with a definite edge to his voice, "Missy told me you were an *old* friend of hers."

"That's right, I am," Jesse said, a white flash of teeth appearing in his bearded face.

"Travis and Doug went to school together," I explained, for want of something to say, watching the two men's measuring stares.

Then Jesse turned to my brother and gave his shoulder an affectionate shake. "Doug, how've you been, buddy?"

Doug's stiff expression softened somewhat as he returned the gesture. "I'm fine. What the heck have you been doing to yourself? I didn't recognize you for a minute. I thought maybe Jim Bridger was trying to kidnap my sister."

Jesse laughed and I looked at Doug with sudden understanding. I had hardly recognized Jesse myself. He and Travis must have had quite a shock, coming through the forest and seeing me caught up in the arms of a strange, bearded man. It was quite a shock for me, too. My ribs still ached from the pressure of those strong arms, but the sensation was far from unpleasant.

"I got into black powder a couple of years ago," Jesse told us. "I've made my own flintlock and a few other things. Last year, I joined one of the local mountain men organizations. I just got back from a rendezvous up in Montana last week."

"Jesse, you've done all that?" I stared up at him in wonder. "Then the tipi we passed in the meadow—it must be yours!"

He nodded. "I worked on it all last winter."

"Will you show me—us, the inside?"

"Sure, but I'd better get these trout up to the cabin first." He bent down and picked up the string of fish, giving them a quick douse in the stream. I grabbed his fishing rod and we set off together through the forest, with Doug and Travis following behind.

Walking beside him, smelling the sunburned pines, and watching for deer along the trail, I felt as if I had never been away at all . . .

Milly Chisholm was waiting on the front porch when we returned and Jesse held up the trout for his mother's inspection.

"Here's supper! Think these'll be enough for everybody?"

"Plenty! Your father's in the kitchen cleaning his two pitiful little offerings," she said with a laugh. "Oh, Jesse, would you mind sleeping in the guest cabin with the boys? Then we can give Missy your bed."

Jesse's bearded face split into a grin as he took the porch steps in one easy stride. "I'll be more than happy to give Melissa my bed any time she wants it."

"Jesse Chisholm, you get in the house this instant!" Milly said in the shocked tones of a mother who has just heard her small son use a swear word for the first time. She shoved his big body into the cabin ahead of her and I could hear Jesse's low chuckle as they went inside.

I wrapped my arms around my stomach and leaned against one of the log supports holding up the porch. The whirling warmth was back again. Oh, Jesse . . . Jesse, what's happening to me?

I turned around with a quivering little sigh and met Travis Young's hard, angry stare. His jungle eyes looked quite dangerous as they blazed into mine.

"I'll see you at dinner!" he snarled and stalked toward the guest cabin.

I stood staring after him for a moment, then bent down for my suitcases. My brother came forward and said with a politeness I didn't often hear, "I'll take those upstairs for you, Sis."

I held the screen door open for him and asked, "Is Travis angry with me?"

36

"You might say his emotions are running pretty high just now."

I picked up my camera case and followed him inside. "Why? What have I done?"

Doug shot me an unbelieving glance. "How about throwing yourself into Jesse's arms for a start, then totally ignoring Travis and me all the way back to the cabin. You were so wrapped up in Jesse, it was like we didn't even exist!"

"I thought you didn't want me to be friendly with Travis!" I reminded him pointedly. "And what's wrong with being glad to see Jesse? We haven't seen each other for four years! And I didn't throw myself into his arms! He was just—well, he was just giving me a hug!"

"Some hug," Doug snorted as we threaded our way around the couch and over to a far wall where narrow pine steps curled up the rustic logs to a small dormer room.

My brother stomped up the wooden steps ahead of me and I said quietly, "Doug, please don't be angry."

He placed my luggage on the landing then turned back to look at me, standing two steps below him. "I'm not really angry. I guess I'm not used to guys reacting to you like this—first Travis is making the moves on you all the way up here, and now Jesse—! When I saw the two of you together like that, I felt like throwing him clear across the stream!"

I couldn't help laughing. "That would have been something to see! I didn't know you could lift Jesse, let alone throw him."

Doug gave me a grudging smile as I stepped up beside him. "Look, Sis, I know how close you two have always been, but—things can't be the same as they used to be. Jesse's a man and—well, you're a woman now. I may tend to forget sometimes, but I'm only your dumb brother."

He opened the door to Jesse's room and set my cases inside, but I hung back to lean against the thick pine railing.

"I don't see what that has to do with our friendship. I know lots of men and women who are good friends."

Doug groaned. "Sometimes, I don't know whether you're incredibly naive, or just plain dense! But you can't tell me that

37

Jesse's so-called hug was like the one Aunt Milly gave you. Think about it, Sis," he said and left me.

I could think of little else as I entered Jesse's room. I leaned weakly against the open door and knew, if Doug and Travis hadn't interrupted us when they did, that scene by the river would have ended in a kiss. The realization carried a startling assortment of emotions in its wake, not the least of which was a healthy portion of disappointment. My mind produced an instant replay of our meeting, this time delaying Travis' and my brother's entrance by several heart-stopping moments.

My imaginings came to a breathless halt. If Travis had seen me kissing Jesse, it would have complicated matters even more. Especially my tidy little goal of somehow getting him to fall in love with me. It suddenly occurred to me that I should be thinking and thrilling over the possibilities of Travis' kiss—not Jesse's.

I sighed and looked about the small, rustic room under the eaves. At the moment, it was impossible to picture Travis' face, let alone his kiss, when every object and furnishing I saw breathed of Jesse's presence. To my right was a double bed with a plain pine headboard. A heavy patchwork quilt done in earth-tones of raw umber, cinnamon and sand covered the bed, and a warm, fluttering feeling accompanied thoughts of sleeping there tonight. Beside the bed, an old-fashioned oil lantern stood on a small night table of knotty pine. To my left was a medium-sized bureau, also of pine. Cool draughts of pine-scented air and golden shafts of mellow sunlight had free passage into the room through an open window on the outside wall, but a sturdy screen prevented the entrance of flies, mosquitoes, and other pesky insects. Directly below the window, a wooden bench served as a window seat. An exquisite Navajo rug cut a colorful swath across one wall and braided rugs warmed the wooden floor, but other than that, Jesse had let Mother Earth do his interior decorating.

I wandered about, delighting in every object. In one corner I found an unusual piece of wood, gnarled and knotted, with an abandoned bird's nest tucked away in one of its twisted branches. On a small corner shelf, I discovered various rocks and minerals, including the perfect specimen of a trilobite. On the bureau, two six-inch geodes served as bookends for as many books as the width of the dresser would allow. I made quick mental notes of the titles. There were several paperbacks on black powder, three thick geology texts and others dealing with backpacking and outdoor survival skills.

My gaze lifted to a flintlock rifle mounted on the wall above the dresser. I know next to nothing about guns, but even my inexperienced eye could recognize the hours of meticulous labor and skill that had gone into the rifle's making. Hanging on a peg beside it was a carved powder horn. I couldn't resist reaching up to finger the smoothly polished bone and for a moment, I felt as if time had slipped back a century, carrying me with it.

"I'll teach you how to fire the rifle, if you like," said a voice just behind me.

My hand sprang away from the powder horn and I swung around to see Jesse standing in the doorway. I swallowed my surprise and managed a croaky, "Hi."

"Hi."

Framed by rustic pine logs, his broad shoulders literally filled the narrow doorway. The same broad shoulders that had carried me along forest trails when my legs were too tired to walk. Suddenly, that time seemed light years away.

We were both staring again and I could feel the color spreading up my neck.

Jesse stepped inside the small room and asked, "Would you like to?"

I nearly choked. "Like to—?"

"Fire the rifle. It's pretty heavy, but if I hold the barrel, I think you could manage."

"I—oh—the rifle! I'd love to! Does she have much of a kick?"

He grinned at me. "Enough."

I smiled back, trying to remember if his left cheek had always had that crease in it when he smiled. I put a hand on the

39

dresser behind me, feeling in need of some sturdy support, and said, "I feel terrible—kicking you out of your room."

"Hey, don't worry about it. I've been spending most nights outside in the tipi, anyway."

"Oh."

"I just came up to get some of my things out of your way. There's plenty of room in the closet and you can have one of the bureau drawers, if you like. Just help yourself."

"Thanks."

Jesse took a few steps toward me and leaned one hand on the dresser top, just inches away from mine. My senses were instantly alive to his nearness and I felt the strongest urge to be in his arms again. For the first time, I was afraid to meet the clear, penetrating blue of his eyes. My gaze slid down to his throat, where the bear claw necklace rested against a curling mat of dark brown hair. This view was no less disconcerting.

Jesse tipped my chin up with a long finger and asked quietly, "So how've you been?"

It never occurred to me to make some pat, insincere reply. The spontaneous honesty which had marked our relationship from the beginning spurred the only possible answer. I met his gaze and said simply, "Lonely."

Gentle fingers touched my cheek. "Me, too."

Something plunked on the roof above our heads, then rolled down the steep side like a marble. A charge of dynamite going off couldn't have had a more explosive effect on my nerves. I jumped back, banging an elbow into the dresser and said, "What was that?"

Jesse managed a shaky laugh. "That spastic squirrel just dropped another nut, that's all. His nest is in the pine tree right outside the window."

We heard an angry 'chrrr!' then the swift skittering of tiny paws running across the roof. I fled to the window and made a pretense of searching the needled boughs. "Is his nest very high up? I'd love to photograph him."

"You can probably get a better shot from outside," Jesse said and when I turned around he was going through the top dresser drawer, removing several shirts and pairs of socks. I sat down on the wooden bench, wondering if my racing heart would ever slow to its natural rhythm. Doug's words suddenly came back to me and I realized he was right. Jesse was very much a man and I was seeing him as such for the first time in my life.

"Mom and Dad mentioned you're really into photography now," he said. "When did that happen?"

"Oh, a couple of years ago. Dad needed some part-time help at the studio, and before I knew it, the shutterbug had bit me." I smiled and added, "Dad's big thing is portraits, but I love doing landscapes and animals—especially wildlife."

Jesse dumped an armful of clothing on the bed, then crossed to the closet and took out a handsome leather jacket, heavy with fringe, and a sturdy pair of hiking boots.

"I can see it all now," he said. "By tomorrow morning, every moose, deer and elk within five miles of here will be lined up outside the cabin saying 'cheese.'"

I burst out laughing and it felt wonderful to laugh with him again. "You're as bad as Doug. On the way here, he was feeding Travis the old bit about me being 'guardian spirit' of the mountains."

Jesse grinned and I realized I was watching for that crease in his cheek to appear. "Well, aren't you?"

I just smiled and shook my head.

He tossed the leather jacket and a few shirts over one arm so he could have both hands free for the load of clothes on the bed. "I'll get out of your way now so you can unpack. If I've forgotten anything, I may have to bother you again later." As he grabbed hold of his boots, a pair of heavy socks tumbled off the pile of clothing to the floor. I quickly retrieved them and stuffed the socks inside one of his boots.

"I feel like I'm the one who's a bother," I told him.

"Tidbit, you'll never be a bother," Jesse said with a steady look and slow smile. "A disturbance, maybe, but never a bother."

And with that, he left me.

41

Chapter 5

"Red Castle . . . the crown jewel of the range."
Wallace R. Hansen

"**D**inner's ready Missy!"

I heard my brother's voice calling me from below and hurriedly checked my hair and makeup one last time in the small, square mirror nailed to the door of Jesse's room.

In all the years we had been coming to Trail's End, I was usually one of the first, if not the first person to appear at the dinner table. Nine times out of ten, Mom had to send me back to the guest cabin to wash my face or comb my hair—minor details I frequently managed to forget. This particular evening I had taken such pains with my appearance, one would think I was preparing for a grand entrance at the Cotillion Ball. Granted, I was not attired in flowing white, but something made me discard my habitual Levis in favor of a dressy pair of brown cords and a cream-colored top.

"He'll never notice," I told the gray-green eyes in the mirror, then gave myself one more lavish spray of cologne before leaving the room.

I paused on the landing to take in the scene below. Doug and Travis were seated on the couch engaged in conversation with Uncle Chuck. Jesse was sitting in a nearby recliner, gently rocking his nephew—but not in the usual fashion. His right ankle rested on his left knee and Barbara's son was perched in the crook of his long legs, thoroughly enjoying this unique position.

"How's little David?" Jesse said, extending an index finger to the child. "How's my tough kid?"

Little David promptly seized the finger offered to him and Jesse grinned. When he bent forward to offer the baby another finger, little David grabbed a fistful of brown beard instead.

"Hey, no fair, Tiger! Come on—let go!"

Jesse picked his nephew up with both hands to look him in the eye. Little David smiled at his uncle and kept a tight hold on the beard. I was smiling myself as Jesse laid the baby in his lap and used both hands to pry the fierce little fingers loose from his beard. When he raised his head, he saw me standing above him on the landing. The light that suddenly kindled in his eyes filled me with a sweet, singing warmth.

Before I reached the bottom of the stairs, Uncle Charles was on his feet and coming forward to greet me with a smile and open arms. I gave his big shoulders an affectionate squeeze and decided immediately that Jesse's embrace didn't resemble his father's any more than his mother's. There is a strong physical resemblance between the two men, however. Uncle Chuck isn't quite as tall as Jesse's towering six feet four inches, but he has the same broad shoulders and rugged bone structure. His eyes are a lighter blue than Jesse's and recent years have added streaks of gray to the warm brown of his hair. But the mere passage of time will never gray Charles Chisholm's personality. His slow smile positively charms the socks off me, I have never once seen him lose his temper, and I love the way he calls Aunt Milly, "Babe."

Uncle Chuck slid an arm around my waist, lowered his eyebrows and his voice and said, "Hey, good lookin'—you wanna have dinner with me?"

"I'd love to!"

"You other fellers'll just have to find your own dates," he told Travis and Doug. "This young lady's spoken for."

Whenever our two families meet around the big wooden table, surrounded by the strength of log walls and the warmth

43

of an old cast-iron stove, I feel sorry for the rest of the world who have never experienced a dinner of fried trout at Trail's End. I'm not sure whether it's the high altitude, Aunt Milly's big black frying pan, or some mysterious combination of ingredients, but cutthroat trout always taste better at the cabin than anywhere else. Perhaps, in order to achieve that subtle nuance of flavor, fried trout must be eaten on unmatched plates and flatware.

I'm sure Emily Post would have a heart attack if she ever saw a table setting at Trail's End. The plates are a conglomorate of melamine, earthenware, and dime-store china, and seldom, if ever, have I had a matched setting of flatware. Even the glasses have a humble genealogy. They come in all shapes, sizes, and colors, and their origin may go back to some long ago milkman who first delivered them as plastic mugs filled with cottage cheese, or to glass jelly jars with cartoon characters painted on the sides. Instead of fine linen, the table covering is shiny, serviceable oilcloth and our centerpiece, a small vase of wildflowers.

Tonight, in addition to the trout, there was a large Pyrex bowl heaped to the top with hash-brown potatoes and a hefty bottle of catsup nearby for all the catsup freaks in the family, like Uncle Chuck, Jesse and me. Barbara had made a special treat in honor of our coming—golden brown scones, still warm to the touch, with curling trails of moist, fragrant steam seeping out of their tender insides. A small glass jar shaped like a beehive was filled with honey, providing the ambrosia for our heavenly meal.

No one at the table was averse to using his fingers now and then—not even Travis, who was eating like there was no tomorrow. Seeing him enjoy a simple family meal so much made me doubly glad Doug had invited him along. It has been a little more than two years now since Travis' parents were killed in an automobile accident, and I couldn't help wondering if times like this were hard on him, even though Travis himself was the first to admit that he never got along with his mother and father— that they had more of a business relationship than actual family life. This detached situation was especially hard for me to understand because my own family has always been the mainstay, the solid center of my life. Doug and Mark can be merciless teases and Mom and Dad might be overly strict and protective at times, but I love them to pieces and I know they love me.

"Hey, short stuff, are you going to hog the catsup all night or give some to me?" Doug asked in his best brotherly manner.

"Be my guest!" I said and poured a red puddle of catsup in his outstretched hand.

Doug wiped his hand on a napkin while Barbara laughed and said, "You two never change!"

Uncle Chuck added, "I wouldn't say that, exactly. Doug's still as ugly as ever, but I have to keep remindin' myself that this pretty young lady beside him is really the 'little Missy' I used to know."

I smiled at Uncle Chuck and across the table, felt the warmth of Jesse's eyes on my face. Color rushed into my cheeks and I glanced quickly at my plate, hoping he wouldn't notice.

Only one week ago I had imagined this very scene in my mind, as if it were a play. Travis was acting out the part I had given him to perfection. He was polite and attentive—Aunt Milly and Barbara were already willing victims of his charm. But somewhere along the way, there had been a few changes in the plot and cast of characters. Jesse's sister—not his wife—was sitting beside him, and it was becoming increasingly difficult to respond to the warm message in Travis' eyes when a much stronger signal was being sent my way from across the table.

Just now, Uncle Chuck was asking Travis about his recent real estate holdings around Scottsdale, Aunt Milly was trying to persuade Doug to eat just one more fish, and Barbara was juggling the baby in one arm and attempting to maneuver a forkful of fried trout into her mouth with the other. Jesse was buttering a scone and I was deboning the pink flesh of my second trout. All very ordinary, and yet there was some kind of current or force humming and vibrating across the table between Jesse and me. I don't know how else to describe it, but I swear, if it were possible to hook that current up to a power

45

source, Jesse and I could have generated as much energy as the Glen Canyon Dam.

"So how was your drive up here?" Uncle Chuck asked Doug. "Which way did you come?"

"I'd planned on taking the road to China Meadows, but Missy had a fit when she found out about the dam construction going on below Bridger Lake," Doug said. "To protect her tender feelings and for old times sake, we took the Chisholm Trail."

Uncle Chuck gave me one of his slow grins. "Now that sounds like my little Missy."

Jesse said, "Pass the honey, please," and our eyes and fingers met as I handed him the small glass jar. The current between us crackled at this physical contact and I wondered why everyone else at the table couldn't see the sparks or feel a sudden charge in the atmosphere.

I forced my eyes away from Jesse's to speak to Uncle Chuck. "Actually, it's a good thing we did take the Chisholm Trail. We found out from some men behind us, there was an accident on the other road with a logging truck, so we would have been turned back or had to wait hours to get through."

Doug wiped a drop of honey from the corner of his mouth and said with a grin, "One small detail my sister neglected to mention is that we were held up on the Smith's Fork Road for well over an hour by something a little more lively than a few logs—300 head of Herefords, to be exact."

Jesse laughed and leaned back in his chair. "Did you have to follow the cattle all the way up here?"

"I thought we might have to at first," Doug said. "You should've seen the guy herding them. All he had were three lousy girls riding herd and those steers were all over the mountainside."

"How did you get through?" Barbara asked.

I gave my brother a wicked look and said, "Doug's lousy girl-sister walked in front of the car and blazed a trail through the herd, that's how!"

"Missy, you didn't!" Barbara couldn't have looked more

horrified if I had just told her I had walked barefoot through a den of rattlesnakes.

"Doug, you shouldn't have let her do it!" Aunt Milly chided him. "What if Missy had been trampled?"

"If you can tell me how to stop my sister from doing something she wants to do, I'll be glad to listen," Doug said calmly and bit into another scone.

Travis gave me one of his smooth smiles and said, "I like my girls with a lot of spirit," then stretched his arm across the back of my chair.

Jesse cleared his throat. "I take it you have several."

Travis' cool air of confidence slipped visibly. Surprise and discomfort suddenly showed on his handsome face, then anger, like swift venom, darted from his jungle eyes. The next moment he was in total control again and I wondered if I had only imagined that startling display.

"Somebody's got to eat this last little trout," Aunt Milly was saying. "Travis, how about you?"

"No, thanks. I don't know where I'd put it."

"Chuck? Jesse? All right, then, who's ready for dessert?" she asked, getting up from the table.

There were several groans but no refusals, so I pushed back my chair to help her clear away the dinner plates.

"Do you folks want milk or coffee with your cake?"

"Milk's fine for me, Babe," Uncle Chuck answered.

"I'd prefer coffee, if it's not too much trouble," Travis said.

"No trouble at all. Missy, you can pour refills on the milk while I make some coffee."

"I think I'll put little David to bed," Barbara said, snuggling the baby who was now sleeping soundly in her arms. "Save me a big piece of cake," she ordered as Jesse pulled back her chair.

"Have you ever seen such a handsome little cuss?" Uncle Chuck said proudly. "Looks just like his grandfather!"

"He looks exactly like his father!" Barbara whispered over her shoulder.

"Where is your husband?" I asked as she was leaving the table. "I didn't get the chance to ask you before."

47

Barbara smiled and we exchanged glances. "David's on a business trip in Denver for a week. He should be able to join us before you and Doug leave."

"Then little David is named after his father."

She nodded. "David Andrew Lawrence II. It's not quite like David in the Bible, but I like it," she added with a teasing smile and left the room.

As soon as the coffee was perking on the stove, Aunt Milly took a knife and divided the applesauce cake into fat squares. I stood on tiptoe to reach a stack of small dessert plates in the wooden cupboard, then set them down on the counter-top.

"Your young man certainly is handsome," Aunt Milly said in a low voice.

"My who? Oh, you mean Travis? Yes, he is."

She lifted out a generous piece, fat with raisins, and eased it onto a plate. "You don't have to play games with me, Missy. He could hardly keep his eyes off you all through dinner. And I could see the effect he was having on you!"

"You—you could?"

Aunt Milly's brown eyes fairly danced. "I may be a grandmother, but that doesn't mean I can't tell when there's a romance brewing."

I smiled and picked up two plates of cake. "Smells like coffee to me, Aunt Milly."

The current was alive and humming as I set a piece of cake in front of Jesse. He looked up into my face and asked, "Would you like to see the tipi after supper?"

I smiled and nodded, suddenly finding it very difficult to breathe.

"Will that be a private showing," Travis interjected, "or can Doug and I come along, too?"

"Naturally, you're both welcome." The coolness of Jesse's voice was a marked contrast to the flammable expression in his eyes. "I didn't realize you were interested in tipis."

"Anything that interests Missy, interests me."

I blushed furiously and nearly dumped Travis' cake in his lap in my confusion, then hurried back to the counter for the rest of the cake, leaving explosive silence behind me.

48

Doug rescued the situation by asking Jesse, "How did you get interested in tipis? I can't see where they would have anything to do with black powder or mountain men."

"There were several mountain men and early explorers who lived in tipis," Jesse said. "Buffalo Bill, Jim Bridger, and Kit Carson, to name a few. Some of them got so spoiled by the comforts of a tipi, they refused to live in anything else. Kit Carson was one of those," he added with a smile. "When John Fremont asked Kit to join his first expedition, he refused to go unless a tipi was taken along. The only problem was, Kit didn't know how to pitch a tipi by himself. You see, his Indian wives had always taken care of that little chore. Luckily for him—and the expedition—a trader happened along with his Indian wife and she taught Kit how to do it."

"Which just goes to show—if you need to know how to get something done—ask a woman!" Aunt Milly pronounced, pouring coffee for Travis and Doug.

"I have to admit, they are kind of nice to have around," Uncle Chuck said, giving his wife's bottom a fond pat as she passed by his chair.

I brought my own piece of cake to the table and sat down. "Well, I don't think it's fair."

"What isn't fair?" Jesse asked me.

"That there were never any women along on those expeditions. Why should men always be the ones to have all the fun?"

"I don't know whether I'd call those early expeditions *fun* or not," Jesse said dryly. "Especially when the men were attacked by Indians and grizzlies, or their supplies ran out."

"I know there were dangers involved, but you can't deny what a thrill and adventure it must have been—opening up the West!"

Jesse's glance was warm. "No, I certainly won't deny that."

"Well, I for one, can live without that kind of adventure," Barbara announced, coming back into the kitchen and taking her place beside Jesse. "Give me a nice soft bed, indoor plumbing and a big piece of applesauce-raisin cake—that's all the adventure I need!"

49

"Amen to that!" Doug said, taking a bite of cake that was far too large to be considered polite.

"I think the mountains are great for an occasional getaway," Travis added, "but I'll never understand why a man would turn his back on civilization to live in the wilderness. Those mountain men must have been a bunch of real misfits."

Jesse ignored the implied insult, but something inside me refused to let the barbed comment go by.

"I wouldn't call someone a misfit who wanted to see what was over the next ridge, or discover the source of a stream," I said, feeling a pulse of emotion hammering in my throat.

"I can relate to the thrill of exploration and discovery," Travis conceded, "but after you've seen what's over that ridge and found the source of that stream—why stay?"

"Maybe those men felt that life in the mountains had more to offer than life in a city," Jesse suggested quietly. "Maybe they wanted peace and solitude more than noise and profits. Or maybe they just didn't like the confinement of streets and houses. I think some men's souls need more elbow room than others."

"What you're saying is, those mountain men couldn't take the pressures of city life, so they ran away from it all," Travis said with a cutting edge to his voice.

"I don't think they were *running away* from anything!" I blurted out. "They were *running to* something! Scottsdale has been my home for twenty years, but I still feel the pull of these mountains whenever I'm away from them. It's almost like the Uintas are calling me—" I broke off, catching Barbara's expression of amused tolerance. I could almost hear her saying 'Poor Missy. She's always been a little strange.'

"Did you bring some good hiking boots with you?"

I glanced up at Jesse's casual question and saw a light like blue fire, burning in his eyes.

"Of course."

"Are you in good condition for a long hike?" he asked next.

I sat up a little straighter as a strange tingle of excitement played about my spine.

50

"I've been jogging at least ten miles a week for months now."

Jesse laid his fork on his empty plate and said, "How would you like to go on a backpacking trip up to Red Castle Lake for a few days?"

"Like to? *Like to!* Oh, Jesse—!"

I wanted to run around the table and hug him, but I couldn't do that in front of everyone else, especially Travis. Oh, why couldn't I be ten years old again—just long enough to fling myself into his arms? Instead, I had to settle for a smile.

"How about you two?" Jesse asked Travis and Doug. "Do you think you could bear to part with some of your creature comforts for a while?"

"How's the fishing up there?" Doug asked speculatively.

"There's good stream fishing almost all the way up the trail and Red Castle is one of the few lakes in the Uintas where you can catch Arctic grayling."

Doug's eyes grew brighter. "Grayling! I'd walk fifteen miles if I thought I could land one of those beauties!"

"Add one more mile and you might get your wish," Jesse said with a chuckle. "Red Castle is about sixteen miles from the Trailhead."

Travis coughed on a mouthful of cake. "Sixteen miles?"

Jesse nodded. "But that's only to the lower lake. There are actually three Red Castle lakes, arranged in stair-step fashion from the highest to the lowest. We can fish all three if you're game."

I breathed an excited sigh. "It sounds incredible! Can I take my cameras along?"

He stiffened slightly at my words, as if a small spasm of pain had just gone through his body. Then he grinned and said lightly, "Sure, why not. I was thinking of taking my horse to carry most of the food and supplies, anyway."

I leaned back against my chair with another rapturous sigh. "This is all too wonderful! I'm so excited, I know I'll never be able to sleep tonight. When do we leave? Tomorrow?"

Jesse laughed. "No way, Tidbit. It'll take a full day to plan the food and pack our gear. You can't take off into the Primitive

51

Area without a lot of careful planning. Besides, you need a day to rest from the drive here. How about if we leave first thing Tuesday morning—day after tomorrow?''

"I guess I can stand the wait somehow," I told him with a smile. "Aunt Milly, you better put me to work tomorrow, scrubbing floors or something to pass the time."

I turned to look at her and noticed for the first time how pale she was, how subdued. I don't think she even heard my lighthearted comment.

"You're sure about what you're doing, son," she said.

Jesse answered her worried expression with a smile. "Very sure."

"That's beautiful country up there," Uncle Chuck said. "I can't think of a better place to go."

A look passed between father and son that I couldn't begin to interpret.

"There are lots of other lakes and places to see that aren't as far as Red Castle," Barbara ventured timidly.

One look from Jesse silenced her. He shoved back his chair and said with a determination that was almost grim, "It's all settled. We're going to Red Castle." Then he left the room.

I watched him go and turned back to the assortment of silent faces around the table. Travis set his fork on his plate and the tiny clang might as well have been an explosion for the effect it produced on Barbara. She jumped up from her chair with eyes suspiciously bright, and took her dishes to the sink. Aunt Milly was sending a silent message to Uncle Chuck from the opposite end of the table.

I caught her eye and asked, "Why don't you want us to go to Red Castle?"

Milly's hasty smile failed to smother the worry in her brown eyes. More than worry. If it didn't sound so ridiclous, I would almost say she looked frightened.

"It's not that I don't want you to go—it's just—"

"Milly was never one for tramping fifteen miles into the mountains," Uncle Chuck explained. "Or Barbara either, for that matter. But that's no reason why the rest of you shouldn't go and enjoy yourselves. Travis, you look like you could use

52

another piece of cake. There's one left on the plate that's just your size."

Travis eyed the lone piece of applesauce cake. "Are you sure? I thought that piece had Doug's name on it."

"I'll flip you for it," my brother said and produced a coin from his pocket.

My question and the necessity of providing an answer to it had just been skillfully juggled out of the way—which made me more curious than ever! I couldn't begin to understand what had changed the casual atmosphere at the table into a moment strung with tension, but I did know it had something to do with Red Castle. If Uncle Chuck and Aunt Milly didn't want to tell me what it was, I knew someone who would!

Travis won the coin toss and accepted the last piece of cake while I excused myself from the table.

"I'll be back to help with the dishes in a few minutes, Aunt Milly. My legs are so stiff from sitting in the car the past two days, I think I'll jog down the road a ways."

Travis half-turned to say something to me, but I was out the back door and gone before he had the chance.

Chapter 6

"Never again leave me to be the peaceful
child I was before . . ."
Walt Whitman

The sun had just dropped
behind the western slopes and although the sky was still a clear
blue, the forest was already wrapped in shadow. Lodgepole
pines loomed in dark silence on either side of the wine-colored
road as I ran by. I had in mind to jog as far as the guard station,
then detour across the meadow and visit the tipi on my way
back. I knew just as surely as the mountain breeze was cool
against my face, that Jesse would be there waiting for me.

I hadn't gone far when I heard a voice some distance behind
me, calling my name. I didn't turn around or slacken my pace
until the voice became louder and more insistent. Then I
realized he was gaining on me and broke my stride to a swift
walk.

"Missy, wait up, will you?"

I stopped so suddenly Travis nearly ran right into me. He
grabbed my shoulders and turned me about to face him. "What
were you going to do—run all the way back to Scottsdale?" He
was breathing hard, but he still managed a melting smile.

"No, I was just going to the guard station and back."

"Really? Somehow, I thought you'd be heading straight for
that damned tipi."

"Travis!"

"Sorry."

The apology was strictly an amenity and we both knew it. I tilted my head back to look into his eyes and said, "You don't like Jesse very much, do you?"

Travis took a steadying breath and let it out slowly. "Not very much, no."

"Why not?"

"Maybe because you like him so much."

"What? Travis, you're not making sense. What does my liking Jesse have to do with you?"

"This," he said and pulled me into his arms.

I have never been kissed so thoroughly in my entire life.

"Travis—"

"I've been wanting to do that all day!" he said fiercely.

"You—you have?"

He smiled suddenly and I saw flashes of amber and green in his jungle eyes. "You don't even realize the effect you have on me, do you?"

"Well, I—it's not something I spend a lot of time thinking about."

He laughed and cupped my face in both his hands. "You're wonderful, Missy! And so beautiful . . . maybe it's the magic of your mountains, but I feel like I'm seeing you for the first time."

His mouth came down to meet mine again and I wondered suddenly what I should do with my hands. They felt so awkward and heavy, just hanging on the ends of my arms. And there was this curious void inside me—an emptiness that I somehow imagined his kiss should fill.

What a stupid thing to be thinking about! Travis Young was kissing me and I was worrying about my hands!

He released me then and asked in a husky voice, "Are you still mad at me?"

I smiled and shook my head.

"That's good!" He slipped an arm around my waist and we began walking slowly up the road toward the cabin.

If I had lain awake every night for a month, I couldn't have imagined a more romantic setting. The sky was blushing with the sunset's rosy afterglow. In the soft light, the green of every leaf and bough became at once more fragile and more intense than anything seen by light of day. Off the road to our left, Jesse's tipi was looming ghostly white on the edge of the meadow. I remembered his promise to show it to me, but as much as I wanted to see the inside, I was even more reluctant to witness further friction between him and Travis.

Then, a scant five yards up the road, two young does emerged from the forest and stood watching us with wide, curious eyes. The next moment their supple brown bodies darted away into the velvety dusk. I sighed and looked up at Travis' handsome profile. This couldn't be happening to me—the girl whose love life was as scintillating and exciting as a first-grade primer. His tawny head leaned down to meet mine and his kiss assured me once again that this moment in time was not a dream, but real and tangible as the arms that held me.

As we came out of our embrace, I was only half aware of movement below us in the meadow. I looked over Travis' broad shoulder and saw Jesse and my brother standing frozen, like the deer, watching us. Hot shame and guilt washed over me and I broke away from his arms.

"Do you want to see the tipi now?" Travis asked, reaching for my hand.

Suddenly, the dream was a nightmare. I couldn't face Jesse. Not now!

"I promised Aunt Milly I'd help her with the dishes," I said in a rush. "But you go ahead if you want to." I started to run.

Travis caught up with me and grabbed my arm. "Hey, girl, don't you ever walk? What's the matter?"

I wouldn't meet his eyes, so he pulled me close against his chest. "You're shaking like a leaf. Are you upset because Doug and Jesse saw us? Is that it?"

I tried to pull away but he held me closer.

"I'm glad they saw us," Travis whispered against my hair. "I want you close to me, Missy."

"Travis, please! I'd like to go back to the cabin. I'm cold."

With a shrug, he released me and we walked in silence the rest of the way. When we entered the back door, Milly Chisholm had both hands in hot, soapy dishwater and Barbara was drying the dishes in the drainer.

"I'm sorry, Aunt Milly. I promised to help."

Milly looked at my flushed face and Travis close behind me, and her brown eyes sparkled. "I've got plenty of help. There's no need for you to do dishes your first night here. Charles has made a nice fire in the fireplace. Why don't you two go in and get warm."

"Sounds great to me," Travis said and with a possessive arm about my waist, he steered me out of the kitchen and into the living room.

Uncle Chuck looked up from Tolstoy's *War and Peace* and gestured to the empty sofa with a smile.

I sat down and Travis sprawled close beside me, stretching his long legs toward the brightly burning logs. "Mmmm, this sure feels good," he murmured as an arm went around my shoulders.

I swallowed and told myself silently, This is what you wanted, Missy Heydon. You've been drooling over Travis Young for months. Now what on earth are you going to do with him?

Travis took one of my hands and raised my fingers to his lips. I straightened up with a nervous little smile and saw that Uncle Chuck was feigning great interest in his book, even though he hadn't turned a single page since we had come in.

"Relax," Travis whispered in my ear. "I'm not going to bite you—yet!" he added with a low laugh and nuzzled my earlobe.

At this precise moment the front door opened and my brother charged into the room. Pride and sheer stubbornness forced me to remain still. After Doug's brotherly lecture this afternoon, I wasn't about to let him know I couldn't handle the situation!

"Oh, hi, Doug! There's plenty of room here on the couch, if you want to join us."

"I can see that!" he growled. "Travis, we still haven't un-packed all our gear from the Blazer. Could you give me a hand?"

"Hey man, can't it wait 'til morning? What's the rush?"

Doug's jaw was one tight line. "We'll have enough to do

tomorrow. Besides, Jesse says it'll probably rain before morning. We've got to unload it now."

"You go ahead," I told Travis brightly. "I'm tired and I still have some unpacking to do myself. I think I'll make it an early night."

Travis relented with a sigh. "Your timing stinks," he said to my brother, then turned to me with bent head and lowered eyelids. I looked down quickly so his kiss only brushed my forehead. "I'll see you in the morning," he whispered and got to his feet.

Before leaving, Doug gave me a tight-lipped look and said, "I can see why you're so tired! You've had yourself a busy little day!" then slammed the front door.

I sank back into the couch cushions, too upset, too bewildered to think. I watched the colors and rhythms of the fire like one in a trance—the brilliant blending of yellows, gold and orange flames danced before my eyes, accompanied by the percussive snap and crackle of dry pine logs. When Uncle Chuck thumped his book shut, I started visibly.

"I don't know as I'll ever finish that book," he said, "even if it is supposed to be a classic. The story's too depressing. I've never been able to figure out why sad stories win all the prizes. I think it'd be real nice if somebody got an award for cheerin' people up instead of adding to their misery."

He got to his feet and stood in front of the big stone fireplace, rubbing his hands together. "Mind if I sit by you for a spell?"

My throat was too tight for me to answer, but I shook my head and he lowered his big frame onto the cushions beside me. We watched the fire in silence for a minute or two, then he said, "I don't know as it'll help much, but if you'd care to talk about what's troublin' you, I'm one heck of a listener. If there's one thing I've learned after bein' married to Milly for thirty-two years, it's how to listen!"

I gave him a little smile and tried to swallow the constrictive tightness in my throat. Looking into the shuddering flames I said quietly, "Uncle Chuck, I think there's something wrong with me—really wrong!"

58

"Now what makes you say a thing like that?"

"Be—because of what happened tonight. It should have been wonderful, but it wasn't. It was awful.!"

"Am I right in thinkin' all this has somethin' to do with our friend Travis?"

I nodded. "For months, I've been hoping he'd notice me—that he'd think of me as more than just Doug's little sister—and now that he has, I don't know what to do! I thought I knew how I felt and what I wanted, but when he kissed me I—I felt so empty inside. I couldn't even think of what to do with my hands!"

"I can see where that might be a bit of a problem," Uncle Chuck said with a smile in his voice. "I always had trouble in the other direction with our Aunt Milly. What not to do with my hands!" he admitted with a chuckle. We smiled at each other and he said gently, "I don't see why that means there's something wrong with you. Maybe Travis isn't the right one."

"You don't understand—it's always like this! I meet someone and as long as things are casual, I'm just fine. But if he starts getting serious or—or physical, I freeze! There's this awful emptiness inside me and I don't feel anything. It scares me!"

His big hand closed about my shoulder. "Honey, there isn't a thing wrong with you that falling in love won't cure. Believe me!"

"But I thought I was—I mean, I thought it would be different with Travis! Maybe it would be if I didn't feel so guilty . . ."

"Guilty? About a kiss?"

The fire hissed and sparks flared as some resin was licked by the flames. I took a breath and whispered miserably, "Jesse saw us! I looked up and there he was."

There was a pause. Then Uncle Chuck said, "Did Jesse say anything to you?"

"No. I didn't give him the chance. When I saw him I broke away from Travis and ran back to the cabin."

There was another long silence, broken only by the soft hiss of a log falling into the flames.

59

"Jesse's pretty special to you, isn't he?"

Under his father's probing glance, I felt the heat of the fire suddenly burning in my cheeks. I looked down at my hands which were carefully smoothing out wrinkles in the sofa's worn throw.

"Jesse's a very special person," I murmured.

Uncle Charles didn't comment on my evasive answer. He just waited with a gentle, patient smile. Finally, I leaned back against his shoulder and asked in a tight voice, "Why does everything have to change?"

"What do you want to stay the same?"

I took a ragged breath and blurted out, "Jesse and me! Everything used to be so—simple between us. Now, whenever he looks at me I can hardly breathe, and this afternoon—when he held me . . ."

"Jesse held you?" his father said very slowly.

"Mmmmm. When we met by the stream. At first, I thought everything would be just the same between us, but then—well, it wasn't anything like the hugs he used to give me."

"I can imagine," Uncle Chuck commented, struggling to keep back a smile and not succeeding. "Maybe I shouldn't ask this, but I can't help wonderin.' Did Jesse kiss you?"

I answered him in a low voice. "No—but I think he would have if Doug and Travis hadn't come looking for me right then."

Uncle Chuck cleared his throat. "Well, this sort of sheds a new light on things." He saw the color staining my cheeks and asked gently, "Are you really so sure you want things to be like they were?"

"I—I don't know. Everything's happened so fast. Right now, I'm not sure about anything!"

Uncle Chuck smiled and patted my hand. "Don't get too up-tight about all this, honey. These things have a way of straightening themselves out. And something tells me you're not the only one who's feelin' some strain!"

"Who's feeling some strain?" Aunt Milly asked, coming in-to the room with Barbara at her heels.

Uncle Chuck answered her with a twitching mouth. "Did I

say strain? I meant rain. It sure feels like rain. We'll probably get some before morning."

Milly Chisholm stared at her husband, a puzzled frown creasing her forehead.

I got up from the couch and gave her a quick kiss on the cheek. "Goodnight, Aunt Milly. You have a wonderful husband, did you know that?"

"I should! He tells me often enough! You're not going to bed already? Where's Travis?"

"He and Doug are unloading the Blazer. It's been a long day," I said with a sigh. "I feel like going to bed early."

"Me, too!" Barbara added emphatically. "Little David isn't sleeping through the night yet and two a.m. comes all too soon for me!" She gave her parents a hug and kiss, then turned to me. "It's wonderful having you here again, Missy! See you in the morning!"

I said my goodnights to all of them and climbed the shadowy steps curving up to Jesse's room.

I had forgotten to close the window when I came down for dinner and as I entered the room, mountain air was pouring in as cold and sweet as water from a spring. I drew a heady lungful and crossed to the window. Through a gap in the pines, I could see the tipi glowing like a huge Chinese lantern against the black night sky. I pulled the window shut with a little shiver, and tried to shut out thoughts of Jesse Chisholm as well.

I didn't bother lighting the oil lamp, but reached for my flashlight instead. One of my suitcases was still lying open on the bed and I rummaged through it for the flannel pajamas I had sewn especially for the trip. Warm nightwear is a difficult item to find in Scottsdale at any time of year, but during July, flannel is strictly an extinct commodity. I considered myself fortunate to find a few yards of lightweight flannel in one of the smaller fabric shops, even though the floral print was somewhat juvenile. I closed the suitcase with a puzzled frown. Where were they? I went to the closet and dragged my second suitcase into the room. A quick check of the contents produced a rising sense of frustration, but no pajamas. Painstakingly, I went through both suitcases again. The pajamas simply were not there. But

61

they had to be! I distinctly remembered seeing them on my bed along with the rest of my clothes as I packed. I had remarked to Mom at the time that they were too large and she suggested I wash the pajamas and put them in the dryer. The dryer! I snapped the locks on both pieces of luggage and returned them to the closet. My flannel pajamas were sitting in the dryer right now, a mere 780 miles away!

It was a standing joke in our family that at least one of us would be stricken with the dreaded "curse of forgetfulness" during the packing for Trail's End. The year Doug left his new Mitchell reel behind was a real corker. Then there was the time Mom packed warm jackets for everyone but herself. But pajamas?

I sat down on Jesse's bed, flashlight in hand. I knew very well I could go downstairs and borrow something of Barbara's or Milly's, but then everyone would find out and I would be the brunt of Doug's jokes for the next two weeks. There were times when I got so sick and tired of being the little sister!

That settled it! I was not going back downstairs. Sleeping in my clothes was one solution to the problem, but a very uncomfortable one. Of course, there was another alternative but if someone happened to come up early tomorrow morning and saw me—horrors! Getting teased about forgetting my pajamas would be a picnic compared to what would happen if anyone found out I had slept nude in Jesse's bed! The very thought of it did disastrous things to my nervous system. I stood up, shivering from emotion as much as the cold, and my gaze focused on the shadowy outline of the pine bureau. Maybe Jesse had something I could wear.

I went to the bureau and directed the flashlight's beam on the contents of the bottom drawer. Long Johns were warm, but not exactly what I had in mind. I grinned and dug deeper. Near the bottom, I found a pair of thick flannel pajamas, soft and worn from many washings. As I picked up the top, something else caught my eye. The corner of a snapshot was peeping out from a small cardboard box. I put down the pajamas to focus the small beam of light on the smiling faces of a tall young man and a freckle-faced girl of nine or ten. Her thin arms were wrapped around his neck in a strangle-hold and he was carrying her in piggy-back fashion.

As I stared at the snapshot, my mind went back to our meeting this afternoon by the river. The rough, bearded face against mine bore little resemblance to the smiling, clean-shaven young man in the photograph. And today, those strong arms had held the soft contours of a woman's body, not the angular shape of a child. With a sigh, I returned the snapshot to its cardboard box. The Jesse and Melissa in the picture belonged to the past, and as sweet as memories might be, they were only that. Memories.

I closed the drawer and with Jesse's flannel top pressed firmly to my breast, went to the window once more. Outside, the Uinta night was black and starless. The only light at all was the glow of Jesse's campfire inside the smooth walls of his tipi.

I undressed in the dark, dropping my clothes on the wooden bench, then wrapped myself in the huge softness of the flannel pajama top. The sheets were icy smooth against my bare legs as I climbed into bed, and I immediately curled into a ball trying to get warm. Turning my cheek against the softness of Jesse's pillow, I wondered for the first time if my desires could ever again be satisfied by a childish embrace.

Sleep was a long time coming.

Chapter 7

"There are things of which I may not speak . . ."
Henry W. Longfellow

The sound of rain woke me in the early hours before dawn. I opened my eyes to soft gray darkness and listened to the steady drumming on the roof above my head, and the wet cadence of the wind in the pines outside my window. Then I burrowed deeper into the bedcovers and slept again.

Sometime between the early morning rain and the sun's rising, a dream came. Hovering on the hazy edges of sleep as I was, none of the dream's details were really clear to me—except a man's voice speaking my name. The warmth of that voice was so vivid, so real! For a moment he was there, reaching out, as close as a caress, then gone.

The shrill chatter of a squirrel brought me fully awake. Jesse's treetop neighbor was giving someone or something a first-rate scolding. I stretched lazily and turned on my side, unwilling to relinquish the warm bed for a hard cold floor.

A boom like a cannon shook the window and brought me bolt upright in bed. What in the name of heaven? I jumped out of bed and dashed across the icy floor to the window. Kneeling on the wooden bench, I peered out the glass but could see no signs of disturbance anywhere. I unlatched the window and pulled it open. A river of fragrance poured into the room —

mountain air, newly-washed, wet pine needles and sharp resin, moist spongy earth—all these and more. I spied the gray fluff of the squirrel's tail whisking through the branches of the pine tree where droplets of rain still clung to needled boughs like crystal tears. Above me, the sky was the color of alpine forget-me-nots, and on the edge of the meadow, the tipi caught the full, smiling face of the sun.

A second boom startled the mountain stillness and the squirrel's scolding turned into screams of protest. I heard hearty male shouts coming from the meadow and realized exactly what those explosions of sound had been. Jesse's flintlock. I should have known Doug wouldn't waste any time getting his hands on that rifle. I might as well forget about photographing any wildlife today. Every animal within ten miles of the cabin was probably long gone by now.

I remembered Jesse's offer to teach me how to fire the rifle and sighed. Ordinarily, I would have been dressed and outside in two minutes flat, but this morning I wasn't sure if I could find the courage to go downstairs—let alone face Jesse and Travis. I let out another sigh, this one of pure frustration and went to the closet for my suitcases.

I pulled on a pair of thick, warm stockings before discarding Jesse's pajama top for my sweatshirt and Levis, then laced up my hiking boots. I probably wouldn't be doing much hiking today, but it wouldn't hurt to break them in a bit before tomorrow.

After making the bed, I grabbed my makeup bag and toothbrush and turned to go. My glance caught Jesse's flannel top lying on the wooden bench in a crumpled heap. Nothing like leaving the evidence in plain sight! I quickly folded the top and returned it to the bottom drawer of the bureau. There! Now no one would ever know. I pushed the drawer shut with a satisfied little smile and straightened up.

The first things to meet my gaze were the empty hooks on the wall above the dresser where Jesse's flintlock and powder horn had hung. I blinked. Then swallowed. Another boom sounded outside and a warm flush shot through me from my toes to my fingertips. I remembered the voice in my dream, the almost tangible feel of a man's presence. Had it been only a dream? I moved toward the door in a daze.

I felt more in control of my thoughts and emotions after a brisk wash in cold water. I gave my hair a vigorous brushing, applied a little makeup and headed down the narrow hall toward the kitchen. I never intended to eavesdrop, but the sound of Jesse's name linked with my own stopped me in my tracks. I pressed a hand against the log wall and stood perfectly still.

"I always assumed Missy knew what happened," Barbara was saying.

"Apparently not, and Jesse said not to tell her," Milly Chisholm replied.

"Not tell her—?"

"That's what he said."

"Sometimes, I don't understand Jesse at all. Why would he want to go back there after—after what happened? I still can't think about it without—"

"He must have a good reason," Milly said and I heard it again, the same thread of fear tightening her voice that had been present last night at dinner. "Your father insists Jesse knows what he's doing." She uttered a sigh and the worried prayer, "Dear Lord, I hope he's right."

"Of course, he's right," Barbara said in an obvious attempt to cheer her mother. "After all, Jesse is thirty-one years old."

"Thirty-one," Milly said with another sigh. "He should be married with children of his own—not wandering around the mountains and living in a tipi. It's not normal!"

"Now Mom, don't start—"

"And that beard!" Aunt Milly went on. "Why he should want to cover up that handsome face with a beard is beyond me!"

I smiled and decided now was as good a time as any to make my entrance, even though my curiosity was at a peak. What was it Jesse didn't want them to tell me?

I called a loud, "Good morning!" from the hall before entering the kitchen and noticed how quickly both women replaced their worried expressions with a smile.

Milly Chisholm was heating water in a big kettle and Barbara was laying out thick bath towels on the table's oil cloth surface. Beside the towels were clean diapers and baby clothes, an infant-sized blue plastic bathtub and an impressive assortment of items: vaseline, baby lotion, powder, alcohol, cotton swabs and soap.

"You're just in time to see little David have his bath!" Barbara said. Her eagerness and tone of voice implied that I was about to witness one of the greatest events of the century, and I couldn't help smiling.

"Where is the star performer?"

She laughed. "Outside, taking a walk with his grandpa."

"My goodness, he really is a precocious child," I said. "Walking at three months!"

Milly poured hot water from the kettle into the bathtub and asked, "What would you like for breakfast, Missy? The boys wolfed down all the bacon but I can fry you an egg and make fresh coffee."

"I'm not very hungry. I'll just get myself some juice and cold cereal, if that's all right."

Aunt Milly sighed as she looked at me. "It seems like just yesterday when you were always hungry! I can't get over how you've changed!"

"You never change, Aunt Milly. It's hard to believe you're a grandmother." I poured some corn flakes into a bowl then helped myself to the carton of milk in the small ice box. The spoons and sugar bowl were in the same place they had occupied for the past twelve years. In many ways, the kitchen at Trail's End was more homey and familiar than the one in my own home. Mom is forever redecorating and moving things around. I don't object to a change now and then, but there is something oddly reassuring about looking for small items and finding them in the exact place you thought they would be.

I sat down at the far end of the table, away from the baby powder and cotton swabs. In between mouthfuls of cereal, I filled Milly and Barbara in on the latest doings with our family. As I finished drinking my orange juice, Barbara asked with a speculative gleam in her eyes, "When are you going to tell us about Travis? You haven't said one thing about him!"

I made an effort to keep a straight face. "Well, let's see. He drives a black Porche, he's filthy rich, and he and Doug were on the swim team at Arizona State before they graduated."

"Not that!" Barbara groaned. "You know what I want to know! How long have you two been going together?"

I laughed and said, "We're not going together! We've never even dated. He's Doug's friend."

"I think Travis has other things in mind besides friendship as far as you're concerned," Milly said with raised eyebrows and Barbara gushed, "I may be a married woman, but honestly, Missy, he is the most gorgeous man I've ever laid eyes on!"

"Every eligible female in Scottsdale has the same opinion," I told her. "I can't imagine what he sees in me."

"Missy, you don't give yourself enough credit," Aunt Milly said as I took my empty bowl to the sink. "Why, even Jesse was saying what a lovely young woman you've become."

My spoon went clattering into the sink, but I managed to save the cereal bowl. I set it on the counter with deliberate care and asked, "What do you mean—*even* Jesse?"

"I think Mom's afraid Jesse's been in the mountains for so long, he's forgotten what the opposite sex looks like," Barbara confided with a laugh. "We've all just about given up hope of his ever getting married again."

I had been staring at a homemade plaque above the sink as if it were a treasured work of art. Now I offered lightly, "Maybe, he just hasn't met the right one yet."

"What about you?" Barbara said and I spun around at her words.

"Me?"

"Do you think Travis is the right one for you?" she asked.

"Oh! Well, I—we really don't know each other very well."

Barbara gave me a smooth smile "There's nothing like a backpacking trip to *really* get to know someone."

The back door opened then and Uncle Chuck entered with a blanketed bundle in his arms.

"Mornin', everybody!"

He gave Aunt Milly a hearty kiss on the lips then passed the baby to Barbara who peeled away the coverings to smile at her bright-eyed son.

"Did Muvver's coot widdow man wike him's walk wif Gampaw?"

I groaned and pulled a face. "Yuck! Whatever happened to Barbara Chisholm—the English major who was always correcting my grammar?"

"I don't know," her father said with a laugh, "but Barbara's been this way ever since he was born. I don't know how the poor little guy's ever going to learn to speak English."

"Never mind what old Gampaw says," Barbara crooned and began undressing the baby for his bath. "Oo dest wuves to hear Muvver talk, doesn't oo?"

I gave Uncle Chuck a pained look and said, "If this gets much worse, I may get sick!"

Milly shoved us both out of the kitchen. "You two go on then. Go on! But just you wait, Missy Heydon! Someday you'll be a mother and I daresay you'll make Barbara's baby talk sound like the King's English!"

Uncle Chuck put an arm around my shoulders as we entered the living room and confided with a grin, "You know, we may like to tease Barbara, but there are times when I'm holdin' that little guy that I start talkin' pretty foolish myself!"

"My folks will probably be just as bad when Mark and Julie's baby finally gets here," I said.

I sat down on the couch and picked up a magazine, idly thumbing through its pages while Uncle Chuck went to the front windows and opened the curtains. Mountain sunshine gladly entered in, filling the room with its golden light.

Uncle Chuck put both hands in his pants pockets and looked out the window. "Milly was telling me last night that Barbara and the baby sort of took you by surprise."

My heart did a somersault but I continued to riffle the magazine's pages. "By surprise?"

He nodded and gave me a close look. "Maybe it's none of my business, but I can't help bein' curious why you thought little Davey was Jesse's baby."

69

I clutched the magazine a little tighter and said with a nervous laugh, "Oh that! It was just a silly mistake."

Uncle Chuck left the window and sat down beside me. I met his penetrating blue eyes and launched into what I hoped would be a convincing explanation.

"You see, I thought Jesse was married. That is, I kind of assumed he was because of what Mom and Aunt Milly said about him and—Sheila." I had to stop myself from adding 'What's-Her-Face.'

"Sheila?" he said musingly.

"You know. That girl from the Northwest. The one he went to visit instead of being here at Trail's End when I—" I broke off as his sandy brows went up a notch. "Anyway, Aunt Milly said he was serious about her."

"Oh, that Sheila," he said with a grin and I knew he had been aware exactly who I was talking about the entire time. "You sure have a good memory. I'd practically forgotten about her. How long ago was that—two years?"

"Three."

"Mmmm. That summer was the last time you came to the cabin, if I remember right. You were how old—seventeen?"

I gave a brief nod and looked down at the magazine in my hands. Three years, and the pain of that summer was still as fresh as yesterday in my mind.

"We all thought Jesse might get married again," Uncle Chuck said, "but when he got back from Portland, he told us it was all over between them. Jesse didn't say too much—just that he knew he couldn't marry her—but I kind of got the idea he was the one who broke things off, and not Sheila."

"He broke things off?" I repeated slowly.

"That's right. Milly was real heartsick about it, but then Barbara met her David and we had a wedding after all. I'm sure we sent you and your folks announcements. It seems strange you didn't know."

"Well, I was away. I was in Tucson with some friends when the announcement came and I—"

He looked at me with those calm blue eyes and I knew I couldn't lie to him. I'm a rotten liar anyway, and with Uncle

70

Chuck it's impossible to tell anything but the truth, the whole truth, so help me. I blew out a shaky breath and confessed, "I threw it away."

"The wedding announcement?"

"Yes. I didn't even open the envelope, or I would have known it was Barbara's and not Jesse's. Like I said before, it was just a silly mistake."

"I don't think it's silly at all," Jesse's father said with his slow smile. "I think it's real interesting!"

The clomp of heavy boots sounded on the wooden porch outside and the front door opened.

"Well, well! Look who decided to get out of bed!" my brother said. "Hope our target practice didn't disturb your beauty sleep."

"I was already awake," I informed him, matching his sarcastic tone with one of my own.

Travis followed Doug into the room and I noticed at a glance the macho male image he presented in tight Levis, down-filled vest and a plaid shirt of deep blues and greens. He flashed me one of his melting smiles and said, "Morning, beautiful!"

My return greeting died halfway as I saw Jesse standing behind him in the doorway, flintlock in hand. Wearing the deeply-fringed leather jacket with the powder horn strung over one shoulder, he had the look of one belonging to another century. Our glances met and held.

"Hey, Jess, when are you going to get those maps so we can see where we're going tomorrow?" Doug asked.

"What?"

"The maps," Doug repeated.

"Oh! I'll bring them down as soon as I put my rifle away," Jesse answered, moving past Travis with his long stride.

I watched him take the stairs to his room as Travis planted himself on the vacant cushion to my right.

"Hey, girl, I'm sure looking forward to tomorrow!" he said meaningfully.

"Hmmm? What did you say?"

"You and Jesse must have the same hearing problem,"

Doug grinned, straddling a nearby chair and wrapping his arms around the back.

"Whatever's wrong with Jesse's ears must be affecting his eyes, too," his father said with a laugh. "I've seen him peel off a pine cone at 100 yards and trim the tail feathers of a magpie flyin' by, but this mornin' he couldn't hit the broad side of a barn!"

I remained silent, feeling a strange fluttering inside, while Doug's laughter joined Uncle Chuck's. "Well, whatever's bothering him, I hope the problem clears up by tomorrow," my brother said, "'cause I'd sure hate to get lost on the trail."

"I keep hoping the fishing up there is worth the hike," Travis said.

"The hike itself is worth it," Uncle Chuck told him. "I'd be goin' with you if it weren't for this damned bursitis in my knees. They stiffen up real bad if I walk too far. You'll have to take lots of pictures for me, Missy, so I can see it all again when you get back."

"I didn't know you'd ever been to Red Castle," I said, remembering Barbara's and Milly's conversation this morning.

"Oh, sure, but not for years now. The last time I was up there, there weren't any fancy trails and bridges the way there are now. In those days, we followed the game trails and river drainages into the mountains. The Primitive Area really lived up to its name back then."

"It's still pretty rugged," Jesse said, coming down the stairs with the maps under his arm. "Once you leave the trails and head across country, the land is just as primitive as it was a hundred years ago."

He pulled a card table away from the wall near the stairs, moved it in front of the sofa, then took a chair for himself.

"What kind of maps are these?" Doug asked, holding the top of one map while Jesse unrolled the other.

"Geological survey maps. They show the exact terrain and elevations of the country, besides identifying trails and lakes. We need the Bridger Lake and Mount Powell quadrangles in order to see all the area we'll be covering to get to Red Castle." Jesse fitted the two maps together and pointed to a patchy

72

island of white amid an undulating sea of green. "Here's the guard station, and Trail's End is just above it—about here. The small, broken lines you see are pack trails. There are two possible routes we can take to Red Castle. One is just south of us and follows the West Fork of the Smith's Fork for several miles. Then it climbs straight up this ridge, cuts across and switchbacks down to the East Fork of the Smith's Fork."

I followed Jesse's lean brown finger as it traced the route and wondered vaguely how I could have known him for so many years without noticing what wonderful hands he had. The backs were incredibly long, with tough, corded veins traveling a tanned path to the curve of his wrist. I shook myself mentally as Travis said with a frown, "I can follow the trail, O.K., but what's with all this 'fork' business?"

"Most of the trails on the north slope follow the streams or drainages," Jesse explained. "Henry's Fork, Black's Fork and Smith's Fork are the main ones, with smaller tributaries branching off like the tines of a fork. That's why you have the Left, Middle and Right Forks of Black's Fork and so on." Jesse's voice was polite and friendly, and about as warm as yesterday's oatmeal. His eyes moved from Travis' face to the maps without once meeting mine. Looking at him, I felt a sick ache begin inside.

"Not too many people are aware of the fact," he went on, "but I think it's kind of interesting that these streams were named after the mountain men who hunted and trapped along them—Andrew Henry, Jedediah Smith, and Arthur Black. In fact, the first rendezvous ever held by the mountain men took place just a few miles from here, where the Henry's Fork meets the Green River."

"Hey, I never knew that before," Doug said in surprise, "and we've been coming up here for years."

"I didn't know myself until I got into black powder and started doing some reading about the area. Nearly every trail has a history—"

"Speaking of trails—" Travis cleared his throat and said in a bored voice, "I thought you were going to show us another route to Red Castle."

73

"Sorry. I get a little carried away, sometimes," Jesse answered coolly, and I felt an almost uncontrollable urge to give Travis a sharp jab with my elbow. "The second route begins at the Trailhead just above China Meadows," Jesse continued, referring to the map once again. "This is the main trail into the area and it follows the East Fork of the Smith's Fork all the way up to the lake. It's a few miles longer, but it isn't nearly as steep. I was thinking we could take the main trail in, then cut across to the West Fork trail on our way out. The packs would be lighter then and it's downhill all the way once we get up the switchback."

"You're the mountain man," Doug said. "You pick the trails and we'll follow. Where will we camp once we get there?"

"There are plenty of good camp sites along the west side of Lower Red Castle Lake."

"How long does it take to get to this lower lake?" Travis asked. "From where I'm sitting, that trail looks pretty long."

"Oh, anywhere from 5½ to 6 hours, depending upon the pace we set. My horse'll be carrying the tents and sleeping bags, plus part of the food, so our packs'll be fairly light. We ought to make good time."

"Whatever you do, don't let Jesse run you to death," his father warned. "My son has a tendency to turn a backpacking trip into an endurance test," he told Travis. "Once he starts headin' into these mountains, there's no stoppin' him! In fact, he's been known to set a pace that would kill a pack mule!"

Doug laughed and I looked at Jesse whose cheeks had turned a ruddy shade above his beard. So far this morning, he hadn't said one word to me. Not one word. I stared at his rugged features as Uncle Chuck went on with a wink in my direction, "And I don't want any of you fellers walkin' so fast you leave Missy behind. Trail or no trail, you could get lost or into trouble if you get separated."

"If that's the case, we'd better give Missy a whistle or tie her to the horse," Doug said. "I've never known anyone with such a lousy sense of direction!"

I was feeling too miserable to attempt one of my usual comebacks, and after several dragging seconds of silence, Jesse said to no one in particular, "Having a good sense of direction isn't nearly as important as being observant and knowing something about the country. The most important thing to remember is, all the streams on the north slope run north out of the mountains. If you follow them and keep walking long enough, you're bound to find your way out."

"I don't know why I'm the only one getting all these special instructions," I said crossly. "I certainly don't plan on getting lost."

Travis put an arm around my shoulders and said, "You just stay close to me, girl, and you'll be fine."

Jesse's mouth hardened and I quickly sat forward, away from Travis' encircling arm. "What do these little squares on the map mean?" I asked, determined to get Jesse to talk to me.

"They're cabins or structures of some kind. Some are pretty much in ruins and others are still in good shape, like the ones above Trail's End," Jesse said and our eyes met above the map. Bittersweet memories came floating back and for a moment, the others in the room simply faded away.

Then Travis asked, "How old are these cabins? Do you think they could date back to the time of the mountain men?"

Jesse blinked and looked at him. "I suppose it's possible. There are old cabins all through these mountains and a lot of them aren't on the maps. I remember one time I was bow hunting somewhere past the Guard Station on the East Fork of Black's Fork. I was just wandering around when all of a sudden I was in a cabin complex. There must have been, say, fifteen to twenty cabins there, plus a big stable and corral areas. No roads went into the place and there weren't any sawdust piles that I could see."

"Was it as large a complex as those cabins on the road by Black's Fork?" Doug asked him.

"Pretty near. It's one of the biggest complexes I've seen. The roof was still on the stable and one of the cabins. I found a few whiskey bottles and there were a lot of old artifacts and rusty metal objects lying around."

"Do you think they could have been built by mountain men?" I asked and Jesse answered me with a shake of his head.

75

"Those cabins are old, but not that old. I found out from some folks in Robertson that they were built by Swedish tie-jackers."

"Tie-jackers?" Travis questioned with a frown.

"Immigrants who worked for the railroad," Jesse explained. "They came to the north slope in the 1850's to cut timber for the railroad. Well, I'd better stop talking and get busy. I've got a lot to do before tomorrow morning."

"Hey, just give me some orders and I'll be glad to help," Doug said.

"Thanks, buddy. You and Dad can get out the tents and sleeping bags while I hunt up the pack frame. Oh, and you better get the rain gear while you're at it."

"How many tents are you planning on taking?" Chuck asked.

"Just the two backpacking tents. Doug and Melissa can sleep in one and Travis and I can share the other."

I sneaked a little sideways glance at Travis and fought back a smile. He didn't look at all thrilled about such a cozy arrangement.

"What do you want me to do?" I asked him.

Jesse gave all his attention to rolling up the maps and answered briefly, "I'll need your help most with the food, but I've still got to finish working out the menus. If there's something you wanted to do this morning for an hour or two—go for a hike, take pictures, whatever—go ahead."

I stared at his bent head and added silently: Fall in the creek, jump off a cliff, whatever—go ahead. Aloud, I said, "I've always wanted to photograph the old cabins above Trail's End."

"Now would be a good time to do it then," Jesse said. "There'll probably be more storms moving in this afternoon." He shoved his chair back from the card table and motioned to Doug. "Let's get going, buddy."

Uncle Chuck looked at my face and coughed. "I guess I better be huntin' up that rain gear."

Travis stood up and stretched his arms above his head with catlike grace. "If there's more rain coming, I think I'll go down

76

to the creek for a little fishing. I'll see you guys later," he said and sauntered out of the cabin.

I was left with a highly volatile mixture of emotions. Anger, hurt, and confusion seethed inside me as I stomped up the stairs to Jesse's room for my camera equipment. Why was I so upset? I had the rest of the morning to visit old haunts and indulge myself in the beauty of my mountains. I should be perfectly happy and content. I grabbed my camera case, tossed in an extra roll of film and slammed the door behind me.

Chapter 8

"On a hill there grows a flower . . ."
Nicholas Breton

The narrow road which leads to the Chisholm's cabins continues south through the forest for approximately one mile before dividing itself into two smaller paths. The right fork becomes a jeep trail which winds its way westward into the depths of the lodgepole forest, while the left fork narrows into a pack trail which cuts through a circular meadow, hops across the stream and continues east, up a steep, forested ridge.

I stood at the junction of the two trails, staring at the left fork where it disappeared into the trees. Three days from now this would be our return route from Red Castle. I felt a little shiver of excitement, wondering what sort of happenings would fill the interim between tomorrow morning's departure and our journey's end. But for now, my course lay straight ahead through the meadow, toward a group of tumbledown cabins on the forest's edge.

My mood and thoughts were much calmer now. A brisk mile walk through sunlit forest and meadow can do wonders for one's disposition. In fact, it is totally impossible to mope or remain angry when the sun is shining on wet meadow grass and fat robins are chortling in the pines, singing songs that city robins will never know. Spikes of woolly yarrow and sunny yellow salsify grew on every side and I was especially careful not to step on the snowy mounds of low-growing phlox. These delicate, white flowers have been a particular favorite of mine ever since Jesse first pointed them out to me and explained that a single, fist-sized clump may be more than a century old.

Like the snowy phlox, the log cabins had occupied this quiet meadow for well over a hundred years. Heavy winter snows had caused the collapse of two of the buildings, but one was still standing, squat and sturdy, with the roof intact. The support beams were as big around as I was and a good foot or so taller.

I was only ten years old the first time Jesse brought me here, and my impressions of the place were scarcely those of appreciation and wonder. There was something so abandoned, so forlorn about the cabins, that I felt uneasy even going near them. Jesse had smiled at my timid steps and fear-filled eyes and taken my hand firmly in his.

"This cabin is like an old man whose family is gone," he told me. "If it seems frightening, it's only because this place is so lonely."

We came often after that, to "keep the old cabin company"—to bring laughter and human voices to the tired log walls that had heard only birdcall and the lonely cry of the wind for so long. And very soon, I wasn't afraid any more. I grew to love and understand the special solitude to be found there at the forest's edge. Sometimes, Jesse and I would bring a picnic lunch. Other times, we came only to talk, sharing ideas, thoughts, and feelings that now seem almost too personal to be put into words.

A shrill little chirring surprised the silence and my eyes found a chipmunk scooting up the cabin walls like a tawny-striped missile. I approached him slowly, unfastening my leather case and easing the camera out of its pouch. The chipmunk checked its flight to note my approach. I smiled at his puffy cheeks which were stretched and stuffed with pine nuts, and got the first shot.

There must have been a bit of ham in the little fellow as well as an assortment of nuts, because he posed like a trooper before scurrying into his nest between the roof and stuccoed logs. After that, I wandered around the area, intent on capturing the mood of the old cabins. The clear morning light and shadows were ideal and I blithely went through a roll of 35mm film.

I was sitting on a fallen log, reloading, when I heard a loud crunching of underbrush and twigs in the trees behind me. I know it's idiotic, but my very first thought was that it must be a bear. Every bone and muscle in my body froze, with the exception of my heart, which was banging away like crazy inside my rib cage. I turned my head slowly, almost painfully, and saw Travis Young emerge from the forest, fishing rod in hand.

I slumped on the log and said, "Good grief, I thought you were a bear!"

Travis grinned and shook an insect away from his blond head. "Don't tell me the 'guardian spirit of the forest' is afraid of bears?"

"I try not to let it get around—with my reputation and all—but they scare me to death! What are you doing here?"

"I wasn't having any luck fishing. As your brother is so fond of saying, all I was doing was drowning worms. I thought it would be a lot more fun watching you. Have I ever told you what a great model I am?"

He set his pole against the log and struck a few Charles Atlas-type poses. I burst out laughing. "Hold that pose! I've got to finish reloading my camera."

Travis put one booted foot on the log and watched me with undisguised interest. "How about some back-to-nature shots? I look great in the raw!"

I raised my eyebrows, hoping he wouldn't notice that my hands were trembling. "I'm sure you do, but unless you want to provide lunch for a few thousand mosquitoes, I suggest you keep your clothes on."

"Mmmmm. You may have a point there."

"I don't, but mosquitoes definitely do!" I said with a laugh and stood up, camera in hand.

I soon discovered Travis was not entirely joking when he said he was a great model. His body lines were pure Olympian and his facial bone structure was a photographer's dream. He posed wherever and however I suggested for a good half hour, then stretched out full-length on the warm grass and called for a break.

"When do I get to take a picture of you?" he asked, picking a long blade of grass and chewing the stem.

"I'm not very photogenic. You don't want a picture of me," I said, sitting down beside him.

"Oh, yes I do! That's a very small payment for my work the past half hour. I usually charge a lot more!"

I swallowed nervously. "I'm sure you do."

Travis raised himself on one elbow and smiled at me. "One picture, O.K., Missy?"

I nodded and handed him the camera. "Where do you want me?"

Travis set my $400 Canon carelessly aside, then his arms reached out for me. "I want you right here," he said.

My senses were startled by his warm mouth and the sudden weight of his body as he eased me back onto the grass. His kiss was deep and searching and for several surprised seconds, I didn't think at all. Then, as the surprise wore off, I had the most curious sensation of being slightly apart from it all. Love in the meadow, sunshine and wildflowers, all the ingredients were there, but I didn't feel the least bit carried away by emotion. If I were, it didn't seem quite logical that I should be so conscious of other things—like the horsefly that just buzzed by Travis' left ear, and the sharp-edged rock that was poking against the small of my back.

There had to be more than this! Frustrated and angry with my own inability to respond, I wrapped my arms around Travis' tightly-muscled back and tried to match the ardor of his kiss. This action had no noticeable effect on my own emotions but produced an immediate response from him. Suddenly, one of his hands was shoving my sweatshirt out of his way and warm, sure fingers were moving up the bare skin of my midriff.

His touch acted like an electric shock on my system and I reached down a frantic hand to stop him. My strength was a poor match against his. I felt smothered by the weight of his body and realized with a sense of pure panic that my struggles were only exciting him further. When his mouth left mine to seek and find the sensitive cord on the side of my neck, I wrenched my head away with a frightened gasp.

Travis' breath was hot against my skin and his voice slurred as he whispered, "Don't be afraid to want me, Missy. It's time you learned how to be a woman."

Through a blinding haze of fear I saw my fingers clutching a handful of grass and the torn stems of some small blue wildflowers. In the brief second that I stared at the flowers, the memory of a long ago afternoon stirred in my mind. Suddenly, it was Jesse's hand I saw, not mine, as he ripped up a handful of fragile blue flax. I could almost hear his voice. The next moment my own voice was crying out, "Travis, stop! Let me go! Let me go!"

The punishing weight lifted and I sat up, trembling all over. I pulled my sweatshirt down, then put my head on my knees, not wanting to look at him.

"There's nothing to be frightened of, Missy. I know you've never had a man before. I don't mind."

He reached out to draw me close again and I recoiled from his touch. "No! I—I can't! I won't!"

Travis stared at me and his jungle eyes were still glazed with passion. His voice was soft and purring, like that of a big cat. "I want you, Missy! And I know you're attracted to me. You can't deny that!"

I took a deep, shuddering breath and choked out the words. "Attracted, yes, but—that doesn't give us the right to—to—"

"To make love?" Travis supplied in a husky voice. "I think you're even afraid to say the words."

"I'm not afraid! At least, not in the way you think I am. Travis, we don't love each other. And even if we did—it's still not right."

"Not right? Missy, we can have something beautiful together. I know we can. Don't spoil it now. There's nothing wrong with me showing you how I feel."

"Yes there is! You're not my husband!"

If I had dumped a bucket of ice cold creek water on his head, I doubt whether it would have had a more dampening effect on his emotions. Travis stared at me for a long moment, then his mouth tightened and he got to his feet.

"I thought you were mature enough for a meaningful *adult* relationship. I can see now I was wrong."

"Adult relationship!" I choked. "My parents have had a 'meaningful adult relationship' for twenty-eight years, but somehow, I don't think that's the kind of relationship you're talking about!" I reached for my camera and struggled to stand.

Travis grabbed my arm and the blaze in his eyes said I had pushed him too far. "Look, little girl! Don't start playing the outraged virgin with me! I never mentioned marriage and you know it! I'm not about to promise something I can't deliver!"

I wanted to laugh, but it came out sounding more like a sob. "That's for sure! You just want to play around—picking flowers!"

Travis stared at me as if I had totally lost my mind. "Picking flowers? What the hell are you talking about?"

"Forget it! You wouldn't understand, anyway!" I shook my arm free from his grasp and staggered past him to gather the rest of my equipment into the leather case.

Travis leaned down for his fishing rod and only the whiteness of his knuckles gripping the pole, gave any indication of his true emotions. His voice was as cool and controlled as ever.

"I'll walk you back to the cabin now."

"No, thanks. I can find my own way back."

"Missy, will you stop acting so damned childish!"

I struggled with my anger as I looked into his eyes. "All right, Travis. I'll try very hard not to be childish if you'll do me just one little favor."

"What's that?"

"Go drown some more worms and leave me alone!"

Reaction was setting in. I was shaking from the inside out as I stumbled along the forest path back to the cabin. Every

83

time I thought about what had happened back there in the meadow, I felt sick—and angry! With myself, far more than Travis. Doug had tried to warn me but I wouldn't listen. What a starry-eyed little innocent I was, believing that Travis might be falling in love with me when the word "love" wasn't even in his vocabulary! And why should it be, when a "meaningful relationship" could handle his physical needs very nicely? Well, it wouldn't satisfy mine. Not now. Not ever! I should have realized what he was after from the beginning, but his flattery and attentions had given my ego a much-needed boost. I forced myself to face the painful truth. I could never love Travis. Heavens, I didn't even like him very much when it came right down to facts. Maybe, I just needed to be in love with someone—anyone—in an attempt to fill the lonely, aching hole inside me that had hurt for so long.

I became aware of a sharp pain between my shoulder blades and stopped to catch my breath and ease the strap of my camera case. It was then I noticed how still the forest had become. Looking up I saw gray clouds rolling in from the west. Thunder grumbled in the distance and a mournful chorus of sighs swept through the pines. I glanced around, trying to determine how far I had come and how much farther I had to go before reaching Trail's End. Doug was right on one more count. My sense of direction was lousy. Probably, if I didn't have the road to follow, I'd be good and lost by now. I picked up my pace, knowing there was a good chance of getting wet very soon.

The rain began with no more than a whisper of sound. One moment the forest was huddled in silence and the next, the clouds had released their burden of moisture. Luckily for me, it wasn't a downpour and there was very little wind. My camera and film were well protected by the waterproof case and somehow, I didn't mind getting wet. I lifted my face to the droplets of water, letting the cool, clean rain wash away the remaining traces of an ugly experience. A little rush of wind sent a cascade of fragrance my way. Vivid paintbrush, starry columbines and lavender-blue lupines growing beside the road were pearled with raindrops and almost unbearably lovely in their delicate, wild way. I bent to pick a stalk of lupine and smiled as the memory returned once more. Only this time, I had more than just a glimpse of that long ago afternoon. I walked on through the rain and lived it all again—the hilltop, the rolling vistas of blue-green sage and Jesse.

We had driven into Mountain View for some food and supplies and on the return trip to the cabin, Jesse stopped the truck so we could climb to the top of a hill and see a view.

I was fourteen—still short and undeveloped, but with all the confusing new urges and emotions of early puberty. And there was something bothering me. Something I couldn't discuss with my mother, who had explained the facts of life to me in the same way she explained everything else—with platitudes and time-worn adages that couldn't begin to help me adjust to so much uncomfortable new knowledge.

As I stood with Jesse, staring out over the endless line of mountains, hills and windy plateaus, I wondered if I dared tell him about *it*. There had never been a time in all the summers of our friendship that he hadn't been willing to listen, but as I looked up at his face—the intense blue of his eyes and the thick brown hair blowing in the wind, I felt more afraid than ever.

Jesse found two rocks that were fairly flat and we each took one to sit on. Then, after a gentle smile and a "Tell me all about it, Tidbit," he simply waited for me to begin.

It was hard. Harder than anything we'd ever talked about before, but somehow I managed to tell him about my friends and the kids at school. A lot of them thought there was nothing wrong with "going all the way." Others said it was wrong unless you really loved someone, then it was all right. One of my girlfriends had been stealing some of her mother's birth control pills, but she got pregnant anyway. The boy wouldn't marry her so she had an abortion. It all made me feel slightly sick and I began to wish sex had never been invented. Why did it have to be so ugly?

Jesse listened to my jumbled outpouring without comment. Even after I finished on a gulping sob, he remained silent for a long moment. His lean cheeks were tinged a shade darker than his tan and he seemed intent on dislodging a rock with his boot. He made several attempts to speak and abandoned them all. I suddenly realized I had embarrassed him and the thought brought more tears to my eyes.

Jesse gave me his handkerchief and said unceremoniously, "Blow your nose, Tidbit." While I did so, he leaned over and fingered the delicate petals of a wildflower growing in the dry, rocky soil of the hilltop. The five petals were sky blue and saucer-shaped, with a tiny gold heart at the center.

Jesse looked into my tear-reddened eyes, and his were as blue as the flower growing near our feet. "Do you remember the name of this wildflower?" he asked.

I sniffed and said, "It's wild flax."

"And I've told you never to pick the wild flax. Why?"

I stared at him and answered promptly, "Because it's so fragile. The petals fall off when you handle it, then it wilts and dies."

He smiled and nodded. "That's right." Then he reached down and yanked up the plant by its stem. Several petals fell off immediately. My eyes flew to Jesse's face in surprise, but he was looking intently at the bruised flower. "A wildflower has no choice whether it will get picked or not," he said. "If someone comes along and sees how beautiful it is and wants it, he'll pick it—like I just did. Then the petals fall off and the flower dies."

Jesse dropped the blue flax and looked at me once more. "You know, Tidbit, you're a lot like this flower. You're soft and beautiful, and someday someone's going to come along and want you very much. When that happens, try to remember— you're not a wildflower. You have a choice. It's up to you whether you get picked or not."

The hilltop faded away and a few salty tears mingled with the raindrops on my cheeks as I realized what a far-reaching effect Jesse Chisholm had had on my life. We were together barely two weeks out of each year, and yet, in many ways he was always with me—blending his presence into my thoughts, molding and shaping the decisions of my life. No other person in the world had such free passage into the feelings of my soul.

Down the road, a tall figure was walking steadily toward me through the rain. My steps slowed, then stopped altogether as we faced each other.

Jesse was bareheaded and droplets of rain glistened in his beard and the thick brown waves of his hair. Although he hadn't been hurrying, his voice was oddly breathless as he said, "I was worried about you."

"I'm sorry. I wasn't keeping track of the time," I answered, sounding breathless myself.

"You're soaked through," he added gruffly, but his fingers were gentle as they lifted a clinging tendril of wet hair away from my forehead.

I think I would have been happy to stand there forever, just staring at him until we both died of pneumonia, if Jesse hadn't smiled and taken my camera case in one hand. With the other, he opened his fringed jacket and wrapped me close inside.

"Let's go home," he said.

The soft voice of the rain whispered around us as we walked in warm, companionable silence. With my arm around his waist and the solid strength of his body so close to mine, I found myself wishing that Trail's End were at least another five miles down the road. All too soon the cabin came into view and Jesse was opening the back door. The aroma of Aunt Milly's homemade soup sent a mouthwatering greeting even before we stepped inside. The big wooden table was set for lunch, but just now the kitchen was empty.

Jesse put my camera case on a chair beside the door, then placed both hands on my shoulders. Looking down at me, he said in a curiously strained voice, "You'd better get out of those wet things."

"I suppose so."

Then, instead of releasing me, the pressure of his hands increased and he slowly drew me closer. I succumbed to his nearness with a sigh and laid my head against his chest. His arms came around my back and tightened. My eyes closed. This was heaven! This was home!

A voice from the kitchen doorway said, "Well! I see you two managed to find each other!"

My head lifted and I saw Jesse's mother staring at us open-mouthed. Her expression was positively thunderstruck. I'm not sure whose cheeks were the rosiest just then, mine or Milly Chisholm's!

Before his mother could comment further, Jesse released me and said once more, "You'd better change out of those wet clothes, Tidbit. Hurry back!" he added with a thread of longing that sent me flying up the stairs to his room.

Chapter 9

"Here rests his head upon the lap of earth
A youth, to fortune and to fame unknown . . ."
Thomas Gray

Strange as it may seem, as I stood in Jesse's room frowning at my bedraggled reflection, my thoughts were not on the offensive episode in the meadow. Nor did I spend any time berating myself for being a näive little fool, which I obviously had been. Rather, the thought came to me that not once in twelve years had Jesse Chisholm seen me in a dress.

I flopped down on his bed and began drying my rain-dampened hair with a towel. There wasn't a thing I could do to remedy the dress situation, but I certainly wasn't going back downstairs wearing a sloppy sweatshirt! I put the towel aside and hunted through the clothes I had brought for something—anything!—that was more feminine, and found a blouse of unbleached muslin. It was peasant style and really too thin to be practical for a trip in the mountains with its drawstring neckline, short sleeves and vari-colored smocking across the bodice. But it was definitely feminine!

By the time I came downstairs, most of the family were already sitting at the table. One look at Barbara's face was enough to tell me that Aunt Milly had already filled her in on the details of a certain incident. We exchanged self-conscious smiles as Doug offered a polite chuckle to the dry punchline of one of Uncle Charles' even drier jokes. When Jesse's father saw me, his interested, "Well, well!" turned my brother's head around. Doug took in my appearance with a frown while Uncle Chuck made the smiling comment, "You must have to beat 'em off with a stick back home."

"Huh?"

"In order to keep all the guys away from your little sister," Uncle Chuck said. "You must keep a good-sized stick handy."

"Oh yeah," Doug mumbled, giving me a suspicious glance. "Too bad I left it at home."

I smiled at Uncle Chuck, completely ignored my brother and turned to Aunt Milly. "I'm sorry if I kept you waiting. Is there anything I can do to help?"

"Not a thing, dear. The biscuits are just about ready to come out of the oven and the soup's on. Besides, I wouldn't want you to spill anything on *that blouse*. It really is lovely," she added, giving me an awkward little smile. "And you didn't keep us waiting. Jesse's not here yet."

"Jesse's here now," said a warm male voice behind me.

All he did was smile and take my arm. All I did was smile and sort of float over to the table. But suddenly, I felt like the two of us had become stars of a new T.V. game show, with the announcer bellowing out: "O.K., everybody! Let's all watch Jesse and Melissa!"

Just because he had changed into a clean flannel shirt that was as deep a blue as his eyes was no reason for everyone to stare at us. And what's so unusual about brushing your hair and putting on a little after shave? It did look like Jesse's beard had been newly-trimmed, but I could be wrong about that. He must have been in a hurry though, because several buttons on his shirt were still unfastened.

The fact that I felt like a dish of butter melting in the sun is totally irrelevant. That sort of thing doesn't show on the outside.

Jesse pulled a kitchen chair out for me and the wooden legs shuddered across the floor in the pregnant silence of the room. I felt like asking Barbara and Doug if they needed something to prop their chins up, but of course, I didn't. Someone had to act normal!

I looked up to smile a simple 'thank you' as Jesse bent over my chair and saw that his shirt had fallen open, revealing a broad expanse of hair-roughened chest. Any attempt to keep things light and casual were promptly abandoned. My emotions, at that moment, bordered on the primitive.

Jesse took the chair next to mine and asked, "Did you get some good pictures of the old cabins?" His voice was casual, but the pulse beating urgently at the base of his throat gave strong indication that he was just as affected by my presence as I was his.

"Yes, I did! The light was wonderful this morning and I got the most wonderful shots of the cabin! And there was this little chipmunk! He was so—"

"Wonderful?" my brother suggested helpfully, and Barbara started to giggle.

Barbara never giggles. Her laugh is as quiet and ladylike as the rest of her. The closest she has come to anything that even remotely resembles a giggle might be a "twitter." But Barbara was definitely giggling now. There is no other word.

"Barbara, those biscuits are ready to take out of the oven now," Milly said, bringing a big tureen of steaming soup to the table. Then, passing by Jesse's chair, she ordered in a fierce whisper: "Button your shirt!"

I love Aunt Milly almost as much as my own mother, but right then I felt like giving her a good swift kick. Thirty-one years old and she says, "Button your shirt!" What was worse, Milly knew very well I had heard her whispered comment and so did Jesse. I wasn't sure about Doug, but his sudden fit of coughing seemed rather suspicious.

Dad has long insisted that I inherited a walloping portion of the "old Nick" from my grandfather Heydon. He must be right because without stopping to think at all, I leaned close to Jesse, put my hand on his knee and whispered just as fiercely, "Don't do it!"

We didn't look at one another, but I felt his smile, and under the table, one of Jesse's hands moved to cover mine.

91

Barbara returned with the biscuits and Aunt Milly took her place at the end of the table, observing her son's open shirt with silent disapproval.

Uncle Chuck bowed his head to offer a blessing on the food and under the table, Jesse's hand tightened around mine.

I had completely forgotten about Travis until Aunt Milly asked Doug if she should save some lunch for him.

"Don't bother," Doug replied. "Travis just got back from fishing and he's really in a foul mood."

"If he's not feeling well, maybe I should take a hot bowl of soup over to the guest cabin for him," Milly said.

"I think all Travis wants right now is to dry out and take a nap," Doug told her. "He had rotten luck fishing and then got caught in the rain coming back."

I blew on a spoonful of soup and said, "That's too bad about the fishing. Maybe the fish had trouble swallowing his line." Doug gave me a questioning glance and I added sweetly, "Or maybe they just didn't like what he was offering."

Our eyes met in full understanding and my brother sighed in obvious relief. "Fish are a lot smarter than most people think," he said with a warm smile. Then, reaching for a biscuit, he added, almost as an afterthought, "You ought to wear that blouse more often, Sis. You look real nice."

After lunch, I packed my clothes and personal items, religiously following the list Jesse had provided. My pack was embarrassingly light, but Jesse refused to let me carry anything in the way of food and equipment, other than my own trail snacks and emergency rations.

"Your shoulders are too small to be bent down by a 30-lb. pack," he told me firmly, and for once, I didn't complain about my size.

As far as photographic equipment was concerned, I had decided to take only my 35mm Canon, plus a telephoto lens and automatic flash. The camera I would carry around my neck in its waterproof case; the rest would hang in individual pouches attached to my belt. This way, I could be ready in a moment for any photographic opportunity that happened along.

The remainder of the afternoon was spent preparing and

packing the food. I had no idea what an exacting, time-consuming process this could be. Each and every item needed to be carefully measured per individual meal requirements and then repackaged from its original container into lightweight, but sturdy plastic bags. Jesse handled most of the complicated tasks and put me in charge of the "gorp"—a ghastly name for gorgeous-tasting trail food. Every pack was to contain ample portions of granola mixed with honey, nuts and raisins. In addition to the granola, Milly provided dried fruit, a few candy bars and a chewy concoction called apricot leather. Jesse also insisted that each pack hold a good-sized ration of beef jerky and pemmican. Jerky is fine, but I looked at the greasy, fat-covered balls of pemmican and shuddered.

"It looks awful!"

"You're going to love it," Jesse assured me with a grin. "This is real Injun food, Tidbit."

I picked up one of the greasy balls and eyed it suspiciously. "What's in it?"

"Dried venison mashed with chokecherries. Then it's covered with suet. I made it myself last winter."

I shuddered again and dutifully packed the pemmican.

Outside, the rain continued in a steady, gray drizzle.

"What'll you do if it's raining tomorrow?" Milly asked Jesse.

"It won't be," was his answer.

"But you're taking along the rain gear, aren't you?" she prodded.

"It's all packed," he told her patiently. "How about you, Tidbit? How's your packing coming along?"

"I'm all finished. At least, I think I am. I probably won't find out until tomorrow on the trail if I've forgotten anything," I said with a laugh.

"It never hurts to double-check," he said, adding casually, "Since we're taking the horse we don't need to be quite as careful keeping the weight down, so there'll be room in our packs for a few items that would ordinarily be considered optional—like *pajamas*."

If I had had any doubts at all about the reality of Jesse's

93

voice and presence in his room early this morning, they were effectively swept away by the potent expression in his eyes.

Color rushed into my cheeks and my voice faltered. "I—uh, sort of assumed we'd be sleeping in our clothes."

"That's fine, if you want to," Jesse said agreeably. "Some backpackers prefer to get out of the clothes they've been hiking in all day, but it doesn't really matter. I'll leave that option up to you," he added with a teasing smile.

I busied myself with wrapping a wire fastener around a plastic bag of granola and prayed Milly wouldn't notice my scarlet cheeks.

Above the steady drip of the rain, we heard the whinny of a horse and Jesse's head turned immediately toward the sound. "That doesn't sound like Saskatoon," he said, listening intently.

"Sas-ka-who?" I asked with a laugh.

"Saskatoon, my buckskin mare," Jesse answered. "I bought her two summers ago from a rancher up in Smithsfield. She's a real frisky little lady—sort of reminds me of someone I know."

Our eyes met above a sack of powdered eggs and I thought, all he has to do is smile like that and I feel like I'm swimming in sunshine. Aloud, I said, "It's a pretty name. What does it mean?"

"Saskatoon is the Indian word for serviceberry."

"Trust my son to name his horse after a plant," was Milly's comment.

We heard a heavy knocking on the front door and a moment later, Barbara was rushing into the kitchen with the baby in her arms and a frightened look in her eyes.

"Jesse, there are some men outside who need your help! Someone's been hurt!"

Jesse dropped the sack of powdered eggs and immediately left the room with Milly and me following right behind.

Outside, a young man in a soggy, down-filled jacket stood shivering and pale on the wooden steps of the porch. A few feet away, another young man, equally soaked and shivering, was sitting astride a big bay horse holding a limp burden in front of him.

I couldn't see the injured man's face, only hair the color of moldy straw which was matted and rain-plastered about his head. A blanket had been wrapped around his shoulders, but even so, it only managed to cover the top portion of his thin body. His legs, hanging bare from cut-off jeans, were exposed to the wind and rain and the flesh was a pasty white.

"Can you t-tell us how much f-farther it is to the guard station?" asked the young man on the porch. "This guy's hurt real bad. I think he's unconscious."

Jesse moved quickly past him to address the man on the horse. "Does he have any broken bones, do you know?"

The rider shook his head and a series of shudders took his body. "I—I don't think so."

"Hand him down to me, then. Slow and easy. We've got to get all three of you inside and out of the rain."

Jesse reached up to grasp the injured man's shoulders as he was lowered off the horse and I saw him stagger back a step from the weight. I think I knew at that moment, even before Jesse pronounced in quiet tones, "He's not unconscious. This man's dead."

Doug and Travis came running up then from the guest cabin and at Jesse's call for assistance, Doug grabbed the dead man's legs. Between the two of them, they carried him up the steps and onto the porch.

Milly's hands were on my shoulders, pulling me back toward the cabin door, but my eyes couldn't look away as they laid him down. Jesse wiped the tangled, straw-colored hair away from a thin face and I found myself staring at the still, silent features of a young man somewhere past his mid-twenties. His eyes were closed and the color of his skin had gone beyond pale to a whiteness that was almost transparent. He was wearing only a cotton shirt, cut-off jeans and one tennis shoe. Other than a few minor scratches, there were no visible wounds that I could see, but his face had a used, empty look.

Jesse pulled the wet blanket away from the man's shoulders

to check the body for injuries and drew a startled breath. "What the crud—? This guy's wearing a shoulder holster!"

It couldn't have been more than a moment that we all stood there staring, while the rain fell and the horses shook their wet manes. But time has an odd way of stretching out the seconds in moments of shock, so that certain images are stamped indelibly upon the mind. I know I will never forget the feel of that moment or the sight of that empty face.

Then Uncle Chuck was at the screen door demanding what had happened and the young man on the horse was slipping off the animal's wet side, moaning, "I think I'm gunna be sick!"

Doug rushed over to give him a supporting arm and Jesse said, "Mom, you better heat up some soup and plenty of hot coffee. You two guys come on inside. There's nothing more we can do for your friend."

Uncle Charles said again, "What happened?" and Jesse answered, "I'm not sure. Hypothermia, I think."

His father backed away from the door so Aunt Milly and Doug could help the other two men inside the cabin.

Travis stepped onto the porch and stared at the dead man. "What's hypothermia?"

"Exposure—when the body loses heat faster than it can produce it," Jesse told him.

"And that can kill a guy?" Travis said with some skepticism.

"You're damn right it can! Sometimes in a matter of hours."

Travis shrugged. "What are you going to do with him?"

"Wrap him up and put him in my truck for now. As soon as those two guys are warmed up and feeling better, I'll take them all down to the guard station."

"I'll go help your mother," I said.

Jesse gave me a nod of thanks and pulled the sodden blanket over the pale face.

In the kitchen, the two men sat huddled in blankets near the wood stove, with the rest of us grouped around the table. Their wet clothes had been stripped off and hung to dry in front of the fireplace. Each man had downed a large bowl of Milly's hot soup, plus several cups of coffee, muttering their thanks again and again. When their shivering had ceased and the color was back in their faces, both men looked measurably better. Looking at the two, I placed them to be in their early twenties, probably close to Doug's age. Both were brown-haired, brown-eyed and amazingly similar in physical appearance. Not so amazing after they introduced themselves as brothers from Evanston, Wyoming, Steven and Bryan Polsen.

"Was the other man a friend of yours?" Uncle Chuck asked.

Both young men shook their heads and the older brother, Steven, explained, "We've never seen him before this morning. Me and Bry were on our way to Red Castle Lake when we found him. I guess it was about a mile up the trail."

Jesse asked, very quietly, "To the big lake?"

Bryan took another gulp of coffee and nodded. "We were camped at the lower lake and the fishing was lousy, so this morning we decided to try our luck up at the big one. Then we saw this guy, just lyin' by the trail."

"Was he conscious?" Jesse asked.

"Yeah, but he wasn't makin' any sense," Steve responded. "He was talkin' real funny and he didn't seem to know where he was or nothin'."

"Was he shivering?"

I looked at Jesse's tense features and felt a little stab of worry. There was something about his face, the expression in his eyes. Something I had seen once before.

Both brothers again shook their heads and Bryan gestured with one hand, trying to explain. "He wasn't shivering, but we knew there was something wrong. He was acting kind of spastic, you know what I mean?"

Jesse nodded. "What about his gear?"

"He didn't have any," Steve said. "The way you saw him is the way we found him."

"Man, that is so weird!" Doug said. "Since when is a black leather shoulder holster standard backpacking equipment?"

"Or tennis shoes," I interjected. "I can't imagine anyone, even a novice, heading into the Primitive Area wearing a pair of sneakers."

97

Bryan gave me a nod. "Yeah, that's what we thought."

"Do you think he was lost, or maybe got separated from his group?" Milly asked.

Steve thought for a moment, then said, "I'm not sure about the group, but I don't see how he could've been lost. Like I said, the guy was right by the trail."

"What did you do after you found him?" Jesse asked quietly.

Steve hitched the blanket closer around his lanky frame. "Well, we figured the best thing was to get him out of the mountains and to a doctor as fast as we could. So we packed our gear and headed out."

Jesse's expression was grim. "And how long were you on the trail before you noticed he was unconscious?"

Steve looked at him and shrugged. "I don't know. It's hard to tell. He was slumped over most the time, but that last hour or so he felt real heavy." The young man gave an involuntary shudder and finished his coffee with a gulp.

Jesse sighed and stood up. "As soon as you guys feel up to it, I'll drive you down to the guard station and you can tell the ranger what you've just told me."

"I'm ready right now," Bryan said with a pale smile.

"I don't know if your clothes are dry yet," Milly said, getting up from the table. "I'll go see."

"It's O.K. if they're not," Steve told her. "Anything'd be an improvement. We sure appreciate the food and coffee, Mrs. Chisholm."

"What'll we do about our horses?" Bryan asked his brother. "Our car and trailer are over at the Trailhead," he explained to the rest of us.

"You're welcome to leave your horses here for now," Uncle Chuck told them. "The rangers'll probably drive you over to get your car and you can come back for the horses later. There's plenty of room in our barn."

"Next time you guys decide to take a fishing trip up here, be sure you pack some rain gear," Jesse said with a hardness that surprised me. "If you'd been out in that rain much longer, you could have ended up like that guy you carried out," he told them and left the room.

For the next hour, I helped Milly finish packing the food. Neither of us was in the mood for much conversation. The sobering presence of death had been too newly felt for me to even get excited about tomorrow's backpacking trip. And the fact that the dead man had been found near Red Castle, somehow made things worse. Milly didn't have to say a word. I could read it all in her face.

I wondered if little David were somehow aware of the tension because he cried and fussed for a solid hour. After we had finished with the food, Milly took the infant from his frustrated mother and rocked him to sleep with that special knack only grandmothers have.

Barbara and I deserted the house for the front porch where we found Doug and Travis sitting on the steps.

The rain had stopped and the clouds were blowing away over the pine-covered ridges to the east. The sun was making its warmth felt once again and the shadows of late afternoon were longer than the pines in the forest. Humming and singing all around us were the vibrant sounds of life—insects, birds, a squirrel's noisy chatter. I stared at the rain-washed forest and the sparkling, sunlit meadow beyond, but all I could see was a young man's lifeless body lying on the porch beneath a sodden blanket.

The roar of an engine forced its way into my thoughts and we all turned as the truck pulled up alongside the cabin. Doug and Travis got to their feet at Uncle Chuck's and Jesse's approach and Doug asked immediately, "How did things go? Did you get everything straightened out?"

"As much as we could," Chuck said. "I don't know as anybody will ever find out what happened to that poor guy. But it's up to the authorities now."

Jesse moved silently past his father to lean against one of the massive log supports of the porch. I had the strongest feeling that he wasn't seeing any of us, that his mind was somewhere else.

99

"He was so young," Barbara commented in a quiet voice. "I wonder who he was?"

"Apparently, it's going to take some time before even the authorities know that," her father answered.

"He might have been able to tell us himself if he'd been taken care of differently!" Jesse said then, with barely suppressed anger.

"What do you mean? Taken care of differently?" I asked.

Jesse stared, unseeing, at the sunlight glinting on the meadow and said tersely, "A hypothermia victim needs immediate treatment. If those two guys had stopped to take care of him at their camp, that man might have made it."

"You don't know that!" Travis contended. "And I think you're being unfair to blame the Polsen's for that guy's death! They brought him out of the mountains to try and save his life—not kill him!"

"I know that, but good intentions don't count for much if you don't have the knowledge to back them up. There's so much they could have done to try and save that man's life. As it was, they not only made his condition worse, they nearly ended up killing themselves!"

"Look, 'mountain man,' it's easy for you to sit back and analyze a situation after it's already happened! The truth is, it might be a little different if you were the one who found an injured person in the mountains and had to carry him out. You never know what you'll do until you're actually faced with a situation!"

Jesse's face blanched at Travis' biting words and I felt the shaft of pain cutting through him as if it were my own. I hadn't seen his eyes look like that since—since that first summer.

Doug said, "Shut up, Travis!" and Barbara looked as if she might burst into tears.

Jesse looked at Travis and said in a flat voice, "You're right. No one knows what he'll do." Then he walked heavily away.

I jumped up to go after him but Doug grabbed my arm. "Not now, Missy. Just leave him alone."

"Doug!"

100

"He's right, honey," Uncle Chuck said gently. "I wouldn't bother Jesse right now if I were you."

I stared at Jesse's father, trying to keep the hurt from showing on my face, while every beat of my heart felt like a painful contraction.

"When is somebody going to tell me what's going on?" I demanded. "I know something's wrong and I know it has something to do with Jesse going back to Red Castle, so don't try to palm off any silly explanations on me. I want to know the truth!"

Uncle Chuck sighed and placed a heavy hand on my shoulder. "I wish I could explain, honey, but I can't. It's something that—well, Jesse would rather tell you himself, and I respect that. Don't push him about this, Missy. Don't push him," he said again, very softly. "I can't say any more than that, except—I think you'll get your answers when you get to Red Castle."

Chapter 10

"Up, over wooded crest
And mossy boulder
With strong thigh, heaving chest
And swinging shoulder."
Arthur Guiterman

At half past seven the next morning, we drove away from Trail's End. Saskatoon was munching the last of her breakfast oats in the horse trailer; Doug and Travis were lounging on the sleeping bags and gear in the camper shell, and I was sitting in the front between Uncle Chuck and Jesse—practically speechless with excitement! Almost from the first moment of waking I had felt it, this heady expectancy, bubbling up inside me like the waters of an underground spring. The palling events of yesterday had blown away with the rain. Blue skies, sunlight sifting through the pines, and an open road were before us! I felt as if I were heading for a special rendezvous in the mountains.

Trail's End was lost in the trees and the Hewinta Guard Station was left behind as Uncle Chuck took the curving forest road to China Meadows and the Trailhead Campground.

Also left behind, were Jesse's buckskins and the bear claw necklace. This morning, dressed in Levis, a plaid shirt and denim jacket, he looked more like the Jesse I used to know. Strange, how just sitting beside him, occasionally brushing against his arm which rested on the seat behind my head, I felt nothing at all like the Melissa he used to know.

Gilbert Meadows passed by. Vast acres of lonely, treeless

green. Then we were into the trees again, winding our way along the rough red road. Yesterday's rain had left it wet and puddled and Uncle Chuck swerved sharply to avoid a rain-filled chuckhole. I slid sideways into Jesse and in reaching out to steady myself, encountered the hardness of his muscled thigh. At the same time, Jesse's left arm came around my shoulders, firmly securing my position against his side.

Life was glorious! My happiness at that moment was all en-compassing, enabling me to see new purpose in all of nature's creations—particularly chuckholes.

We drove past China Lake and Uncle Chuck asked Jesse, "Did you remember to put fresh batteries in the flashlight?"

Jesse smiled and nodded. His father had been running down various items on the packing list all morning and this was the second time he had asked about the flashlight.

A short distance beyond China Lake, we reached the junction and turned right, driving past a small pond and lush meadows with deep, willow-banked channels that were a favorite feeding ground for deer, elk and moose. At the south end of China Meadows is the area known as the Trailhead. Here, the Forest Service have provided outdoor grills, a few tables and an outhouse. In addition to the large parking area, there is a stone ramp for unloading horses.

While Jesse led Saskatoon out of the horse trailer and the rest of the men began unloading the truck, I grabbed my camera and walked past the main parking area towards the lip of a hill. To my left was a pine-covered knoll, dropping steeply down to a marshy meadow. Directly ahead, the dirt road led the way down a sage-covered slope to a sturdy log fence which zig-zagged along the perimeter of a dense border of pines. This was the Trailhead. The end of man-made roads and barriers. Most of China Meadows and the surrounding campgrounds were long familiar to me as we had come often to fish the lakes and streams over the years. But I had never been farther than the log fence. For some reason, that fence had been the boundary to my mountain world. Very soon now, those limits would be left behind and I would walk into a wilderness I had heard about but never seen.

I took a few pictures of the meadows below, where a golden mist hovered over thick clumps of willows, then Doug walked up to me and said, "Hey, Sis, we're all set and Jesse's just about got the horse packed. You'd better use the 'John' while you've got the chance. It's going to be three days before we see another outhouse."

So much for the "poetry of earth." I looked at my brother and smiled. With Doug, life was always plain prose.

I turned to follow him back to the parking area and noticed for the first time, two vehicles parked unobtrusively under the pines, a few yards away from the dirt road. I grabbed Doug's arm and said in a choked voice, "Oh, no! They're here!"

"Who's here?"

I pointed to the brown pickup truck and dark blue van with two empty horse trailers behind. "Remember those men behind us on the Chisholm Trail? That's their truck and van! I know it is!"

"Oh, for crying out loud! What if it is?"

I tried to ignore the little jabs of fear pricking inside me and shrugged away my previous words. "Oh, nothing. I just wish they weren't up here, that's all."

Doug laughed and shook his head. "You're unreal, you know that? You're absolutely unreal!"

We walked over to where Jesse and his father were tightening the ropes on Saskatoon's pack and Travis was putting on his backpack.

Doug called out, "Hey, Travis, take off the pack! Jess, you might as well unload that horse and get him back in the trailer."

"What are you talking about?" Travis asked with a puzzled grin.

"There's no sense in us going anywhere," Doug told them with a resigned shrug. "These mountains are just too full of people. Jess, you should've made reservations!"

I laughed and gave my brother a shove. "Doug, will you cut it out!"

Jesse grinned at us and said, "I hadn't noticed too many crowds this morning. Where are all these people?"

"Around the road a little ways. At least, their cars are.

104

Missy spotted the truck and van that followed behind us on the road the other day," my brother explained, giving Travis a wink. "I think she's afraid that blond guy's gonna jump out from behind a bush or something."

Jesse gave the knots securing Saskatoon's pack one more pull and asked with interest, "What blond guy?"

"It's really nothing," I said before Doug could launch into another one of his stories. "When we were stuck behind that herd of cattle, some men drove up behind us. They were kind of rough-looking and they didn't—" I trailed off, hating to let myself in for more of my brother's teasing.

"They didn't what?" Jesse persisted, ignoring Doug's broad grin.

"They didn't strike me as the backpacking type," I said.

"Maybe they were construction workers on the dam," Uncle Chuck suggested. "I've seen a few rough types myself since they started building that dam down below us."

Somehow, I didn't think so, but I gave quick vocal agreement to Uncle Chuck's comment as he hugged me and offered fatherly instructions to be careful. For a moment he looked as if he wanted to say more, then he smiled and handed me my backpack.

I buckled the straps firmly about my hips as Uncle Chuck turned to Jesse. "Have a good time, son, and we'll see you back at the cabin day after tomorrow."

Jesse nodded and took Saskatoon's halter rope. Then he looked at me. "All set?" Excitement added a husky pulse to his voice and heightened the blue of his eyes.

"All set!"

Uncle Chuck waved good-by at the top of the hill as we walked down the sage-covered slope toward the log fence. We stopped briefly to look at a large wooden map near the entrance to the Trailhead, then all the barriers were left behind as I followed Jesse up the trail and into the trees.

For the first two miles or so, we climbed steadily along a ridge of heavy timber. The trail was rock-strewn and narrow enough that we were forced to walk single file. Far below us, unseen but in harmonious voice with birdcall and the fresh morning breeze, was the river. We saw no animals, but were frequently assured of their presence by fresh deer or elk droppings along the trail.

Lodgepole pines grew thickly on both sides of the trail. Some were young giants, feeling their way toward the sun. Others were tired patriarchs, leaning heavily on the firm roots of a younger generation. There were scarecrow trees, scorched reminders of a sizzling encounter with summer lightning. And then there were the fallen ones—dry, dead pines completely stripped of bark and bleached a bony white—skeletons of a previous forest whose time was no more.

We had been on the trail exactly one hour when we reached a large bridge which spanned the Smith's Fork river. Made of heavy timber and painted steel, it was solid, sturdy and incredibly ugly.

Jesse grinned and cited the bridge as a prime example of one of the improvements the Forest Service had made on north slope trails.

"I admit, it's kinda nice not to get your feet wet crossing the river," Doug said. "But it's a shame it's so pug-ugly!"

I drank from the canteen Jesse handed me, then said, "It doesn't fit in at all! Why did they have to paint it orange?"

"I'll be sure and tell my boss that you don't approve of the color scheme the next time I see him" Jesse said with a laugh.

"Does your job with the Forest Service include things like this bridge?" Travis asked him.

"Yeah, I get my fingers in a lot of different pies. Geologists do a lot of field work, aerial photos and maps, and then apply that information to help solve problems with the land."

"What kind of problems?" I asked, passing the canteen to Doug.

"Landslides, soil stability, road construction, bridge sites, things like that. Geologic surveys are pretty important when it comes to providing information for timber harvesting and watershed studies."

"Don't tell me you're to blame for that dam construction going on below Bridger Lake!" I accused him.

Jesse gave me a shame-faced grin. "I was wondering how long it would take you to figure that out."

"Jesse Chisholm!"

"That's what happens when the 'guardian spirit' stays away from the mountains too long," he teased and gave my hair a gentle tug. "O.K., guys, our five minutes are up. Let's get moving."

A short distance beyond the bridge, the trail moved out of the forest and the land opened up into a broad, almost treeless area. Grass was sparse and the soil was nearly as purple as the rocks strewn across the landscape. It was as if nature's paint-brush had suddenly gone wild. Yellow stonecrop, scarlet gilia, and pale lavender flea-bane were all blooming together and I couldn't walk by without taking a few pictures. The vistas were breathtaking. Ridges of dark pines, blue sky that was almost hard in its brilliance and the occasional glimpse of snow-capped mountain crests far above timberline.

In the minute or two that I lagged behind, Jesse and Saska-toon kept on going and when I looked up, their figures were rapidly diminishing in the distance. I realized in a moment why Uncle Chuck had warned us about Jesse's long-legged stride. His pace wasn't overly fast but every step was as smooth and steady as a machine. I snatched one more picture of him and Saskatoon against the brilliant skyline, then ran like blazes to catch up.

Doug had taken my place behind Jesse, but Travis turned back to wait for me.

"Want me to ask that 'mountain man' to slow down a little?" he said with a smile.

I shook my head and panted, "No, I'm fine. I just need to catch my breath."

Travis' voice was as warm as his smile and he had been polite and friendly all morning, but I knew very well I had been relegated back to the ranks of Doug Heydon's kid sister. Well, that was fine with me! As far as Travis Young was concerned, I was only too happy to remain "little Missy" forever!

The mood of the landscape changed with every passing mile. I knew we were climbing, but the slope was so gentle as to be almost unnoticeable at times. We left the open area behind and once more the forest was pressing close against the trail. This land wasn't dry and rocky like the area we had just passed through, however. Pine needles were puddled in feathery swirls along both sides of the wet trail and I could see small, boggy meadows amid the trees.

Up ahead was another man-made surprise. To prevent hikers from taking short-cuts across the meadows and eroding the landscape, the Forest Service had built a corduroy trail through the boggy spots. It was similar to a western-style boardwalk and constructed of heavy timber. Unlike the gaudily painted bridge, this was one addition to the wilderness I highly approved of.

I gave a cry of pleasure as the wooden trail made an abrupt right turn near a large, wet meadow. Blooming amid the grass were hundreds of purple, elephant-head flowers. I called to Jesse and asked him to stop a moment, then went totally mad as only a photographer can, in capturing the wild beauty before me.

"Will you look at that!" Travis exclaimed, examining an individual flower and smiling over the precise resemblance to an elephant's head.

"Who says the good Lord doesn't have a sense of humor," Doug said with a grin.

"If I told some of my friends that I'd seen a meadow full of purple elephants, they'd think I'd been snortin' the sauce," Travis laughed and we moved on.

We had been walking for about two hours when Jesse began looking for springs. We still had plenty of water in our canteens, but there is nothing like pure mountain water to really quench one's thirst.

The river was on our right now, still hidden by a thick cover of undergrowth and trees, but more vocal in its presence. We passed by one stream that crossed directly over the trail because Jesse wasn't satisfied with its source. Then we came to a second, smaller stream. Jesse left the trail and climbed up the wooded hillside a short distance to check the stream's source.

He returned moments later, pronouncing the water safe to drink.

We knelt on the damp grass, cupping our hands to capture the clear, cold water and drank eagerly of its sweetness. Jesse emptied his canteen and refilled it from the spring. I did the same and during our five-minute rest break, snapped another half dozen pictures.

Below the little stream, I found a thick patch of Indian paintbrush in an astounding variety of shades. There was dusky rose, burnt orange, lemon yellow and chartreuse, as well as the familiar scarlet. Tucked in among the paintbrush were tiny wild daisies and yellow buttercups.

Jesse smiled at me and said, "Save some film for Red Castle."

"I've got gallons of films!" I told him and bent to capture the mountain symmetry of clear water flowing over rounded stones.

We had been hiking for a little more than three hours and ten miles were behind us when Jesse registered our names at the Primitive Area sign-in box erected by the Forest Service. My enthusiasm was still stronger than my fatigue and the prospect of six more miles ahead of us seemed a pittance. The weather was warm and sunny. We had long ago abandoned our jackets and tucked them into our packs. Our hunger was appeased by granola and Milly's apricot leather. I found it amusing to see how long a distance I could cover while chewing one piece. Sometimes, I caught myself chewing in time to the pace of my feet and had to laugh.

The trail was reddish brown now and very narrow, with thick grass springing up on both sides. For the most part, it hugged the very edge of the forest, following every bend and curve of the trees. I was so used to keeping a steady pace, I nearly walked right into Saskatoon's broad rump before realizing Jesse had stopped and was pointing through the trees to a large, open meadow.

"Look! There! Do you see them?" he asked in a whisper.

I smiled and nodded. Some thirty yards away, a doe and her twin fawns were grazing in the tall grass, sunlight warming their soft brown pelts. We watched as the mother browsed for a few seconds at a time, then lifted her head, big eyes wide and watchful. Something, I'm not sure what, alerted her to our presence and suddenly she was bounding across the meadow with her young following close behind.

A short distance farther on, Jesse pointed out a narrow trail which forked to the right through the meadow, and indicated this was the route we would follow on our return trip. I gave it only a moment's glance, preferring to look ahead where the main trail was leading us deeper and deeper into the mountains. All too soon this day would be only a memory, but for now, the morning was still young and I wanted nothing more than to live this journey one step at a time.

We said little as we walked and I found it a peaceful change to observe the silence of the wilderness. Thoughts flowed more freely without the civilized interference of telephones, radios and traffic. There was time here to reflect, to ponder, and to understand. Agnostics and atheists might find credence to their beliefs in the sterile climate of stone and cement, but I defied any man to enter this mountain world without acknowledging the hand of the Creator. There was peace and a sweet sense of purpose in everything I saw. It was in the sunshine on the meadows, the dappled shade under the pines. It was in every flower and the very air itself. No wonder they came and stayed, I thought, reflecting on those long ago mountain men whose feet had touched the same soil mine were touching now. No wonder.

I had completely lost track of the time, when Doug called up to Jesse, "My stomach is demanding to know when we're going to stop for lunch!"

"There's a good place not too far ahead," Jesse answered over his shoulder.

"How far is 'not too far'?" Travis asked warily.

"Oh, about a mile or so."

"A mile I can handle," Doug said, "but that 'or so' has me worried."

Jesse grinned. "We should be pretty close to the next bridge, and that's where you'll get your first view of Red Castle.

I'd planned on stopping there for lunch, unless you're too tired." He looked at me with sudden concern. "Have I been pushing you too fast? We can eat here if you like."

"I'm not that tired. Let's go on to the bridge!" I told him recklessly.

I wouldn't have admitted it for the world, especially with Travis and Doug puffing along behind me, but that last mile seemed at least five miles long. The Smith's Fork was our constant companion now, and at one point the river divided itself into a veritable avenue of streams, with little streets of water crossing and intersecting themselves at all angles. The timber wasn't as dense in this region and our view extended for greater distances, but still, the elusive Red Castle was no where in sight.

To the south, I noticed a buildup of puffy white clouds and silently hoped we wouldn't be walking through rain before long. Then, just when I was beginning to give serious consideration to the idea that Red Castle was only a myth, the trees parted and the trail moved out of the forest. Down a small green slope, we saw a wooden bridge spanning the Smith's Fork and our steps automatically quickened. My eyes were on the bridge and my mind was centered on lunch until Jesse stopped and said, "There she is. There's Red Castle."

Rising out of dense ridges of pine forest to the south, with scarfs of white cloud on either side, was a massive, wine-red mountain.

"It really does look like a castle," I said in amazement.

"But it's not red," Travis commented. "It looks more like lavender or purple to me."

"The color depends on the time of day and the way the light hits the mountain," Jesse said quietly. "I've seen the castle when it was very red."

"I wouldn't care if it was pink with yellow polka-dots," said my ever-sensitive brother. "It's there and we're here—and I'm hungry!"

He and Travis crossed the bridge and eagerly shed their backpacks, but Jesse stood a moment longer, ignoring Saskatoon's impatient nickers, to stare up at the turreted walls of ancient stone. It was a magnificent sight and yet, strangely forbidding—almost menacing in size and mood.

I glanced away from the castle into Jesse's bearded face and saw a grimness in the tight line of his mouth and a bleakness in his eyes that cut through me. Something prompted me to move closer to his side and slip my hand in his. He jumped a little, as if he hadn't been aware of my presence, then his fingers tightened around mine.

"I'm glad you're here," he said.

I tried to smile away the loneliness in his eyes and answered softly, "Me, too."

He sighed then and said in a more normal tone, "Let's go eat!"

We devoured the thick hoagy sandwiches Aunt Milly had made for us in a matter of minutes. The men made short work of two sandwiches apiece and had me wishing I had asked her to pack me an extra one as well. I never remember food tasting so wonderful. We finished up with fresh fruit, then Jesse agreed to a ten-minute rest.

"It's better to take short, frequent rests rather than one or two long ones," he cautioned us. "That way, your muscles won't start stiffening up."

"What muscles," Doug groaned. "Right now, even my bones feel like tired jello." Neither he nor Travis needed a second invitation to stretch out full-length on the grass, arms over their faces.

I sat near the stream and Jesse did the same, locking his long arms around his knees. Neither of us felt the need to talk, choosing instead to listen to the liquid voice of the river. The air was warm and soft, freshened by a tender breeze that barely ruffled the tops of the pines. Blooming on the edge of the bank was a large cluster of spectacular magenta flowers, but I didn't have the least desire to pick up my camera and start taking pictures. Somewhere in the world, men and women were at work, wars were being fought, people were loving, dying, being born. But all that seemed an eternity away from the peace of this moment.

I glanced away from the stream with a sigh of contentment

and discovered Jesse's eyes on my face. I gave him an awkward little smile and said, "What are you thinking about?"

"That your hair looks like wild honey when the sunlight catches it that way."

The idle peace I had been feeling was effectively interrupted by the hard pounding of my heart. My awareness of our surroundings blurred and faded as all my senses became fine-tuned to the nearness of one man.

Jesse picked a small daisy growing in the grass between us and tucked it in my hair. My gaze lowered from the blue of his eyes to the curve of his mouth and I felt a deep ache inside to experience his kiss.

"Hey, our ten minutes are up!" Doug called loudly. "When are we going to get moving?"

Jesse sighed and said under his breath, "Your brother was right! These mountains are too crowded!" Then he got to his feet and untied Saskatoon's rope from a low-growing bush.

Doug brought me my backpack and took note of the flower in my hair with a frown and the low-growled comment, "Watch yourself, Sis. He's too old for you."

I touched the daisy's soft petals with trembling fingers and walked past Doug without saying a word.

For perhaps a quarter mile, the trail hugged the lower fringes of the forest, following the stream's uphill course, then suddenly, it made a sharp, right-angled turn and began climbing the ridge. Jesse led the way up the switchback and Saskatoon's occasional whinnies echoed hollowly through the quiet space of the forest. The vegetation wasn't nearly as dense as it had been closer to the river and the pines were spread much farther apart. Looking up, I could see the zig-zag pattern of the trail high above us. It was by far the steepest climb we had yet encountered and we were all too breathless for any conversation. Finally, we reached the top of the ridge and the trail leveled out once more. Looming directly in front of us was the awesome splendor of Red Castle.

Alpine meadows were opening up on either side and wildflowers were everywhere, as were columbines, paintbrush, buttercups, starflowers, daisies, and dozens of others I didn't have names for. Up ahead, I could see a cataract of white water spilling down a rocky slope. The sound of the river grew in mighty crescendo as we neared the falls, then diminished as the red trail moved on.

I felt almost breathless with the splendor of it all—and with running to catch up after frequent stops to take pictures. Jesse indulged my photographic madness by slowing the pace, and after hurrying up a gentle slope, I found him and the others waiting for me at a small bridge and fork in the trail.

"The left fork heads around the base of Mount Powell and over to the south side of the lake," he was explaining to Doug.

"Which one is Mount Powell?" I asked him.

Jesse stretched an arm toward a bony ridge of reddish-purple rock whose summit was still capped with snow. Then, instead of taking the lead as he had the entire journey, he motioned for Doug and Travis to go ahead and matched his lengthy stride to my smaller steps. The trail was much wider through the meadow, enabling us to walk side by side. I was looking up at the turreted walls of Red Castle when I felt the warmth of his hand enclose mine, and I didn't need words to tell me that whatever Jesse had to face up here, we would face together.

Chapter 11

"What is he but a brute
Whose flesh has soul to suit . . . ."
Robert Browning

Fringed by radiant alpine meadows and deep pine forests, Red Castle's lower lake sits at the rocky base of the mountain itself. The lake was much larger than I expected; according to Jesse, a good thirty-five acres in size. As we followed the trail along the lake's northern side, I watched the sun and wind tease the rippling surface of the water until it glittered like a mass of gold and silver coins. Cloud shadows suddenly obscured the treasure and I cast an anxious glance beyond Red Castle's lofty pinnacles where a heavy buildup of gray-white clouds smudged the blue sky.

"I hope it doesn't rain," I said as thunder rumbled in the distance.

Jesse gave me a reassuring smile. "I don't think it's headed our way."

He led us past the tents of a few campers to the far end of the lake. Here, we left the trail and followed him up a gentle, flower-starred slope. Jesse glanced around a level area near a cluster of giant pines and gave a satisfied nod. "This ought to do. We'll camp here."

We were far enough away from the lake not to be overly troubled with mosquitoes and off the main trail so as to ensure complete privacy. I looked about in delight and unbuckled my backpack. My shoulders felt light enough to soar away.

"You guys can fish or do whatever you want while I unload the horse and make camp," Jesse said as Doug and Travis relieved themselves of their backpacks.

Doug stretched his arms above his head. "I'll help you unload, then we can all go fishing. Man, I hope those graylings are good and hungry! Hey, Travis-my-man, would you care to place a little wager on who hooks the first one?"

"What sort of wager did you have in mind?" Travis asked with a calculating gleam in his hazel eyes. He bent to take something out of his backpack and the next moment he was on his knees with a hand over his eyes.

"Travis, are you all right?" I asked quickly.

"Yeah, I just got dizzy for a minute, that's all." He made an attempt to stand and staggered backwards.

Doug grabbed Travis' arm and said, half-joking, "Hey, buddy, did you spike the canteen while I wasn't looking?"

"It's probably the altitude," Jesse said, noting that Travis' tan had taken on a bilious green tinge. "We're close to 11,000 feet up here, and it gets to some people more than others. You'd better lie down for a while."

Travis stretched out on the grass with a groan. "Sorry, Doug. I guess the fishing'll have to wait."

Jesse looked away from Travis and turned to me with worried eyes. "How are you feeling, Tidbit?"

"Wonderful!"

"Not light-headed or anything?"

I smiled into his eyes, not entirely sure how to answer his last question. Being close to him, feeling the warm pressure of his hand on my shoulder, I felt very light-headed—but it had nothing to do with the altitude.

"Missy's always a bit light-headed," Doug grumbled, unscrewing the top of his canteen and offering a drink to Travis.

"Is something bothering you?" Jesse asked him. "You've been acting kind of edgy all morning."

Doug tossed a pointed glance in our direction, then shrugged. "Skip it. I guess I'm just tired."

"Well, I'm not!" I said bluntly. "And I'd love to go fishing! I just hope my pole isn't at the bottom of the pack!"

116

Jesse laughed and gave my shoulder a squeeze. "The fishing equipment is right on top. If you'll hold Saskatoon's head and say a few pretty words to her, Doug and I will get this pack off her back."

I held the halter and patted the buckskin mare's velvety black muzzle while Jesse untied the ropes. Watching him, I felt the current between us begin to sing and hum until it was as vibrant and alive as the birdsong in the pines. Jesse bent to unfasten the cinch under Saskatoon's belly and I swiped at a mosquito that was hunting for a place to land on his neck. My fingers barely brushed the warm brown of his hair, but the brief moment of contact was enough to stir a vague longing within me. Whatever happened to the casual familiarity we once shared? Somewhere along the way it had been replaced by desires and emotions that almost frightened me with their intensity. I clutched the mare's halter a little tighter and tried to think of other things—the prospect of an afternoon's fishing, seeing Red Castle at sunset—anything except the fact that I wanted so badly to touch and be close to Jesse Chisholm.

Some five minutes later, I walked down the grassy slope toward the lake, fishing rod in one hand and bait box in the other. When I reached the water's edge, I laid my gear down to smear on a fresh coat of insect repellent, then took off my hiking boots. The grassy bank felt delightfully cool and soft to my tired feet.

There was the same old excitement in hearing the whir of the line as it sang across rippling waters, and listening for that tiny plunk as the baited hook sank into the blue depths. I glanced from one end of the lake to the other and took selfish pleasure in the fact there wasn't another soul in sight. Red Castle was my only companion. Directly across the lake, the wine-red mountain looked down on my simple mortal pleasures and I smiled into its forbidding face.

The base of the castle was blanketed in rock rubble and its deeper crevices were still lined with snow. The ramparts and massive buttresses had been intricately carved and chiseled by nature's master sculptor—weather. Gazing at the ancient red walls, I wondered how many millenia had gone into its making.

117

A sudden jerk on my line diverted my attention back to the lake. I gave an excited gasp as the line tensed and jerked again. I lifted the rod ever so slightly and thrilled to the sudden pull and tension this produced. I began reeling in, struggling with my excitement and mentally repeating the instructions Jesse had given me dozens of times. My enthusiasm and eagerness had resulted in the loss of many a trout over the years and I was determined not to lose this one.

A silver gleam flashed in the sunlight above the lake's surface and I knew the fish must be a good size. When the line was short enough and the fish fairly close to shore, I swung it onto the grass and reached for the wriggling body. I had never seen a trout like this one. Its color was a shimmering, silvery gray and the dorsal fin was more than twice the size of the rainbows and cutthroats I had seen. With the slippery scales firm in hand, I knelt on the grass and gave the fish's head a hard whack on one of the red rocks bordering the shoreline. The trout jerked convulsively. I shuddered and gave it one more whack for good measure, realizing all over again that this was the one part of fishing I would never get used to.

"Well, well! If it isn't Smokey the Bear's little helper!"

At the sound of that drawling voice, my body jerked almost as convulsively as the fish I had just caught.

He was mounted on a big brown gelding and behind him, thin legs straddling the back of a sorrel mare, was the Chicano. The tall blond urged his horse off the trail and down the slope in my direction. My heart began to pound with thick, suffocating beats, and even if I had been able to think of something to say, my throat was too dry for speech. I swallowed and tried to ignore the men's approach, giving all my attention to removing the hook from the fish's mouth.

"Been puttin' out any forest fires lately?" the blond asked, to which the Chicano replied with a low chuckle, "I think this little one could start a few fires!"

The blond reined his horse a few feet from where I was kneeling and said in a low tone, "Hey, doll, you can light my fire any time you want!"

My fingers began to shake and I gave up on the hook. I left the rod on the ground and got to my feet.

His blue eyes were even more pale than I remembered and just now there was a hot white gleam in their depths that made my stomach crawl. The breeze was blowing his long yellow mane around his face and he brushed it back with an impatient hand.

"What's the matter, little lady? You don't look too happy to see me."

I made an attempt to move past him, but he quickly turned his horse to block my escape. "If you don't mind, I was just going back to our camp," I said coldly.

His thick lower lip curled into a smile and he gave a nod to the Chicano. "Now, do you think that's nice, Tony? Here we are, wantin' to be polite and friendly, and the little lady won't even say hello."

Weasel-black eyes slid over my face and the Chicano's mouth parted in a crooked yellow smile beneath his mustache. "I think the little one is afraid of you," he said in heavily-accented English.

"I'm not afraid!" I said and met the blond's heavy-lidded gaze. "I just don't enjoy having your horse breathing down my neck! So back off and let me by."

"I never back off from something I want," he said and to prove his point, urged the brown gelding forward a few paces.

I backed away and made another attempt at getting around him. The blond gave his horse a swift kick in the sides, forcing me even closer to the water's edge.

"What kind of stupid game are you playing?" I demanded.

"Lady, I don't play games!" There was no amusement in the smile he gave me and once more he urged the horse forward.

I didn't budge until the animal's head was only inches from mine and my stocking feet were teetering on the rocks with water lapping over them. I put a hand on the horse's muzzle to steady myself but the animal gave a nervous snort and shook his head, knocking me off balance. I stumbled back into the lake and frigid water covered my feet well past the ankles.

119

The Chicano gave a snickering laugh and suddenly, I was as angry as I was frightened! No matter how cold the water was, I was ready to stand in the lake all day long rather than yield one more inch!

Seemingly from out of nowhere, a man's tinny voice was saying: "Moser, this is Hicks. What's your ten-twenty?"

I looked around, startled, and saw the blond reach for what appeared to be a portable CB-radio attached to his belt. I noticed then that the Chicano was carrying a similar unit.

"Moser, do you read?" the voice demanded.

The blond pressed a switch and answered, "I read you. We're across the lake. Over."

There was cool authority in the voice and the command: "I want you and Sanchez back at camp. Now!"

"We're on our way."

The man called Moser returned the radio to its leather case and motioned for the Chicano to leave. Then he looked down at me. "I sure hate to leave—just when things were gettin' interesting—but I'll see you later, doll!"

Chapter 12

"I love these two, the mountain and the man . . ."
Glennys Sabuco

I walked very calmly out of the water and sloshed up the grassy bank as Moser and Sanchez took the trail around the far end of the lake. The blond lifted his hand in a cocky farewell salute, but I looked straight ahead, pretending not to notice. Then, when there was a good forty-yard distance between us, I broke into a terrified run and headed straight for camp. It didn't matter that my feet were wet and icy cold, or that my legs were shaking so much I stumbled and grazed my hand on a rock. All that mattered was getting away from those pale blue eyes and that ugly yellow smile.

I burst into camp and saw Jesse and Doug sitting on a log chewing beef jerky. Travis was snoozing in one of the two bright green tents they had set up. The first thing my brother said was, "What'd I tell you, Jess? I knew she'd come tearing back here like a scared rabbit!" He began to laugh and I completely fell apart.

"Don't you dare laugh at me! Don't you dare!" I screamed. "What kind of stupid brother are you, anyway?" I sank to my knees on the grass and began to cry.

"What the heck are you cryin' about? Hey, come on, Sis, don't cry like that!"

"I'll cry if I want to!" I flung back at him. "You don't care what happens to me!"

The next thing I knew, Jesse was kneeling beside me and his arms were wrapping me close against his big chest. "It's O.K., honey. Go ahead and cry if it helps."

He held me and stroked my hair while I soaked his shirt front with my tears. "I was so scared! I tried not to let them know, but—oh, Jesse! I was so scared!"

"What happened? Doug pointed out that tall blond and the Mexican when they rode by us a few minutes ago. What did they do?"

I shuddered and sat down and Jesse reached for a handkerchief in his Levis pocket. I wiped my eyes, then put my head on my knees, feeling slightly sick and still a bit shaky.

"Your stockings are dripping wet!" Doug said. "And so are your pantlegs. What'd you do—fall in the lake?"

I sniffed and flung him a cold glance. "No, I did not fall in the lake! Your *friends* decided to play some cute little game and forced me into the water!"

"What? How did they do that?"

"The blond did it—with his horse!" I told him. "He wouldn't let me by and he kept forcing me backwards."

Jesse reached down and began to pull off my wet stockings. "Your feet are like ice!" he said, then turned to Doug. "Why don't you make yourself useful and get Melissa a dry pair of socks."

Doug moved to do his bidding, looking more shame-faced by the minute.

"What happened?" Jesse asked me again, worry and anger flashing in his eyes. "Who are those guys, anyway?"

"The blond's name is Moser. And I heard the man on the CB calling the Chicano—what was it? Sanchez, I think."

"The man on the CB?" Jesse questioned with a frown.

I nodded as Doug dropped a thick pair of woolen socks in my lap. Before I could pick them up, Jesse grabbed the stockings and started putting one on my foot.

"You don't need to do that!" I protested.

He ignored me and pulled on the second stocking, saying,

"I want you to tell me exactly what happened—everything, O.K., honey?"

I looked into his eyes and smiled a little. "O.K."

One of his hands reached out to cover my knee and I felt a little rush of warmth replace the shivering fear of a moment ago. "The two of them, Moser and Sanchez, rode up behind me while I was fishing, so I didn't notice them at first until—My fish!" I burst out, suddenly remembering. "I left my fish down on the shore!"

"Doug will go get it, won't you Doug," Jesse said, and it was an order, not a suggestion.

My brother cleared his throat and nodded.

"Would you bring my rod back, too?" I said.

"Sure. Anything else?"

"The bait box."

Doug started down the slope and I called after him, "Oh, I forgot my hiking boots! They're on a rock near the bait box."

Doug stood on the trail a moment longer. "You're sure that's all? The fish, the pole, the bait box and your shoes?"

I smiled at him. "That's everything."

Doug shook his head and walked down the grassy slope.

When I finished relating the incident between me and the two men on horseback, Jesse asked thoughtfully, "Can you remember exactly what the man on the CB said to Moser?"

"I'm not sure. I was so scared at the time—"

"I know, honey, but try—if you can."

I bent my head, hoping he wouldn't notice the blush creeping along my cheekbones. As nicknames went, I preferred his newest for me even more than Tidbit.

"Let's see. The first thing he said was, 'Moser, this is Ricks.' No, it wasn't Ricks. Hicks! That was his name. 'Moser, this is Hicks. What's your—'" I sighed in frustration. "I'm sorry, Jesse. I think it was a number or something. Ten-forty, ten—"

"Ten-twenty?" Jesse suggested.

"Yes! That's it!"

"That's CB talk for 'what's your location,'" he explained. "What did Moser tell Hicks?"

"He said, 'We're across the lake.' Then Hicks ordered him and Sanchez to come back to their camp and they left."

Jesse rubbed the back of one hand across his beard. "What do you mean, ordered them back?"

"Well, it wasn't so much what he said as the way he said it. He just sounded—in charge." I looked at Jesse. "Isn't it kind of unusual, taking powerful CB units on a backpacking trip?"

"Not really. Hunters and hikers are starting to use them more all the time now."

"Oh. Jesse, do you think they're really—" I broke off, wondering if I dared give voice to my thoughts.

"Really what?"

"I don't know how to say this without sounding ridiculous."

His blue eyes were completely serious as they looked into mine. "I don't think anything you say is ridiculous. Go ahead."

I gave him a look of silent gratitude, then asked. "Do you really think they're just backpackers?"

Jesse stared at me for a moment, then picked up a grayed branch of dead pine. "I don't know. They could be I guess . . ."

My eyes must have betrayed the fear I was struggling to hide, because his hands suddenly dropped the wood and gripped my shoulders instead.

"Look, it doesn't matter who or what they are, because they're not coming near you again! From now on, I'm not letting you out of my sight—understand?"

His fierce male protectiveness made me feel extremely fragile, but I thought his last statement needed some clarification. I cleared my throat and said, "Not ever? There are times when a lady needs her privacy."

Jesse's grin conceded my point and his hands relaxed their hold. "Just make sure you take a good-sized stick along the next time you visit the powder room. Agreed?"

I sighed and smiled. "Agreed."

Below us, Doug was trudging up the slope with my paraphernalia in his arms. We got to our feet at his approach and

Doug called excitedly, "Hey, Missy! Do you know what you caught?"

He dropped my hiking boots on the grass and held up the fish for Jesse to see. "Will you look at this! She hooked a grayling! This flippin' fish is at least fourteen inches!"

Jesse laughed and hugged me and I felt like running right back down to the lake and catching a dozen more if I could be assured of a similar response.

Travis poked his head out of the tent flaps and asked with a yawn, "What's all the excitement?"

"Melissa hooked the first grayling," Jesse told him. "She wins the wager!"

"No fair!" Travis said, crawling out of the tent. "Guardian spirits aren't eligible! That fish probably jumped on her hook and begged to be caught!"

Doug laughed and asked, "How are you feeling? You're looking a lot better. Not quite so green around the gills."

"I feel better! That sleep must have been what I needed. Man, I was dead to the world!"

"I've got all our fishing equipment ready," Doug told him. "I'm ready to hit the lake any time you are."

"You're on!"

"Hold it just a minute!" Jesse interrupted as the two made a grab for poles and bait. "I was just telling Melissa that I don't want her to be left alone as long as those dudes are camped across the lake from us. I think it'd be a good idea if we all kept an eye on her, O.K.?"

Doug nodded soberly as Travis asked, "What dudes?"

"Those guys behind us on the road the other day," Doug filled him in. "The blond gave Missy a bad time a few minutes ago. I saw the hoofprints down at water's edge," he said to me with an apology in his eyes. "I never thought they'd pull a stunt like that. Sorry, Sis."

"And I'm sorry I yelled at you. I didn't mean to."

"Let's get down to the lake then," Doug said with a grin. "No way is my kid sister going to be the only one who lands one of those silver babies!"

We spent the remainder of the afternoon fishing, and

although Doug and Travis landed three good-sized cutthroats apiece and Jesse caught four, I was the only one to hook the elusive grayling. After my first catch, however, I didn't get so much as a nibble. Finally, I gave up and stretched out on the grassy bank for a few minutes' rest. The air was almost still and the sun was warm on my face and arms. I closed my eyes, listening to the placid lapping of the water against the shoreline and the high, lonely call of a bird.

Something light and cool tickled my cheek and I brushed it away with my hand. A moment later, something tickled my nose and I gave it another swipe.

"Melissa."

I opened my eyes and saw Jesse's bearded face just above me. His eyes were a mirror of the mountain sky and he was watching me with an expression that fairly melted my bones.

"Have I been asleep?"

"For over an hour." He leaned over and stroked my cheek with a long blade of grass and I had to suppress the urge to reach up and draw his brown head down to mine.

I knew then that I loved him. Strange, that it should come this way—the knowing and the sureness. And yet, not so strange. Loving him had been part of me for a long, long time. Only the realization was new.

"Doug and I are going back to camp to get a fire started and clean the fish," he said. "Want to come with us?"

"Mmmm. I guess so—if I can convince my body to move." I closed my eyes, afraid he would read the love there too easily.

"You've got five seconds," his smooth voice said next to my ear. "If you're not up by then, you know what'll happen next!"

I opened one eye. "You wouldn't dare! You know I hate being tickled!"

"One, two—"

"I can't get up if you're leaning over me!"

"Three—"

"Jesse!"

He laughed and said, "That's a problem you'll just have to work out for yourself. Four—"

I put my hands on his chest and made an attempt to push him back, but he quickly grabbed my shoulders and we rolled together in the grass.

The fingers of one hand lightly tickled my side and I gasped, "No fair! You didn't say five!"

We laughed and rolled over once more, arms and legs entwined.

"Aren't you getting a bit *old* for 'fun and games' in the grass?" came a sarcastic comment.

Jesse and I looked up to see Doug standing over us with clenched fists and anger burning hot in his gray-green eyes.

"I've got a few years 'til retirement," Jesse said with amusement.

Doug bristled. "Look, I know you said to keep a close eye on Missy, but don't you think you're carrying things just a little too far?"

My face was hot with embarrassment but Jesse didn't act the least bit upset. We disentangled ourselves, then he offered me a hand and we both stood up.

"I'm glad to see you're feeling a little more protective towards your sister," Jesse said, calmly brushing some grass off his pantlegs. "It's about time."

"About—about time!" Doug sputtered. "I never thought I'd see the day when I'd have to protect her from you, and I'll be damned if I'm gonna stand here an' watch—"

"Simmer down, buddy. Simmer down," Jesse said with a chuckle. "What you need is some exercise. Chopping firewood'll do wonders for letting out all those pent-up feelings. I think we'll both feel better after hacking away at a big log. Then maybe we could have a little talk. What do you say?"

Doug made a restless movement, then wiped a hand across his face. "O.K., but don't get too close to my ax!"

"Douglas Heydon!" I cried out, finally finding my voice after staring open-mouthed during their entire exchange. "Do you have any idea how ridiculous you sound?"

Doug had the grace to look faintly apologetic as Jesse asked me, "Do you want to do some more fishing or are you coming with us?"

I glanced down the shoreline where Travis was perched on some red rocks which jutted out into the water. "As long as Travis is here, I think I'll try for one more. I can't believe there's only one Arctic grayling in this entire lake!"

Jesse grinned and plucked a few blades of grass out of my hair. "O.K., but don't wander off."

I smiled into the warm blue of his eyes. "Don't worry. I won't!"

I fished for another forty-five minutes or so, but my heart really wasn't in it. Instead, it was soaring away, somewhere among Red Castle's lofty pinnacles. I felt like singing, shouting and skipping across the lake all at the same time.

Travis made his way over to me and said, "I'm ready to call it quits if you are."

"That's fine with me."

I began reeling in as Travis gave me a cryptic glance and said. "You're in way over your head. You know that, don't you?"

"In over my head?"

"You and Jesse."

I grabbed my line and attached the hook to one of the eyes on the rod. "I don't know what you're talking about."

"Oh, yes you do! Remember on the drive up to the cabin, when I said if you ever looked at a man the way you were looking at those mountains, heaven help him? Well, little Missy, I've seen the way you look at that mountain man—only he's not the one who needs help. You do!"

"Travis, I don't want to—"

"Whether you want to listen or understand doesn't matter. There are a few hard facts you need to know!"

"And you're the hard facts expert, I suppose?"

"Somebody's got to face reality," he said with a twisted smile. "You're in love with an image, Missy—not a man! You look at those buckskins and the flintlock and his tipi—even his damn name sounds like some outlaw or trapper or something!"

"Travis, I know what you're trying to tell me, but it just isn't true! I've known Jesse for years! We've—"

"You've known him for a few weeks at a time, here in the

mountains! But what's he like away from here? What do you really know about him or the way he lives? There's got to be something weird about a man who's never married and spends all his time wandering around the mountains wearing buckskins. It's like he's trying to live in the past or something."

I stooped down for the bait box and said quietly, "Jesse was married a long time ago, but his wife died."

"What happened to her?"

"I don't know all the details. Jesse never talks about her and I haven't wanted to pry. All I know is that she was killed on their honeymoon in the mountains."

"What'd I tell you?" Travis said with a smooth smile. "He is living in the past! Jesse doesn't need you or any woman. He's married to the mountains!" His voice lowered and he took a step toward me. "Don't be a fool, Missy! He could never make you happy. Forget him!"

I stared into his jungle eyes, feeling a dry ache in my throat and said, "I can't."

Travis put both hands on my shoulders. "I could help you forget him—if you'd let me!"

I twisted out of his grasp as his head bent closer and fled up the slope toward camp.

*   *   *

I tried to forget what Travis had said—put it completely out of my mind—but like the sting of a bee, the pain of his words continued long after the stinger was removed. My love for Jesse didn't change or diminish, but the joy of realization was smothered by sudden doubts and fears. How did Jesse feel about me? Was I still "little Missy" to him? What if I had been misinterpreting his actions and assuming too much?

The brilliance of afternoon faded and soft twilight settled round the brooding walls of Red Castle. A thin veil of gray smoke was rising above the tops of the pine trees across the lake. It would have been a pleasant sight if I hadn't known whose campfire it was. Our own campfire was burning bright and with the sun's passing, we all felt the need of its warmth.

Doug brought me a sweater and placed it around my shoulders. Then, noticing where my gaze was wandering, he said, "Don't worry, Sis. I don't think we'll see them again."

I looked up at him and smiled. "I hope not."

He gave my shoulders a squeeze and sat down beside me on the log. For the moment, we were alone. Travis was back down at the lake, determined to catch one more before dark. The sight of fish jumping out of the silver-gray waters for insects had proved to be too great a temptation for him. After dinner was over, he grabbed his rod and fairly flew down the slope.

Jesse was up the grassy hillside a few yards away from camp where Saskatoon was tethered. I watched him as he brushed the mare's creamy tan coat and felt my doubts rise once again. All evening he had been unusually quiet and pensive, not saying more than a dozen words to me. I looked away with a sigh and said to Doug, "What did you and Jesse talk about this afternoon?"

"Oh, this and that."

"Could you be a little more specific?"

"I could, but I won't."

"Was it about me?"

Doug grinned and poked at a blackened branch with the tip of his boot. "Now what makes you think we'd be talking about you?"

"Doug, if you want to watch your sister die by inches, just keep it up!"

My brother continued to poke at the branch until it fell into the orange flames with a soft hiss, then he said, "Let's just say, Jesse and I reached an understanding."

His voice was completely serious and I stared at him closely. "What kind of understanding? About what?"

"Man, you are merciless! You know that?"

I smiled. "So I've been told. What kind of understanding?"

Doug relented with a sigh and a shrug. "It's kind of hard to explain—but it's funny how you think you know someone and then, well—you find out you're totally wrong." Doug looked beyond me to where Jesse stood in the gray dusk with his horse. "I've never really understood Jesse or the life he leads—being alone so much, and now, all this mountain man stuff. But after talking to him, I can see why he's lived the way he has all these years—and why he's never remarried."

My throat went dry and my mind flashed over Travis' words: "He lives in the past. Jesse doesn't need you or any woman. He's married to the mountains."

I thought of the young bride Jesse had lost somewhere in the mountains and my heart sank.

"Any more questions?" Doug asked.

I pulled my sweater closer around my shoulders and stared into the fire. "No more questions."

Darkness comes quickly in the mountains and we were all too tired to stay up and wait for the moonrise. Jesse and Travis said goodnight to us as Doug and I crawled inside our small tent. Silently, I unlaced my boots and just as silently, climbed into my sleeping bag. I turned over, facing the side of the tent, and waited until Doug had switched off his flashlight before releasing the flood of tears that had been threatening to break all evening. It hurts like anything to cry quietly, but with Jesse's tent only a foot away from ours, I had no choice. My throat ached and burned and my chest was tight from holding back the sobs, but at least the tears were silent. No matter how many there are, tears can fall without a sound.

"Hey, Sis!" Doug whispered. "What's wrong?"

When you can't say 'everything,' there's only one answer left. I swallowed and said, "Nothing."

"Are you sure? You've been so quiet all evening."

"It's been a long day. I'm just tired."

My voice broke and I felt Doug's hand on my back, attempting an awkward pat of comfort.

"Goodnight, Sis."

"Goodnight."

Long after the tears had stopped, I lay awake, eyes wide open to the inky blackness. The night couldn't be black enough to suit me. Black described the state of my emotions exactly.

Beside me, Doug's breathing was even and deep. The longer I listened, the louder it seemed to get until I thought my nerves would shatter and break! I turned over and tried wrapping the

131

sleeping bag around my head. It didn't help. I couldn't sleep and I couldn't bear lying there a moment longer. I slithered out of my bag a few inches at a time and felt the surrounding darkness for my sweater. My fingers found the touch of cold yarn and I slipped my arms into the sleeves. I didn't bother putting on my boots, but crawled out of the tent on all fours, then stood up in my stocking feet.

The stars! The stillness! And the sweet, cold air! I drew in deep lungfuls and gazed up where the night sky was ablaze with light. At home, the stars always seemed so cold and remote, but here in the mountains, the night was glittering and alive! I moved away from the sheltering pines to see the full spread of sky and my eyes found the Shining Trail. I have always loved the Indian name for our more prosaic Milky Way. Years ago, Jesse and I had stood under this same sky and he had explained how the Indians believed that the Shining Trail was the route departed spirits took to reach the home of the Great Spirit. Tonight, I gazed up at that celestial pathway and thought of Jesse's wife. What had she looked like? I shivered and realized with a strange sense of sadness that I didn't even know her name.

Somewhere up the black hillside, a stealthy rustling stirred the underbrush and my body froze. The rustling stopped and once more the night was completely still. Then it came again, like furtive footsteps moving toward our camp. I held my breath and listened with dry, paralyzing fear as the night visitor advanced ever so slightly, only to pause as if he, too, were listening.

When the noise came again, I backed up two steps and whispered in the direction of the tents, "Jesse!"

The rustling sounds moved further down the hillside and I jumped back with a gasp. "Jesse!"

There was sudden movement in the tent behind me, then a tall figure was at my side.

"Melissa? What's the matter?"

I clung to his brawny waist and whispered, "There's someone out there!"

The light rustling came again and Jesse tensed, putting an

arm firmly about my shoulders. Then he switched on his flashlight and searched the hillside above us.

The circular beam surprised some movement near a large bush and caught the graceful head of a young doe. The deer's head lifted and her eyes gleamed red in the light as she stared directly at us. Then she calmly went back to browsing the tender leaves of a woody bush, as if our presence were only a minor distraction.

My tenseness left me in a long, shuddering sigh, then I began to laugh. "It sounded exactly like footsteps," I said to Jesse. "I was sure Moser and his crew were sneaking down the hillside, all set to ambush us."

He chuckled and switched off the flashlight. "Serves you right for prowling around alone out here. I thought I told you not to wander off."

"I know, but I couldn't sleep."

"Neither could I."

Something in his voice started my heart pounding and I realized suddenly that I was still hanging on to his waist. I let go and stepped away with the trembling observation, "There's a glow on the eastern ridge. The moon'll be up soon."

Behind me I heard a thud as the flashlight hit the ground. I half-turned in surprise. The outline of Jesse's head and broad shoulders was barely distinguishable as he reached for me, then his mouth sought and found mine in the darkness.

The emptiness inside me was filled to overflowing. We kissed, clung together, then kissed again in desperate gladness and I never once wondered what to do with my hands. To hold him close, to touch his face, to feel the strength in his shoulders and neck—I was weak with happiness.

My legs began to shake and Jesse lifted me easily into his arms, his mouth never leaving mine. His kiss deepened and my lips parted under his with a moan. We were both trembling as he set me down outside my tent.

We stared at each other through the darkness and I reached for him once more. Several kisses later, we said goodnight and crawled inside our separate tents. After wriggling into my sleeping bag and listening to Jesse do the same, I lay smiling in the darkness. No matter what Travis said, Jesse Chisholm did not kiss like a man who lived in the past!

Chapter 13

"The Future I may face now I have proved the Past."
Robert Browning

Mist—rising from the lake; cool swirls of white vapor drifting in the stillness of early dawn. Across the calm water, furry borders of pines were tipped with light. Red Castle and the surrounding ridges seemed completely void of depth and dimension. Sharp crags and rocky turrets dissolved in a soft blend of color, mirroring the lake's shade of blue-green. The sky above was palest saffron.

I pressed the shutter release button and captured in a fraction of a second, the timeless beauty of a mountain dawn. Moments later, the sun rose over the ridgeline and when its gold spilled into the lake, the mist was gone in a matter of seconds.

I had awakened early and climbed the hillside behind our camp to photograph a Red Castle sunrise. The sun waits for no one and I knew if I had taken the time to wash or change clothes, the moment I now had on film would have been gone forever. I took a few more shots, then put the lens cap on my camera and headed downslope towards camp.

There was still no movement in either tent. It isn't possible to tiptoe in clunky hiking boots, but I gave it a first-rate try, stepping quietly across the dewy grass. I left the camera on my sleeping bag and reached for my backpack, watching Doug's tousled head for any signs of waking. Rather than hunt for the

135

items needed, I took the entire pack and headed for a little spring I had found the evening before. It was only a short distance from camp and almost completely hidden by a thick cover of brush and trees. I picked my way around bushes and wildflowers, listening for the sound of water to identify the spring's presence. A lazy trickling to my left led me slightly upslope and I found the spring, gurgling pure and cold out of the hillside. Wildflowers were like sprinklings of stars in the wet grass beside the water and moss grew thick and slippery on the purplish-red rocks.

A small bird piped a shrill staccato as I knelt and discarded my jacket and wrinkled blouse. Shivering, I gave my face, arms and neck a thorough scrubbing with soap and washcloth, being careful not to rinse or get any soap in the spring itself. Then I rubbed my chilled skin back to life with a towel. I stuffed the soiled blouse into my pack and pulled a cotton-knit t-shirt over my head. It was short-sleeved and collarless and I knew I would have to be liberal in my use of insect repellent today, but for now, I hated to smear on the smelly stuff when I felt so fresh and clean from my spring water wash. I got out a tiny bottle of perfume instead, then sat down on a dry rock to do my makeup and hair.

I have never been one to primp and fuss with jars of creams and cosmetics and I had packed only the bare essentials for the trip, but Doug had still laughed and poked fun at what he called, "woman's ridiculous vanity." Looking into the compact's tiny mirror, I applied lipstick in the same peachy shade as my top and felt a desperate desire to be beautiful in Jesse's eyes. I stared at the small nose, the wide, gray-green eyes and frowned. I looked so young. There was absolutely nothing sensual or seductive in the face looking back at me. I added a touch of mascara to lashes that would never be lush and long, then closed the compact and reached for my brush and comb.

It took a few minutes to get all the tangles from my hair, but at least there was enough natural curl in it to eliminate the need for permanents and nightly curlers. I held a long, waving strand to the sunlight and smiled over Jesse's comparison the day before. Maybe he didn't mind if I weren't glamorous or sophisticated.

I returned my things to the backpack and picked up my jacket. Beside its denim folds, a patch of wild daisies were snuggled in the long grass. On impulse, I picked one and tucked it in my hair.

The sun was well above the ridgeline as I walked back to camp and insects hovered in a golden haze down by the lake. Our tents and the trunks of the pines nearby were still in deep shade, but the higher branches were brushed with gold. I set my pack on the ground and leaned against the scratchy trunk of a lodgepole, listening to the silence and drinking in the pure morning air.

A moment later, the flap of Jesse's tent was tossed aside and he crawled out. My lips parted as he got to his feet and stretched. His shirt was more than half undone, with the shirt-tails hanging outside his Levis, and his thick brown hair was mussed and tousled. I wondered, suddenly, what it would be like waking up beside him for the rest of my life, and the thought made me catch my breath.

Jesse turned at the sound and saw me standing under the pine tree just behind him. There was a small moment of self-conscious silence as each of us took in the other's appearance. He ran a hand through his hair and I said softly, "Good morning."

He didn't answer right away. A bee hummed a zig-zag path between us through the golden air. Jesse's blue eyes moved over my face, resting a moment on the daisy in my hair, then holding my gaze with suffocating intensity. Somewhere in the pines, a robin began to sing. He was chirping so loudly, I almost missed hearing the low-spoken words, "I love you, Melissa!"

I'm not sure if I really doubted what I had heard or whether I was just too much in shock to make any sense. All I could do was stare at him and stutter, "W-what did you say?"

He swallowed and said with some difficulty, "I wasn't going to tell you—that is, I hadn't planned on saying anything yet, but I—" He paused and his eyes spoke volumes. "I just

137

can't wait any longer to tell you how I feel. I've loved you for so long!"

I took a wavering step toward those blue eyes and whispered, "I love you, too! I think I always have."

We reached for one another and love exploded between us, shattering me to the very core and at the same time, making me whole for the first time in my life. All the years apart, the frustrations and uncertainty, evaporated like the mist on the lake in the warm sunlight of our love.

I leaned back against the tree and Jesse kissed my eyes, my face, and my lips, murmuring his love with every kiss. I couldn't hold him close enough.

When he bent his brown head to kiss the pulse beating frantically at the base of my throat, my knees went weak. Gently, he lowered me to the ground and through the dappled sunlight under the pines we looked into one another's eyes. I reached up and put both hands on his chest, spreading my palms and fingers into the dark, curling hair. I felt the shudder that quaked through his strong body and said in quiet wonder, "All these years, I thought it was the mountains calling to me—pulling me back here—but it was you! All this time, it was you . . ."

His fingers were trembling as they touched my face. "I'll never let you go again, Melissa!"

Somewhere through the golden haze of his kiss, a voice came to us, saying almost plaintively, "Is it safe for me to come out yet? I don't think I can wait much longer!"

We turned to see Doug's head venturing out of the green tent flaps and quickly scrambled to a sitting position. Jesse tucked his shirttails into his Levis and said, "You can come out now."

Doug tossed an embarrassed glance in our direction. "Sorry for the interruption, folks, but—uh, you know how it is!" He got to his feet and made a dive for the trees beyond camp.

Jesse and I watched him go, then collapsed on the ground and laughed till our sides ached.

We cooked breakfast together, laughing over nothing and sharing smiles of love that melted my heart like bacon grease in a hot frying pan. Doug observed the entire scene with grinning nonchalance that made me think he wasn't entirely surprised by the turn of events.

I brought him a plate of scrambled eggs and bacon and said accusingly, "Something tells me you knew how Jesse felt about me before I did!"

Doug accepted the plate and bit hungrily into a piece of bacon. "I told you we reached an understanding! Up until last night I just couldn't see you two together. I don't know why, but the whole idea made me pretty darn mad!"

"I noticed that! What changed your mind?"

"Well, Jesse presented certain facts in such a logical way that I decided things might work after all."

I looked at Jesse who was on his haunches before the campfire, turning the bacon. "What kind of logical facts is my brother talking about?"

Jesse glanced up from the frying pan. "It's very simple. I told Doug he was going to have me for a brother-in-law whether he liked it or not, so he might as well shape up and get used to the idea."

"Oh, you did! And the two of you went right ahead and settled everything without so much as asking how I felt about—about—" A warm flush shot through my veins with the comprehension of his words. "Jesse, do you— are you—?"

He stood up and asked, "How many pieces of bacon do you want, Mrs. Chisholm? Two or three?"

I threw my arms around his neck and pulled his head down to mine.

"Bacon's burning," Doug commented.

Jesse's mouth left mine just long enough to say, "You turn it," then his arms pulled me close.

Travis woke up a few minutes later and eyed our breakfast hungrily. "Hey, why didn't you guys tell me breakfast was ready?"

"I figured your nose would get the message across sooner or later," Doug said. "Don't panic, man! We left plenty for you."

"Well, keep it hot!" he grumbled, giving Jesse and me a

139

suspicious glance, then headed for a cover of pines above camp.

When Travis returned, I got his plate and dished out generous portions of eggs and bacon. "There's some dried fruit, if you like, and a packet of hot cocoa mix. The water's in the kettle."

"Cocoa?" Travis groaned. "What happened to the coffee?"

"I never pack any on backpacking trips," Jesse told him. "There's no food value or energy in it, and up here, you need all the energy you can get."

Travis made a face as he ripped open the packet and dumped the brown powder into a cup. "I haven't had cocoa since I was ten years old."

"Shut up and eat," Doug said cheerfully. "We're heading up to the big lake this morning and if you don't piddle around all day with your food, we'll still have some time to fish here before we leave. Man, I've seen some beauties jumpin' out there!"

I sat back down next to Jesse and asked, "Can I get you anything else?"

"Not to eat, but it's been at least five minutes since I had a kiss."

I smiled and lifted my lips to his.

"Maybe I ought to grow a beard," Doug commented, rubbing a hand over his day's growth. "If it produces results like that, it's worth a try!"

I turned to smile at my brother and saw Travis' face as he stared at Jesse and me. The mask had dropped completely and there was anger and jealousy, as well as total surprise in his expression. Travis caught my glance and the mask slipped smoothly into place.

"I take it congratulations are in order," he said stiffly.

"Melissa and I are going to be married," Jesse told him, and I felt a lovely warmth inside just hearing the words.

Travis didn't bother to comment. He gave me a long look, took a gulp of cocoa, and pulled a face.

I cringed a little, wondering why I had ever been attracted to him.

140

Doug filled the uncomfortable silence by asking a shade too brightly, "When do we leave for the big lake?"

"There's no rush," Jesse answered. "I thought I'd pack us a lunch first, then we can take our time and relax once we get there."

"How far away is this lake?" I asked him.

"A little over two miles."

"Over two miles! That's a round trip of nearly five miles!" Travis complained. "What's this upper lake got that the lower one doesn't?"

"Well, it's nearly five times as large and sits right in the middle of a glacial cirque," Jesse began.

Travis crushed his paper cup with his boot and said, "Forgive me, if glacial cirques don't turn me on. You guys go ahead. I'm staying here."

I looked at him in surprise. "Travis, are you sure?"

"Positive! After yesterday, I'm in no mood for a five-mile hike."

"Maybe that isn't such a bad idea," Jesse said evenly. "The elevation's close to 12,000 feet up there, and altitude sickness isn't anything to mess around with."

Doug smiled, but disappointment was plain on his face. "Hey man, if you want to stay put, that's fine. We can fish here this morning and then take it easy."

"You don't need to stay behind because of me," Travis told him. "I'm a big boy now. I can take care of myself. Besides, I think those two need a chaperone more than I need a babysitter."

Doug grinned and nodded. "You have a point there, but I still hate to leave without you."

"Hey, don't make such a big deal about it! If I get bored, I can always sit around and drink cocoa!"

After breakfast, Doug and Travis decided to try their luck one more time at the lake. I stayed behind to wash the dishes, feeling besottedly domestic, while Jesse packed our lunches for the hike. The chill of early morning was gone and the sky was a radiant blue with only a few high clouds. I paused in the midst of scrubbing the frying pan to watch a hummingbird as it

141

darted among the bushes and flowers just a few yards away.

Suddenly, the little bird flew straight up in the air like a jeweled missile. When he was so high I could scarcely see him against the blue, the bird turned and plunged joyfully toward the earth. I grabbed Jesse's sleeve and pointed as the hummingbird soared once again.

Together, we watched the tiny bird perform his feats of aerial skill over and over, and I murmured, "That's just how I feel this morning. Don't be too surprised if you see me soaring and swooping today."

Jesse pressed a lingering kiss on my lips. "I'll have to keep a tight hold on you then, because I want you right here with me!"

A few minutes later, the camp was put in order and I sat down outside the tents to load my camera.

"While you get your stuff ready, I'll go fill the canteens," Jesse said. "Be back in a minute, honey!"

I smiled and nodded, then bent over the camera, carefully removing the roll of exposed film and tucking it away in my case. I was unwrapping a fresh package of film when a male voice called from the trail below our camp, "Mornin', little lady!"

I must have jumped a foot. Both camera and film tumbled off my lap into the grass. I glanced up to see the tall blond give me a surly grin and doff his hat, a ridiculous ten-gallon affair with a gaudy orange feather in the band. His companion this morning was the big bearded man. Both men were carrying a knapsack of provisions behind their saddles and this time, my eyes were instantly aware of the CB radios attached to their belts. And something else. Both the ox and the blond wore powerful binoculars around their necks.

With a pounding heart, I retrieved my camera and film, then cast an anxious glance toward the trees where Jesse had gone.

"Come on, Moser, we better git goin'," the big man grunted. "We ain't got time to mess around with no dames."

I held my breath and waited, but the tall blond kept a tight

142

hold on his horse's reins and stared straight at me. Then he swung a long leg over the horse and dismounted.

"You go ahead, Clyde. I'll be along as soon as I get a good morning kiss from the little lady, here."

"You'd better go," I said as Moser started up the slope in my direction.

He grinned. "But I don't want to go—and there's no one here to make me. We saw those other two guys fishin' down at the lake, so it's just you and me, doll!"

Jesse suddenly appeared out of the trees. "I wouldn't be too sure about that," he said.

Moser halted in obvious surprise and his pale eyes narrowed as they took in Jesse's size and strength.

There was a charged moment of silence, during which Jesse laid the canteens on the ground and picked up the ax which lay near the stones of the campfire. Then he said to Moser in a voice I had never heard before, "Get on your horse and get out of here! I don't want to see your face around this camp again!"

Moser stood his ground and answered Jesse with a sneer. "You can't tell me what to do!"

Jesse walked calmly down the slope, ax in hand, and the big man on horseback muttered nervously, "Come on, man! We ain't got time for no trouble! We gotta get movin'!"

The blond considered this with a frown, then backed away and mounted his horse. The two men rode off down the lakeside trail and Jesse watched until they were completely out of sight.

I took a few deep breaths, trying to release the clenching tension inside me before getting to my feet.

Jesse turned to me with concern. "Are you all right, honey?"

I nodded and gave him a shaky smile. "I'm glad you're on my side. I had no idea you were so dangerous!"

"Come here, and I'll show you how dangerous I can be."

My heart was racing again, but for an entirely different reason. "Are you going to put the ax down first?"

"Absolutely!"

*　　*　　*

143

Being in love does strange things to one's perspective. We hiked for a good mile and a half through ancient groves of Douglas fir and Engleman spruce, where sunlight filtered softly through needled branches a hundred feet above our heads. We saw deep, snow-fed pools hidden away near Red Castle's rocky base. And I didn't take a single picture. In fact, I didn't even think about it until Doug asked if I had remembered to bring the telephoto lens.

By that time, we had left the forest behind and were climbing over a bleak landscape unlike anything I had seen around Trail's End. Conifers were more scarce here, and noticeably shorter in height. Foliage, in general, wasn't as thick and lush as it had been at the lower lake. The surrounding ridges and meadows supported a thin covering of green, but more prominent were the layers of exposed bedrock which had been thrust up to the surface, like bones of the earth.

Rocks were everywhere, massive blocks and chunks of precambrian sandstone. The oldest rocks in all the earth. At times, the trail nearly disappeared among them, but Jesse led the way upward with quiet sureness.

I don't know why, but the change in landscape brought about a definite change in Jesse's mood. The higher we climbed, the more distant and detached he became. His comments were few and impersonal and his affectionate teasing ceased altogether. I could see the loneliness of the windswept heights in his eyes and felt helpless to know what to do.

As we neared timberline, we were confronted by a massive ridge of red stone which stood like the mighty wall to an ancient city of the gods. Eons of the earth's history had been carved into its seamed and weathered face, and Jesse told us it was nearly 1,000 feet high. Gazing up at the wall's gigantic proportions, I have never felt so small and insignificant.

Then the trail made a sudden curve to the left and we began climbing a giant's staircase of roughly hewn rock. Red Castle Peak loomed ever nearer on our left and the massive wall was to our right, as we followed the only passageway into the heart of the castle.

We paused at the top of the rocky stairs to give our legs a

144

rest and catch our breath in the thin air. Before us was the crestline, the backbone of the Uintas—sheer sides of exposed bedrock and glacially sharpened arêtes. Nestled in a deep, glacial bowl below the mountain ridge was Red Castle Lake. The sun was on the water and the lake shone like a blue jewel in a rocky crown. We were well above timberline now, and there were no trees or bushes around the lake, or anywhere in the glacial amphitheater. Only sparse grass, a few wildflowers and strange tablets of red stone. Some of the rocks were perfect rectangles. Others were piled neatly on one another with green and yellow lichens growing in the cracks. Looking at the stones scattered across the lonely landscape, I had the eerie feeling they could have been giant building blocks left behind by the mighty Titans of long ago.

There was a feeling about the place. I'm not sure if mere words can describe the mood of that high valley. It was wild and beautiful, certainly. But desolate, too, and austere. Time itself had a different meaning here. I found myself thinking not in terms of minutes and hours, but eras and epochs where man had no place or existance.

I shivered in a gust of wind and turned to Jesse. He was staring at a rocky ledge some distance to the left, very near the forbidding face of Red Castle itself. Near the brink of the ledge, purple rocks formed a wall that was so precisely laid out and proportioned, as to appear man-made.

Jesse's expression was one of grim determination and the look in his eyes almost frightened me.

"Jesse? What is it? What's wrong?"

He dragged his eyes away from the rocky ledge to look down at me, then gathered me close in his arms.

"It's all right," I whispered. "Whatever it is, you don't need to tell me if it hurts too much."

Jesse's arms held me tighter and over his broad shoulder I saw Doug standing quite still, a look of mute sympathy on his face.

I knew then. I'm not sure how, but I believe there are ways knowledge can be given without the use of words.

"That's where she died, isn't it?" I said softly.

145

He nodded and I swear I could feel some of the pain and horror leave his body. Without another word, we left the rocky ledge behind and took the gentle slope to the lake.

At first glance, Red Castle Lake appeared smaller than the lower one, but as we drew closer, I realized it was several times larger. The shoreline was rocky rather than smooth, with many of the rocks jutting out into the water. Some were large and flat enough to provide fairly comfortable seating. I curled up on one such rock and used another for a back rest, while Doug collected his pole, grabbed the bait canteen and moved a discreet distance along the shore.

I patted the rock's warm surface and looked up at Jesse. "There's room here for you, too."

He smiled and eased his length down beside me. For a long moment we listened to the rhythmic lapping of the water against the rocky shore and the sigh of the breeze as it curled the lake's surface into rolling curves of blue silk. Then he said, "Carol and I were just fifteen when we met."

"Carol?" For so long, I had carried only a vague image. Now, suddenly, she had a name.

"Carol Anderson," he supplied, giving me a careful glance.

I met his eyes and asked easily, "What did she look like?"

Jesse glanced over the lake, frowning a little, as if it were hard for him to remember and I felt a sudden surge of joy, followed by a twinge of guilt.

"She had brown hair and she smiled a lot," he said finally.

"Was she taller than I am?"

The corners of his mouth twitched slightly. "Yes, quite a bit."

"How did you meet?"

"At a Valentine's dance in school. It was girls' choice or I wouldn't have gone."

"Did she—did Carol ask you to go with her?"

"No. She asked my best friend, but he got sick at the last minute and asked Carol if she'd mind if I filled in for him. She wasn't too happy about the whole thing, but she finally agreed to go with me."

"And at the dance, you fell madly in love and Carol decided to keep you around permanently," I said with a little smile.

Jesse stared at me. "How did you know that?"

"Because I love you—and because she'd have to be crazy not to fall for you."

His glance was warmer than the sun on my face. "I love you, Melissa!"

I just smiled, then stared out at the lake. I didn't trust myself to touch him yet. There was still too much to be said.

Jesse wrapped his arms around his knees and continued, "We went together all through high school and I gave her a diamond on Valentine's Day in our senior year. Both our families were pleased but hoped we'd wait at least a couple of years before getting married. Two years sounded like two centuries to us. We lasted seven months and got married the first of August—on Carol's eighteenth birthday. Neither of us had any money, so my folks suggested that we honeymoon at the cabin."

I looked down quickly as a stab of jealousy cut through me. It hurt to think of Jesse and his bride sharing all the intimacies of love in the one place where we had always been together. I bit my lip and realized with some shock that I had been seven years old at the time. Seven years old! A grubby little kid with mousy hair and missing teeth. At that time in my life, I didn't even know there was such a person as Jesse Chisholm. What right did I have now to be jealous of someone and something that happened nearly thirteen years ago?

I realized suddenly that Jesse was looking at me with tender concern. It was almost as though he knew my thoughts. "Do you mind—too much?" he asked quietly.

A wave of love flooded over me so I could hardly speak. I shook my head and murmured, "No."

"Are you sure? I don't want you to feel—"

I reached out and touched his arm. "And I don't want you to feel like you have to justify loving her to me. Carol had her place in your life and I—" I swallowed and finished in a small voice. "I don't ever want to take that place."

Jesse silenced my feeble efforts at nobility with a hard kiss.

147

"Just in case you didn't know, I never have and I never will love anyone the way I love you!" He kissed me again and said, "I didn't think I could face coming up here again—but with you—" He sighed and held me closer. "I feel like I've finally put the past to rest."

We leaned back against the rock and I laid my head on his chest. I felt sheltered and safe and totally secure in his love. Now was the time to ask the question.

"What happened to her, Jesse?"

He didn't answer immediately. One of his hands absently stroked my hair, while the other pulled me closer to his side.

"The year before Carol and I were married, I hiked up here for the first time with Dad," he said quietly. "I fell in love with the place and wanted her to see it. Since we were coming to Trail's End for our honeymoon, we made plans to hike up to Red Castle and spend a day or two. We spent one night at the lower lake, then left for this lake the next morning. We fished for a while, then fell asleep in the sun."

I stared at the lake's gleaming surface, trying to rid my mind of the painful images his words evoked. Until today, Jesse's wife had never been real to me. I can't honestly remember feeling anything more than mild curiosity toward the person who had shared his life for such a brief time. But now—now I saw a tall girl with brown hair, sleeping quietly in his arms . . . in this very place. The rocks would have been warm and smooth then, the way they were now. The lake, austerely beautiful in its lonely setting . . .

I turned my face against Jesse's chest and shut my eyes, trying to push the past away, not wanting to hear more. But his words continued, softer now, and more halting than before.

"Thunderstorms can hit pretty hard and fast during August. When we woke up, lightning was already flashing around the peaks. We started out right away, but Carol said she wanted to take some pictures from the ledge. I should have stopped her—I tried—but suddenly she was running ahead of me—toward the wall that goes along the edge of the cliff. It happened so fast—all I remember is a blinding light and a sizzling

148

crack." He took a breath and said in a low tone, "It went right through her."

"You mean—lightning?"

Jesse gave a short nod and I felt the tightness in his chest. "I was close enough that the force of the bolt knocked me down, too. I'll never forget the sound of it. I thought the whole mountain had exploded. I wasn't out long though, because the air was still crackling when I came to." He swallowed and said hoarsely, "She wasn't breathing when I got to her and her hands were badly burned where she'd been holding the camera. I should have given her mouth-to-mouth resuscitation right then, but I panicked. If I'd just stopped to think—but lightning was flashing all around us and I knew I had to get her off that exposed ledge—" He stopped and struggled for control. "She was gone before I got her back to camp."

"Oh, Jesse—"

"Then the rains came and it was too late to get out of the mountains before dark, so I—I put her in our tent and waited until morning."

My mind flashed the stark image of an eighteen-year old Jesse keeping vigil beside his dead bride during the long black hours of the night, and I couldn't suppress a shudder.

"Did you—carry her all the way back to Trail's End?" I asked in a dry voice.

"No. Only the first nine miles. Then I met a ranger and he took her the rest of the way on his horse."

Only nine miles. My lips formed the words, but no sound came out.

"I tortured myself with guilt for a whole year after that," he went on. "I couldn't get her face out of my mind. Sometimes at night, I'd remember how it felt, carrying her out, and my body would start to ache all over again. My folks made me come back the next summer. I didn't want to, but they forced me to face Trail's End and the mountains, thinking it would help bring me out of my depression. It only made things worse until—until I met this little 'tidbit' of a girl with freckles on her nose and the spunkiest eyes I'd ever seen in my life." His voice

149

thickened and I tried to blink back the tears, but they came rolling down my cheeks just the same. "She made me realize what I was doing to myself and my family—then she opened my eyes to life again."

Jesse wiped my tears away with his fingertips and when I looked into his eyes I saw only the future. Our future.

Chapter 14

*"Wherever we go in the mountains . . .
we find more than we seek."*
John Muir

For the remainder of the morning we fished and explored the rocky shoreline. Doug was never more than an arm's length away. After leaving us alone for that first hour, he must have decided he was neglecting his duties as chaperone, because I have never seen my brother so annoyingly attentive.

We ate lunch around one o'clock on a large, rocky slab about ten feet from the water, and Doug hovered over us like a pesky insect the entire time. I finished my apple, aching to be alone with Jesse and wishing someone would invent a flyswatter for big brothers.

"When are we going to head back to camp?" Doug asked. "I hate to leave Travis on his own all day."

Jesse glanced up at the sky where continents of white clouds were drifting across an endless sea of blue. "I guess we should be starting back soon. Aren't you going to do any more fishing?" he asked hopefully.

"Naw. I'm beginning to think there isn't one flippin' fish in this whole lake. I'll start packing our stuff, if you like."

I caught Jesse's eye and knew his frustration was the same as mine.

"I've got a better idea," Jesse told him. "Melissa and I will do the packing and you can take some pictures."

"Huh?"

Jesse picked up my camera and handed it to Doug. "Here. Go shoot something! I don't care what it is, just so long as it's far away from here!"

Doug accepted the camera with a twitching mouth. "You know one of the things I've always liked about you, Jess? You're so subtle—just like getting hit over the head with a rock!"

Jesse grinned. "Don't tempt me, buddy."

"O.K.! O.K.! I know when I'm not wanted."

I laughed and gave Doug the small case with my telephoto lens and a box of extra film. "Here. You might need this."

He trudged away with a deeply wounded air, then called over his shoulder, "Where'll I meet you?"

"At the top of the ledge!" Jesse called back. "In a half hour or so."

When Doug's figure was only a small speck against the rocky slope, I knelt on the slab of wine-colored rock and began putting the leftover food into the backpack. Jesse folded his jacket into a pillow of sorts and stretched out full-length, linking his hands behind his head. I snatched a sideways glance at his muscular body and rugged face. The sun added glints of gold to his hair, and a healthy copper tinge along his cheekbones made the blue of his eyes even more intense. He turned, suddenly, and looked at me.

"Why don't you leave that for now."

Except for the soft whisper of the wind, there was nothing to break the silence of the glacial valley.

I moved beside him, feeling unusually awkward, and Jesse's strong brown hands closed around my shoulders.

"Do you realize this is the first time we've been alone—really alone—since you came?" he said, making an attempt at lightness. "I can't believe it's finally happened!"

I drew a shaky breath and placed a tentative hand on his chest. "And I can't believe this is really *us*—together like this . . ."

152

"I think we could both use some convincing," Jesse said.

It took quite some time before either of us felt thoroughly convinced. His love awakened feelings and desires in me that I never knew existed. I lay trembling in his arms, close to his pounding heart, but not half as close as I wanted to be. My body yearned to know his and in those moments I discovered an agonizing truth. There is no test or challenge in saying no to someone you don't want, but to hold back when every bone and fiber is aching for fulfillment is a bittersweet decision. And yet, there was no other decision. The things I wanted most to give him were not yet mine to give—not until we belonged to each other. When that time came, there would be no holding back, only love.

I sat up, trying to release the frustrations inside me, and wrapped my arms around my knees. "Maybe we better go look for Doug."

"If that's what you want."

I looked at his face, the lines of strain around the mouth and the love burning in his eyes. "You know what I want," I whispered. "If I told you how much . . ."

The wind sighed through the high valley and we neither moved nor spoke. Our control at that moment was too fragile to risk even a touch.

Finally, Jesse put an arm across his forehead and stared at the sky. "You know, it's kind of funny. I didn't think anything could be harder than being without you these past four years—wondering how you were, what you were doing—if you ever thought of me . . . But sometimes, having just a little can be a lot worse than having nothing at all."

"Oh, Jesse—" I closed my eyes and put my head on my knees.

"I'm sorry, honey. I shouldn't have said that. I'm only making things harder for both of us." He drew a long breath and added in a lighter tone, "I've been waiting for you for so long, you'd think I'd be used to it by now."

"How long? When did you know how you felt about me?" I asked, still not looking at him.

"Four years ago—when you were sixteen."

153

My head jerked up. "But—that was the summer you acted so cold and—indifferent!"

He gave a short laugh and raised himself on one elbow. "Indifferent? I was in shock! When you left Trail's End the summer before, you were still my little Tidbit. I wasn't ready for the changes in you, physical and otherwise," he admitted frankly. "We'd always been close and affectionate with each other, but that summer I found myself wanting to hold you and touch you in ways that were a lot more than friendly! I didn't know what to do and it made me angry. Especially when you kept telling me about all the different guys who had taken you out during the year! I wanted to bust their heads in!"

I couldn't help smiling. "And all the time, I thought I was boring you to tears."

"To make things worse," he continued, "your mother took me aside and delivered a first-rate lecture about the difference in our ages and laid down the rule, in so many words, that I was to keep my hands off!"

"Jesse, you're kidding!"

"Would I joke about my future mother-in-law? She must have guessed how I was beginning to feel about you and I can't really blame her for worrying. I was twenty-seven then and you were only sixteen."

I rubbed my cheek against the back of my hand and sighed, remembering. "Mom treated me to a lecture, too. On the way home I was crying my eyes out because you had acted so different, and she kept telling me it was only a matter of time before we outgrew each other. I insisted she was wrong, but inside, I was scared silly you would forget all about me."

Jesse smiled and shook his head. "Believe me, I tried! I went out with more girls that year than all the rest of my life put together! And I purposely stayed away from Trail's End the next summer."

"Is that when you met Sheila-What's-Her-Face?" The name slipped out before I realized what I had said, and Jesse lay on his back, laughing.

"Who told you about her?"

"Your mother! She was positively glowing about the whole

154

thing. And so was my mother, come to think of it." My smile faded and I looked into his eyes. "When you weren't there that summer, I thought I'd die. I've never hurt so much in my life!"

Jesse's mouth tightened with emotion and he said, "Come here, Tidbit."

I put my head on his chest and his arms came around my back, warm and strong. "Why didn't you marry her?" I asked in a whisper, loving the feel of his body so close to mine.

"She wasn't you," he said against my hair. "I cared about her, but—it just doesn't work when you have to try to fall in love. I couldn't keep pretending to myself, or to her, so I broke things off. I decided to tell you how I felt the next time you came to Trail's End, but you didn't come back—" His arms tightened around me and he asked, "Why, Melissa? All these years I've wondered. Why didn't you come back?"

"I thought you were married."

"What?"

I lifted my head slightly and said, "When I found out about you and Sheila, I couldn't face going back to Trail's End. Then a while later, Barbara's wedding announcement came and I thought it was yours, so I threw it away without even opening the envelope." I could see the amazement in his eyes as he struggled to take it all in. "All these years, I've been trying so hard to forget you! If only I'd known!"

Jesse stared at me. "You mean, you came up here thinking that I—that I was married to Sheila?"

I nodded, laughing a little. "It sounds funny now, but I even thought Barbara's baby was yours!" He grinned and I told him, "You should have seen my face when Barbara started to nurse him and I realized my mistake!"

We kissed and laughed, then kissed again.

"With so many misunderstandings, it's a miracle we got together at all," I said.

Jesse gave me a close look. "Since this seems to be the time for clearing up misunderstandings—what about Travis?"

I drew a pattern on his chest with one finger and said hesitantly, "Well—he's really Doug's friend."

"Doug's friend was kissing you two nights ago."

"I know." I sighed and looked into his eyes. "I guess I was trying to fall in love, too. I was so lonely! I'm not sure I would have had the courage to come back to Trail's End if Doug hadn't invited him along. He was my moral support to face you and Sheila," I explained in a small voice.

"Then I guess he's worth something," Jesse allowed, "but I sure had one hell of a night after that little scene! I thought I'd lost you for good!"

"I'm sorry, Jesse! I don't know what else to say—except I was stupid and confused."

"I was a little confused myself," he said in a husky tone. "Especially when I went upstairs the next morning to get my flintlock and saw you asleep in *my* bed—wearing *my* pajamas!"

I bent down and kissed his brown throat. "Is that all you felt when you saw me—just confused?"

"Lady, you almost had company that morning!" he growled softly as both hands curved and tightened around my shoulders. He turned then and rolled on his side, taking me with him, so we lay facing each other.

"Are you going to tell me why you were wearing my pajamas, or do I have to keep guessing? I've come up with about four million reasons so far and they're probably all wrong." His tone was light and teasing, but sparks of blue fire glittered in his eyes.

I smiled and put my arms around his neck. "Do you remember the Heydon's 'curse of forgetfulness?"

Jesse's expression was blank for a moment, then he grinned. "You didn't!"

"I did! My flannel pajamas are probably still in the dryer back home unless Mom's discovered them."

We laughed together, then he asked with an interested lift in his voice, "Why didn't you tell Mom or Barbara? They would've been glad to loan you something."

"I know, but then—well, Doug would've found out and you know my brother—" Jesse smiled and put his lips to my forehead as I went on in a quieter tone, "I was so frustrated and confused that night—trying to understand my feelings and what was happening to me. I didn't realize it then, but I needed

156

to be close to you—or at least something that was a part of you . . .''

Jesse's arms tightened around me and he whispered, "Melissa, darling, if I'd known . . ." Then we were lost in another kiss.

Suddenly he released me and sat up. I stared at him as he took a deep breath and blew it out again.

"Come on!" he said, "We better find your brother before all my good intentions go down the drain!"

We finished packing our things and left the lake without a backward glance, walking hand in hand past the silent stones and awesome walls of the castle.

Looking at Jesse's rigid expression, I said lightly, "I've been thinking. As soon as we get back to camp, let's take a poll of all the campers in the area."

He gave me a puzzled look. "Why?"

"So we can find out if there are any ministers or ship's captains around."

Jesse laughed and some of the tightness left his face. "Aren't you forgetting a few things, like blood tests and a marriage license?"

I waved these aside. "Minor details."

"I plan on taking care of those 'minor details' just as soon as we get back," he promised, giving my hand a squeeze.

We had just reached the giant's staircase when we saw Doug running toward us at breakneck speed. He was coming from the direction of the rock wall near Red Castle's west face. Jesse and I exchanged worried glances, then ran to meet him.

"The ledge," he panted as soon as he reached us, then leaned over with his hands on his knees, struggling for breath in the thin air.

"Take it easy," Jesse cautioned. "Whatever it is can wait a minute. Try taking some slow, deep breaths."

Doug shook his head and gasped, "I saw a plane! There's a plane down there—in the trees—below the cliff!"

I blinked and stared at him. "A plane? Doug, are you sure?

He nodded and gestured for us to follow him. "I'm sure! I saw the wings through the telephoto lens!"

157

The flashes of white were definitely recognizable as the wings of a small plane. They lay, several yards apart, in a tall stand of timber. The fuselage was completely hidden by the trees.

From our vantage point on the ledge, we had been able to look down several hundred feet to the fringes of a forest about a quarter mile away where the plane had crashed. Finding the plane on the ground was another matter. We followed the trail for some distance, then cut into the trees near a marshy meadow and worked our way downslope toward the rocky base of the castle.

The forest keeps its secrets well, and it must have been close to an hour before we found the wreckage. The plane was lying on its side in a thick cover of pines, wingless and with the propeller torn off. Jesse reached the cockpit first and looked inside.

Doug said, "Is anyone—?" and Jesse shook his head. Then he gave a low whistle and motioned to Doug.

"Come take a look."

My brother poked his head through the open door and I heard his quick, indrawn breath. "I'll be damned!"

I stood behind them with cold hands and a pounding heart. Now that I knew there were no mangled bodies inside, I ventured closer and asked softly, "What is it?"

Jesse looked at me. "Drugs. Mostly marijuana. The whole fuselage is crammed full of the stuff." He stepped back so I could look, too, and my jaw dropped at the sight. There must have been hundreds of pounds of marijuana, all neatly wired and baled, inside the small plane. But that wasn't all. Near the pilot's seat, a brown cardboard box had been torn open and small cellophane bags containing a whitish powder were strewn about.

Doug picked up one of the plastic bags and stared at the contents. "What do you think it is? Cocaine—heroin?"

Jesse gave the sack a peremptory glance and shrugged. "I don't know—but we'd better not touch anything!"

Doug nodded and tossed the bag inside the plane. "This

stuff has got to be worth at least a million! How long do you think it's been here?"

"It's hard to say, but my guess is, not more than a few days," Jesse answered.

The wind sighed through the tops of the pines and I backed away from the wrecked plane with a shiver. "I wonder what happened to the pilot?"

"Man, I can't see anybody walking away from something like this," Doug said.

We all looked at each other and Jesse said, "Maybe we ought to take a look around."

I found the tennis shoe barely three yards from the plane, wedged under a dead tree root. I picked it up and saw once again the straw-colored hair, the thin body, and the used, empty face.

"Jesse—?" My voice was scarcely more than a dry croak. I cleared my throat and tried again. "Jesse, I've found something!"

He and Doug came running and I held up the shoe. "The man those two hikers brought out of the mountains—he must have been the pilot!"

Doug stared at the shoe, then turned to Jesse. "I remember now—the Polsens said they found him near the trail to the big lake! It has to be the same guy!"

Jesse nodded. "We're going to have to report this to the authorities as soon as possible."

"Don't you think they know about the plane crash?" I said stupidly.

"Drug runners don't usually file a flight plan," Jesse answered.

I swallowed and stared at the tennis shoe. Ever since I had found it, my mind had been centered on a young man brought out of the mountains, not a cargo of illegal drugs.

"It still seems strange that nobody knows about the crash," Doug said with a shake of his head. "I thought all planes were equipped with some kind of device that set off a distress signal or something."

"They are, but this wouldn't be the first time a crash

locator didn't work," Jesse told him. "I'm sure the authorities don't know about this plane."

"But somebody must," I said.

Jesse nodded. "Yeah. The drug runners. They might not be aware of its exact location, but you can bet they know the plane went down."

The silence of the forest turned ominous as Doug gave voice to my thoughts. "Do you think they're looking for it?"

"I can't imagine them writing off a million dollars without at least trying to find the stuff—especially if the authorities don't know it's here," Jesse said.

"Moser—and those men," I said flatly.

"Oh, come on, Sis! I admit those guys are tough-lookin' dudes, but that doesn't mean they're criminals!"

"Moser and the big bearded man were both carrying powerful binoculars this morning," I told him. "And the big man kept telling Moser they didn't have time to fool around—that they had to get going."

Jesse put an arm around my shoulders and said thoughtfully, "None of us have seen all four of them together. They must work in pairs."

Doug stared at him. "You mean—you think those guys—you really think they're—?"

"I don't think we can afford to take any chances—do you?" Jesse countered.

Doug moistened his lips and his face was pale. "No—no, I guess not."

Jesse took the shoe out of my clenched hands and tossed it away. "Come on! We've got to get back to camp. We're getting out of here tonight!"

"But we don't have time to hike out before dark," Doug said. "It's already after four o'clock!"

"If we have to, we can spend the night somewhere along the trail," Jesse told him. "I'm not going to risk spending another night at the lake. We've got to put as many miles between us and those creeps as possible!" He grabbed my hand and motioned for Doug to follow, then stopped in his tracks. "Wait a minute!" Jesse threw a backwards glance at the wreckage and said to me, "Do you have any pictures left on that roll of film?"

I checked the camera. "Yes. Two or three."

"Before we leave, it might not be a bad idea to get a few pictures of the plane. You never can tell, it might come in handy as evidence."

As I adjusted the settings on the camera, there was a sudden creaking in the branches behind us and Doug swung around with a nervous gulp.

Jesse said, "It's only the wind," but my brother took another careful look around.

"What direction was Moser headed this morning, by the way?"

"Toward the west end of the lake, I think," Jesse told him. "But it wouldn't hurt to keep your eyes open!"

I snapped a shot of the plane's exterior, then moved closer to get a picture of the cargo, focusing on the cardboard box and its spilled contents. I pressed the shutter release and took a sharp, second look at the floor beside the pilot's seat. Peeking out among the plastic bags and bales of marijuana, was the smooth, rounded nose of a revolver.

"Jesse, look!"

He peered over my shoulder and I pointed to the gun.

"That explains the empty shoulder holster," he said. "Let's hope there are some good fingerprints on the gun. Did you get a picture of it?"

"I'm not sure, and that was the last frame on the roll."

"What you've taken should be fine," Jesse said and steered me away from the plane. "Now let's get out of here!"

Chapter 15

"I must go, I must run
Swifter than the fiery sun.
And all my fears go with thee!"
Francis Beaumont & John Fletcher

It was five o'clock by the time we reached the lower lake. The afternoon was still warm and I could see three fishermen casting their lines into the blue-green water. One of them, a young man in his teens, waved a friendly hello as we walked past. It seemed odd, somehow, to wave and smile in return. We climbed the gentle slope to our camp and Saskatoon whinnied a greeting. Travis was no where to be seen.

"Where is he?" I said, fighting back tiny pricks of alarm. "He wasn't down at the lake or we would have seen him."

"Will you calm down!" Doug snapped. "He's right here, asleep in the tent."

"Wake him up," Jesse said. "I'll fix us a quick bite to eat, then we can pack up and head out."

If it had been up to me, we would have forgotten both the eating and the packing and run the entire sixteen miles back to the Trailhead. Waves of fear and panic were crashing around inside me, the kind that sweep away both reason and common sense. All I wanted was to run—away from the forbidding face of that red mountain and especially from the men camped across the lake. Instead, I dropped down on a log and watched as Jesse got out the backpacking stove and two packages of dried stew. His movements were calm and unhurried.

"I was going to cook biscuits tonight, but maybe we can make do with gorp instead," he said, and the steadiness of his voice helped ease some of the fear inside me.

"Is there anything I can do?"

"Just one thing."

I gave him a questioning glance and he replied gently, "Try to relax, honey. We're going to make it back just fine."

"I know. It's silly to feel so scared inside. I'm sorry."

He left the stew to give me a kiss and I held myself tightly against him.

"You are the tastiest little tidbit," he murmured against my neck. "I'm tempted to have you for dinner instead of this stew."

I laughed a little and he said, "That's better. Feel like making us some lemonade? There's some powdered mix in the food bag over there."

I nodded and snatched one more kiss before letting him go.

Doug was kneeling beside the tent, giving Travis' shoulder a shake. "Hey, wake up, man! Is that all you know how to do— sleep?"

Travis cocked one eye open and yawned. "You guys were gone long enough! What kept you?"

"Man, you are not going to believe this, but we found—I found—" he corrected himself exultantly, "—a plane! I spotted the wings through the telephoto lens and then we hiked down to it and—"

"The plane!" Travis cried, scrambling out of the tent and grabbing Doug by the arm. "Are you serious? You guys really found it? Where?"

I dropped the packet of lemonade and stared at Travis. Jesse was staring, too.

Doug blinked and said, "Hey, wait a minute! Who's telling who about this thing, anyway? How did you—?"

Travis laughed and bent down for his hiking boots which lay on the ground just outside the tent. "This is incredible! Man, are Hicks and Moser going to be surprised when we tell

163

them! They've been looking for that plane for three days now, and you guys walk right into it in one afternoon!"

A chill knifed down my back and I looked at Jesse whose pose had suddenly gone rigid. His voice was low and even.

"Hold it just a minute, friend. When did you talk to Hicks and Moser, and how do you know they're looking for a plane?"

Travis sat down on a log and yanked a hiking boot on one foot. He ignored Jesse's question and glanced at me with a pleased smile on his face. "Boy, you sure had those guys figured wrong, little Missy!"

I made an effort not to cringe at his pointed use of my nickname and asked, "What do you mean, figured wrong?"

"Come on now," Travis said smugly. "You know you thought they were first-class thugs. Well, they're not—they're agents! Undercover agents for the 'narc' squad. That plane you found is carrying a cool two million in cocaine besides marijuana."

Travis' bland announcement produced the desired response. Doug and I were both knocked speechless.

Jesse put the packets of stew into a pan of boiling water and asked carefully, "Why should they tell you who or what they are? I can't see narcotics agents blowing their cover to anybody who passes by."

"They didn't blow their cover—I did!" Travis answered hotly and tied the laces on his boots with an angry jerk. "I was fishing the other side of the lake and saw Hicks and the Chicano having a beer near their camp. It was around noon and I was pretty thirsty, so I invited myself over. Hicks, the older guy, was kind of surprised to see me. He and the Chicano were going over some maps and I guess they didn't notice me until I got into their camp. Then a minute later, Moser and Bushman called in on their handy-talkies—"

"Bushman?" Doug questioned.

"The big guy with the beard," Travis explained, enjoying himself thoroughly. "Anyway, the two of them called in to report they hadn't had any luck finding the plane and were on their way back to camp."

I brushed a persistent fly away from the paper cups where I

was mixing the lemonade and listened in stunned silence as Travis went on, "Hicks looked pretty uncomfortable and I knew I'd overheard something that was none of my business. I was going to make my apologies and leave, but Hicks said since I'd heard that much I might as well know the rest."

"And that's when he told you they were undercover agents?" Jesse said.

Travis' tone was challenging. "Yeah, that's right."

Jesse only said, "Go on. What happened after that?"

"Well, Hicks told me they'd received a tip about a plane loaded with drugs that had gone down in the Red Castle area, and they were anxious to find it before the drug runners had a chance to come in and make off with the stuff."

"I'll bet they were," Jesse commented. "I suppose they showed you some I.D."

"No, and I didn't ask for any! What'd you expect me to do—demand to see their badges and diplomas?"

"No, I just wondered. Were you still at their camp when Moser and Bushman showed up?"

"Yeah. We had a few beers together and a few laughs. Those guys are all right—once you get to know them," Travis added with a frowning look at Jesse. "Before I left, Hicks asked me not to say anything about them to other campers. Naturally, they don't want anybody else getting wind of what they're up here for."

Jesse smiled a little as he stirred the stew. "Naturally."

Travis didn't miss the sarcasm. "What's that crack supposed to mean?"

"It means I don't believe those guys are cops."

Travis shoved back a tawny strand of hair and his jungle eyes blazed with anger. "Are you calling me a liar?"

"Not you—them," Jesse said easily and dished the stew onto four paper plates. "Doug, do you want to get those sacks of gorp and a couple of packets of catsup? We've got to get moving if we're going to make it out of here tonight."

"What? Are you crazy? We've got to get over to Hicks' camp and tell him about the plane!" Travis exploded.

165

Jesse handed him a steaming plate of stew. "We're not telling anybody anything until I'm satisfied that those guys are really who they say they are—so calm down and eat!"

Travis slammed his plate on the ground. "I don't take orders from anybody—especially high-minded know-it-alls! I've had just about all I can stomach of you, Chisholm!"

Jesse smiled but there was no amusement in his eyes. "You're not exactly one of my favorite people either, kid. But that has nothing to do with what's at stake here."

Travis sat there fuming while I passed around the cups of lemonade. Doug tossed the packets of catsup and gorp to Jesse, then sat down on the log next to Travis. He accepted a plate of stew and eagerly blew on a forkful of potatoes and meat.

"Hey, this stuff isn't half bad," he said, giving Travis a nudge with his elbow. "Especially when you're hungry!"

"Are you going to sit there and let him tell you what to do?" Travis demanded.

Doug glanced at his friend's untouched plate and said, "There's a fly in your stew."

Travis gave the insect an angry swipe and picked up the plate. We ate in tense silence for a few minutes, then he said, "I suppose you know it isn't possible to make it back before dark?"

Jesse shrugged. "It won't hurt to spend the night on the trail."

Travis swallowed a mouthful of stew and said, "What makes you so damn sure they're not cops? You don't know a thing about them—you've never even talked to them!"

"Well, I have!" I put in. "And nothing you could say will ever convince me that Moser is an undercover agent!"

Travis gave me a deprecating glance. "Why?" Because he's got the hots for you? Since when is a guy a criminal if he makes a pass at a good-looking chick? Besides, he was just giving you a bad time. He didn't hurt you, did he?"

"No, but—"

"Well, then? How can you sit there and pass judgment on the guy when you don't have any facts? I tell you, we've got to get over there and let them know about that plane!"

"Speaking of facts," Jesse said. "You haven't given us one yet to back up your story. All you have is Hicks' word for who they say they are. What makes you so sure he wasn't lying through his teeth?"

Travis was slightly taken back, but only for a moment. "Man, if you'd seen their camp and talked to them, you'd know! Those guys are organized! And set up! They've got maps and equipment—I mean, they really know what they're doing!"

"So do drug runners," Jesse stated flatly. "Face it, buddy. We have no way of knowing for sure who those guys are—and I'm not about to risk any of our lives trying to find out!"

"What is this 'risking our lives' bit?" Travis said with a sneer. "There's something you need to face, *buddy*! It wouldn't be good for your big mountain man image to admit that I'm right and you're wrong! I'd spoil all your fun—blazing the trail, saving the girl from the bad guys, and all that crap!"

Jesse was very still beside me. Then he laid his empty plate on the ground and looked Travis squarely in the face. His eyes were like glittering chips of blue ice.

"Travis, if I'm wrong about those guys, you can call me ten kinds of a fool and I won't give a damn! But there's one thing you better get straight—we're packing up and getting out of here tonight—*all* of us! Even if I have to tie you across the horse!"

Travis spit out a vulgar curse and tossed his plate of food away. "I'd like to see you try it!"

I jumped up and grabbed him by the arm. His muscles were taut and coiled under my fingers. "Travis, please! Can't you at least try to understand? It doesn't matter who's right or who's wrong! It just doesn't matter! And arguing like this is only wasting time. Please—even if you don't agree, come with us! Maybe you are right, but we can't take that chance!"

It seemed like minutes instead of seconds that I stood staring into those jungle eyes, seeing the fiery flashes of gold and green, and feeling the animosity and frustration raging within him. Then, suddenly, the control was back and his expression was cool and confident once more.

"O.K. I'll come. But not because I think you're right about

167

any of this! I want to see the look on your boyfriend's face when he realizes he's made an ass out of himself—hiking sixteen miles out of the mountains to report a plane crash when the authorities were right across the lake."

I have never come closer to slapping a man's face as I was right then, but Jesse only answered mildly, "Whatever turns you on, kid! Melissa, would you put away the food? I'll get Saskatoon and start putting on the pack frame. I want to be out of here in the next ten minutes."

"I'll take care of the sleeping bags and tents," Doug said, giving Travis a nod and meaningful glance.

Travis shrugged and looked at the tents with a resigned sigh. "I'll give you a hand with those in a minute—as soon as I water a tree," he said and headed downslope toward a cover of pines.

Doug and I exchanged glances as Travis walked away and my brother delivered his opinion of his friend's behavior in a few choice expletives.

I ran to retrieve Travis' plate of food from the bush where it had landed, then stuffed the paper garbage into a plastic bag. The only items that needed washing were our utensils and the pan Jesse had used to heat the stew. These, I hurriedly rinsed with cold water.

Moments later, Jesse came down the hillside leading Saskatoon. Doug had two of the four sleeping bags rolled up and the tents down.

"Let's pack out all we can on the horse," Jesse said. "We'll make better time and won't get so tired if our packs are lighter."

"The food's put away and ready to go," I told him.

"Thanks, honey. Doug, what time is it?"

"Ten minutes to six."

Jesse looked up at the sky where a hazy cloud cover was obscuring the late afternoon sun. He frowned and said, "It's going to be a dark night if those clouds stick around."

"Do you think it will rain?" I asked him.

"No, but I doubt we'll make it back to Trail's End before

dark." Jesse glanced around then and asked, "Where's Travis?"

Doug's expression was blank. "He was here just a few minutes ago. He made his excuses and went to visit the trees."

"Which way was he headed?"

Doug pointed to the group of pines below camp and Jesse said tersely, "You better go find him!"

Doug dropped the foam pad he had been tying and ran toward the trees where we had last seen Travis. He searched the area, calling Travis' name, but there was no response. My heart began a heavy, hard pounding.

Doug ran back to us and gulped, "I can't find him anywhere! You don't suppose he'd be stupid enough to—"

"How long has he been gone?" Jesse demanded.

I shut my eyes and tried to think. "Five minutes—maybe a little longer."

Doug was looking like someone had hit him in the stomach with a two-by-four. "Jess, I—if I'd thought he'd pull anything like this—!"

"Forget it! I should have known his ego wouldn't let him give in."

"What are we going to do now?" My voice sounded childishly small and thin to my ears.

Jesse began untying the pack frame with swift, angry jerks. "We're getting out of here! Now!"

"But those guys have horses!" Doug said. "There's no way we can outrun them!"

"If they're stupid enough to run their horses at this altitude, we won't have anything to worry about. Those animals'll be dead after the first mile," Jesse told him. "At least we've got a head start. Let's make every minute count!" He threw the pack frame off to one side and said, "Put on your warmest jackets and stuff your pockets with trail food. We're leaving everything else behind. If they see our tents and gear, they might not realize we've gone and that'll buy us a few more minutes."

I grabbed my heavy jacket out of my pack and asked, "What should I do with my camera and film?"

"Put 'em in my backpack," Jesse said quickly. "But you and Doug leave your packs here." He reached into the food bags and tossed us each some dried fruit, granola and jerky, then put on his backpack and buckled the straps around his lean hips. "You ready, Tidbit?"

I gave him a shaky nod and he said, "Give me your foot then and I'll give you a boost up."

"Why? I don't mind walking."

Jesse grabbed me by the waist and swung me effortlessly onto the mare's back. "We'll make better time if you ride," he said shortly. "There's no way your legs can keep up with mine."

I settled myself astride the horse and Jesse grabbed the halter rope, heading for the lakeside trail at a swift walk.

Doug ran alongside him. "Wouldn't it be safer if we stayed away from the trails and cut cross-country?"

"Probably, but there's a lot of deadfall on the ridge just above us and I don't know whether I could get the horse through it. Besides, we're not taking the main trail. The Bald Mountain trail cuts off just before we get to the switchback. It's the long way home, but Moser and his crew will never think to look for us there."

Doug blew out a relieved sigh and Jesse looked back at me. "Keep a sharp eye on our rear, O.K., honey?"

I nodded and clung to the buckskin's heavy mane.

It seemed like forever instead of fifteen scant minutes before Jesse's long-legged stride had put the lake behind us. Saskatoon didn't approve of the pace and was continually balking and jerking on the rope. Even Doug was hard-pressed to keep up with him and I was thankful my legs didn't have to try. The only time Jesse slowed at all was in crossing the streams. Between the lower lake and the switchback, there were three fair-sized streams cascading directly across the trail. On the hike up, I had paid them little heed, enjoying the diversion and easily leaping from one stone to another in my eagerness to reach the lake and our journey's end. Now, each one loomed as a time-consuming obstacle course.

I kept a nervous watch on the trail behind us as Jesse led Saskatoon carefully across the first stream. We had covered a little more than a mile and still had the widest stream, plus a long stretch of open meadow to cross. Evening shadows were lengthening on the forest trail and the air was calm and quiet. The scene was all wrong for a get-away. There was absolutely nothing in the landscape that hinted at danger. And yet I knew the danger was very real and somewhere on the trail behind us.

We reached the second stream some twelve minutes later. In most places it wasn't more than a foot or so deep, but there were enough deep holes pocketed between the rocks to make the going risky and slow. I hadn't remembered it being nearly so wide or the bank so steep. Between us and the opposite side was a full twelve feet of rushing water. Saskatoon balked and shied away from the stream, but Jesse finally managed to cajole her into the water. We picked our way across and I cringed every time the mare's hooves slipped on the smooth stones. With an ungainly lurch, Saskatoon achieved the opposite bank and I relaxed my fierce hold on her mane.

Jesse picked up the pace once more and pointed to the thinning trees ahead. "We're nearly to the meadow!"

Then from behind, came a startled cry and a splash. I looked back to see Doug half-sprawled, half-lying on the steep bank. He was dragging one foot out of the water and his face was pinched and white.

Jesse tossed me the halter rope and ran back to him. "What happened?"

"I slipped on a damn rock," Doug said through his teeth, and grabbed Jesse's arm. "I'll be O.K. Come on, we've gotta keep moving!"

Jesse frowned. "Hold on. Are you sure you can walk?"

"Sure! I just turned my ankle a little, that's all." He smiled and shook off Jesse's supporting arm, but I could see the whiteness around his lips as he took a few mincing steps.

"Oh, Doug, who are you trying to fool? You can't walk ten feet on that ankle, let alone ten miles!"

Jesse bent down beside him "Maybe I'd better take a look at it."

"We haven't got time!" Doug groaned, as Jesse loosened the laces on his boot.

171

"Then Saskatoon will carry you both," Jesse told him matter-of-factly. "Hop up, buddy. You're riding from here on."

Jesse hefted him up to the mare's back and Doug grabbed hold of my waist, biting back a cry of pain.

"It's already swelling," Jesse said. "I don't think it's broken, but you've got a bad sprain."

"Skip the examination, Jess, and let's get moving!"

Jesse gave a grim nod and pulled Saskatoon forward once more.

When the meadow opened up around us, I felt as vulnerable and visible as a deer. Jesse accelerated his pace to a loping run on the level stretches of the trail and I marveled at the stamina that kept him going. In minutes, we reached the bridge. Behind us was mountain silence, an empty trail and the brooding face of Red Castle. I shifted my gaze to the trail ahead where the red path narrowed, then dipped downhill. Soon the air was vibrating with the sound of rushing water and I knew the falls must be near.

I strained to see, then cried, "There it is! There's the signpost and the fork in the trail!"

Doug gripped my waist a little tighter. "Thank God, we're going to make it!"

Jesse broke stride to give me a breathless smile and snatch one more look at the trail behind us. His big chest was heaving and perspiration was running down his neck in rivulets. Instead of relief, I saw a sudden, slight tensing in his body.

"They're coming!" he got out before yanking the rope and breaking into a dead run.

I barely had time for a hurried look over Doug's shoulder, but that scant second caught the silhouettes of two men on horseback framed against the backdrop of dark pines and alpine meadow. The scene held perfect balance of composition and light, looking for all the world like a calendar photograph. Sunlight glanced off the ruddy flanks of the horses and their heads were curved in a graceful arch. Suddenly, the picture sprang into life as Moser and Bushman urged their horses into a full gallop.

172

Barely fifty yards ahead of us, the trail forked and the trees waited as a shadowy refuge. Forty yards. Thirty.

Everything was pounding around me. The horses' hooves, the plunging force of the waterfall, my head and my heart. Doug's hands gripped my waist with bruising force and his breathing was ragged and harsh in my ears. But no more so than Jesse's. After pushing hard for more than two miles, his strength had to be nearing an end, and the weight of the backpack was slowing him down.

I flung a desperate glance over my shoulder and saw Moser's long yellow mane whipping the air and Bushman's massive legs mercilessly kicking his horse's sides. They were gaining on us with every second.

Jesse reached the fork in the trail and the silent pines were only yards away when he suddenly tossed us Saskatoon's rope and yelled, "Get into the trees! Hide!"

"No!" I screamed. "No! Jesse, don't—!"

But he was already breaking away and veering to the right in an attempt to direct the two men away from Doug and me.

Doug slapped the rope against the mare's neck and gave her flanks a brutal kick. Saskatoon broke into a startled gallop and I screamed again, "No! Doug, stop! We can't leave him!"

"Keep your head down and hold on!" he yelled in my ear and urged the horse forward with another hard kick.

The mare's coarse black mane stung my cheeks as I wrenched my head around to see Moser turn his horse and make straight for Jesse. Watching his desperate flight to the trees, my heart hammered out the message: "You'll make it! You'll make it! You've got to make it!"

Suddenly, Moser reined in hard and jumped to the ground. He was reaching for something. Then his arms were extended, elbows taut, with both hands gripping a revolver. The first shot sang out and Jesse never missed a step. A second shot and a third ruptured the air and I saw Jesse's strong body twist with a sudden, surprised jerk. He went down on his face and lay still.

"No! Jesse—!" I grabbed the rope out of Doug's hands and yanked the mare's head around, then everything happened at once. There was a thunderous boom. Saskatoon screamed and

173

stumbled. I went sailing over her head, rolled in the grass and landed in a thick patch of low-growing spruce.

The air was alive with frightened screams and whinnies, but it wasn't Saskatoon. I lifted my head and saw Bushman's horse rearing in pure terror. A heavy revolver flew out of the big man's hands as he struggled to control the animal.

The scene spun and whirled around me as I staggered to my feet. I put a hand to my head and saw Saskatoon lying only a few feet away. Blood was spilling out of a huge, gaping hole in her side and the ground beneath her was dripping crimson. Nausea rose in my throat and I choked back the bitter fluid. The mare's beautiful eyes were glazed with pain and looking to me for help. Listening to her thick, dying gasps, I felt another wave of nausea and a cold, shaking weakness in my bowels.

No more than a yard away from the dying horse, Doug's twisted body lay agonizingly still.

Shock and pain. Grief and a numbing kind of disbelief held me in a motionless void. My eyes went helplessly to the spot so near the trees where Jesse had fallen. Moser's tall figure was striding confidently toward him, gun in hand.

Life and movement came surging back and I screamed, "No! Don't you touch him!"

The distance between us was too far for me to see his face clearly, but the rangy blond head jerked immediately in my direction, then to Bushman who was still fighting to quiet his horse. I heard Moser's rasping shout, "Get the girl! Don't let her get into the trees!" I saw Bushman give his horse an angry, frustrated kick. With a wheezing groan, the animal collapsed beneath him and lay on its side, gasping for breath. Bushman cursed the exhausted animal and got to his feet while Moser grabbed the reins of his own horse and leaped on its back.

The wind stirred the tops of the pines as he galloped toward me and its whining voice seemed to whisper Jesse's last words: "Get into the trees! Hide!"

I turned and ran.

Chapter 16

"Thou comest! All is said without a word."
Elizabeth Browning

Panic was spurting through my veins but something, call it instinct or even inspiration, plotted my course. I kept to the thickest cover, dodging and darting through the pines as swiftly as a deer. Moser had no choice but to leave his horse behind and take up the chase on foot.

The ground beneath my running feet wore a thick carpet of soft pine needles, and the earth was still fairly moist from recent rains. Except for the unavoidable crack of a dry twig or fallen branch, my flight was amazingly silent. Far more so than my heart which was pounding a hard, wild rhythm inside my chest. Flashes of green meadow appeared between the brown trunks on my right and avoiding them, I plunged deeper into the forest. What I thought was the wind roaring through the trees, suddenly emerged as a stream, some six feet across. I flew from stone to stone, reaching the other side without wetting even the bottoms of my boots.

I ran on, hoping the sound of the tumbling water would mask the direction of my escape. For years, the forest had been my friend, now it was a refuge—a sanctuary. I flattened my back against the trunk of a lodgepole to catch my breath and heard heavy splashing in the stream behind me.

I raced away, giving no thought to direction. Distance was all that mattered. Without warning, the trees thinned and I ran right into a trail. But which trail? Everything looked the same. I glanced around for three helpless seconds then plunged down the trail at a punishing speed, taking advantage of its smooth, nearly-level grade. Then I cut into the pines once more.

The taste of blood was in my throat and I couldn't seem to draw in enough air. I dodged behind a sturdy trunk and forced my lungs to take slower, deeper breaths. From behind, came the brittle crack of dry wood crumbling under booted feet. He was closer now.

The chase began again. No matter how well the trees hid my presence, the sound of my escape was constantly giving Moser my direction, as accurately as any compass. My own ears were tuned so acutely to the crashing sounds of his pursuit, I was only half aware of the peaceful flow of water, coming from somewhere below me. Without consciously making a decision, I fled downslope toward the river. The volume swelled even as the ground fell away in a steep, forested ridge. Something about the place was vaguely familiar. When I saw the red trail cutting its way down the slope in a zig-zag fashion I realized I had come to the switchback. There was little comfort in knowing where I was because the area was devastatingly open. The trees were yards and yards apart instead of a few feet.

I tried to think, to picture in my mind the way we had come. Beyond the switchback was the river and the bridge. But how far? And wasn't there an open stretch near the bridge? Or was it on the opposite side?

The heavy crashing behind me insisted I find cover—and soon! I ignored the switchback trail completely and took a plunging course straight down the ridge. My knees were shaking and weak from the steep grade. My hiking boots felt like heavy blocks of cement, but I couldn't stop running. Suddenly, the ground was racing up to meet me faster than my feet could go. The curling root of a dead pine snatched at my ankle and I went tumbling down the hillside. I rolled perhaps twenty or thirty feet, grabbing at bushes to try and break my fall. The whirling stopped and I got to my knees, gasping for breath.

Above me, there was silence. Then a snap. I leaned over, holding my sides and listening. He must have been listening as well because the forest was hushed and still for an agonizing fifteen seconds. Then I heard the soft crunch of booted feet, walking slowly now, somewhere on the trail above me.

I struggled to my feet and glanced around in desperation, mouthing the silent plea: Help me. Please, help me!

Something insisted that I follow the river, not downstream, but up. My chest was hurting me with every breath and my legs were trembling like aspen leaves in the wind. Half-stumbling, half-crawling, I made my way toward the edge of the stream. Here, willows and other bushes made a wild, almost impenetrable hedge. I pushed my way through them, mindless of the scratches and whip-like branches that slapped my arms and legs. Where now? My mind was screaming the message: run! run! But through the panic, a stillness somewhere inside gave the quiet direction: Here. Hide.

Not even five feet away, the river bank jutted out in a rounded knob of land, completely grown over with willows and wildflowers. The view around that tiny knob was effectively blocked by the tangled screen of green and brown.

I edged my way around the slippery bank, hanging onto the willow branches and trying to keep from stepping into the stream. My left foot slid into the water, but at least it was shallow, no more than a foot or two in most places. I reached the hidden side of the bank and discovered a small hollow where the spring runoff had cut deeply into its curved sides. Willow branches arched well over the washed-out area, dabbling their leafy tips in the water, but the ground underneath appeared to be dry. I crouched low, ducked under the willows, and crawled in on all fours, molding myself to the contours of the bank. The willows made a leafy, protective canopy over my head and all along the bank, mountain bluebells nodded in the fading light.

I pressed a hand to my pounding heart and waited, straining to hear the sound of footsteps and praying not to. Nothing. Only mountain water playing soft melodies to the silent trees. The silence was almost worse than the crashing sounds of his pursuit. Even allowing for the voice of the stream, I should have been able to hear something if he were nearby.

I shut my mind to the discomforts of my cramped position and the constant ache of complaining muscles. Time passed. I fought back the temptation to sneak a quick look by counting. I didn't want to think, or remember, but the image of Jesse's fallen body kept superimposing itself over the regiment of numbers marching through my brain.

After counting to 600, I decided I might risk a look around. My legs were so stiff and cramped, when I tried to move, I couldn't. I reached out to grab a willow branch for support and heard a tiny click, the hum of static, then a voice which couldn't have been more than five feet from where I was hiding.

"Hicks—this is Moser. This is Moser. Over."

My heart gave a frightened jerk and my arm froze in its extended position.

The response was rather tinny, but Hicks' voice was as commanding as ever. "Did you stop them?"

"The big guy with the beard is stopped permanently! I got him just before he got into the trees. Bushman shot the horse out from under the girl and her brother."

Slowly, I drew my arm back to my side and covered my face with my hands.

"Are they alive?" Hicks demanded.

"I didn't have time to check the brother because the girl took off through the trees and I had to go after her. But I think he was unconscious. Bushman has him."

"What about the girl?"

There was a moment of loaded silence, then Moser said, "She got away. I chased her as far as the bottom of the switchback, then lost her." Moser waited for Hicks to respond and when no comment or instructions came, he said uncomfortably, "She'll never make it out before dark. She didn't have a pack or any food. I wouldn't worry about her. She won't be any trouble to us."

"I'm not worried about the girl!"

Hicks' voice was livid with anger as he delivered a blistering opinion of Moser's actions and performance for the day. Moser inserted a few choice comments of his own that gave me a sick feeling in the pit of my stomach. Having two older brothers, I have been exposed to some locker-room language from time to time, but nothing like the ugly stream of filth I was hearing now.

Finally, Hicks' voice gathered some control and he asked with a coldness that was almost more frightening than his anger had been, "So how's a dead man and an unconscious kid supposed to show us where the plane is? Tell me that, Moser!"

Moser didn't answer.

The cry of a bird echoed through the forest and I closed my eyes. My throat ached but I couldn't cry. There was nothing left inside me to cry or feel ever again. Only emptiness.

Moser asked in a voice that was almost subdued, "What do you want me to do now?"

"Get back to Bushman and make sure he doesn't get any trigger-happy ideas with the brother. Then bring him back to camp. You and Bushman better hope that kid's all right—understand?"

"I understand. I'll see you back at camp." Moser's answer could only be described as submissive, but after switching off the radio he told Hicks exactly where to go and what to do once he got there. After that, there were a few seconds of silence, then what sounded like the dry crack of breaking branches somewhere on the hillside above me.

My position under the bank denied me both sight and sound. The only sense I had to determine Moser's presence was feel. I waited, counting slowly to one hundred before attempting any movement. Even then, I hesitated, waiting another full minute. Something wasn't right. Something about his conversation with Hicks was pricking my subconscious and urging caution. Another long minute passed. Daylight was fading and the hushed mood of evening cloaked the forest. Even the movement of the stream was muted and soft.

Moving an inch at a time, I uncurled my stiff arms and legs from the hollow and took a few deep breaths. There wasn't a joint or muscle in my entire body that didn't ache. I grabbed hold of a willow branch and got to my knees. The cold fear of Moser's presence was still throbbing inside me. I wet my lips

179

and stared at the mountain bluebells on the grassy bank. I had to leave sometime. It might as well be now. The very moment I was going to rise, something moved in the willows a few feet away. I swallowed a startled gasp and glimpsed a dark, mounded shape waddling in my direction through the maze of branches. The porcupine passed within inches of me, taking note of my presence with the flick of one eye, then ambled up the bank and out of sight.

Before I could move another inch, Moser's voice barked out, "All right, little girl! The game's over. I can hear you, so forget the hide 'n seek and come on out!"

A chilling cold spread through my veins but I remained motionless. So this was why the feeling of his presence had remained so strong. He must have known all along that I was hiding somewhere nearby. Telling Hicks that he had followed me to the bottom of the switchback had been an outright lie. Moser couldn't have missed hearing my fall down the ridge and that would lead him directly to the stream. I hadn't had nearly enough time to reach the bottom of the switchback and he knew it. The only thing he hadn't known was exactly where I was hiding. So he had decided to wait. Well, he was going to have to wait a little longer!

From above, I caught the tiny snapping sounds which marked the direction of the porcupine's slow waddle.

Moser gave a satisfied grunt. "That's right, doll! I can hear you, so just come on—What the hell?" His voice lifted in surprise and I felt like blessing every one of those pointed little quills.

A piercing crack suddenly shattered the air and I clapped both hands over my ringing ears. The shot reverberated through the forest and for one wild moment I wondered why I wasn't dead. Then I heard Moser's angry curse and noisy departure as he stomped through the brush and up the hillside.

This time, all my senses assured me he was gone, but the relief was so weakening it was some time before I found the strength to stand. Shivering and cold, I crawled through the screen of willows and climbed up the bank. The first thing to meet my gaze was a bloody mass that had been a porcupine only moments before. Moser's bullet had caught him in the head and at close range. I staggered away and leaned against a tree, retching violently. The vomiting racked my insides, but when it passed I felt strangely calm. Weak, shaking, with a burning throat and a vile taste in my mouth, but calm nonetheless.

I wandered along the heavy undergrowth lining the bank until I reached an open place that was grassy and fairly level. There, I knelt and bathed my face and hands, noticing for the first time, the jagged tears in my jacket and Levis, the angry red scratches on my hands and legs. I cupped my hands and drank from the stream, not caring one way or the other if the water was pure. It was cold and eased the raw pain in my throat.

Nothing could ease the raw pain inside. What to do . . . where to go . . . Kneeling on the bank, I closed my eyes and offered the quiet prayer, "Dear God, please help me—" I didn't know what else to say. Finally, I lifted my head, got to my feet and started up the hillside.

Finding the switchback trail was no problem, but I knew I couldn't retrace my flight through the forest. The only way to find Jesse would be for me to go back to the fork in the trail by the waterfall and start looking from there. I had to find him. Nothing else mattered. Not the oncoming night and prospect of spending it in the open. Not even the fact that Moser and Bushman had Doug. All I wanted was to be with Jesse.

My thoughts were a jumbled mixture of images and emotion as my plodding feet moved slowly up the switchback. Only yesterday, Jesse had led the way up this trail, his broad back and long legs always before me . . . What was I going to tell Aunt Milly? She never wanted him to go. She had been frightened of Jesse's return to Red Castle from the beginning. I saw it once again, the wine-red mountain, the ancient turrets of stone with snow-filled crevices. Then Jesse's face, bending over me, his eyes deeper than the waters of the lake. It wasn't fair! To have his love for barely a day wasn't fair! Never to know the joy of belonging to him . . . to give him sons and daughters. What was it he had said this afternoon? . . . only this afternoon? It

181

felt like another lifetime. What was it . . . sometimes it hurts worse having just a little than having nothing at all.

I dropped down on my knees in the middle of the trail and began to cry. Hard, racking sobs that tore at my chest and echoed through the forest stillness. I cried his name again and again, and the wind seemed to whisper back the words of his farewell: "Don't cry, Tidbit. I'll be here waiting for you—just like the mountains . . ."

The tears fell harder. There was a knot in my breast where my heart used to be and I wished fervently, for the first time in my life, that I could die.

"Don't cry, Tidbit—"

The voice. Would I ever stop hearing his voice?

"It's all right, darling. Please don't cry. Everything's going to be all right now!"

Through tear-blinded eyes, I looked up and saw a bearded face bending over me. I had to touch its brown softness to believe he was really there. His cheeks were as wet as mine.

"You're alive—oh, Jesse! You're alive!" I sobbed and went into his arms.

It was a time for touching, not talking. I needed no answers to questions, no explanations; only the reassurance of his heart beating next to mine and the solid warmth of his arms. My life had been given back to me. When I put my arms around his neck, he flinched suddenly, and I drew back to look at him. A red stain was spreading through the left sleeve of his jacket, just below the shoulder.

My eyes widened as they took in the size of the wound, but he said quickly, "It's O.K., honey. I would've been a lot worse off if he'd got me in the leg."

"But—you're bleeding!"

"I've lost a little blood, but at least the bullet went clear through."

"Jesse, we've got to stop the bleeding! Is the first aid kit still in your backpack?"

"Yeah, but—I'm not sure where my backpack is." He gave me a thin smile and said, "I took it off somewhere in the trees because of my arm."

182

I bit my lip and looked into his eyes. "When I saw you go down, I thought—"

"I know, honey, and thank God, so did Moser. He's a crack shot and that last bullet hit me square in the back."

"But how—?"

"Something in the backpack caught the bullet instead of me, but the force of the shot was enough to knock me down. Moser probably would have finished the job if you hadn't yelled at him when you did. When he took off after you, I crawled into the trees." His expression tightened into worry. "How did you get away from him? I was coming down to look for you when I heard a shot, then a few minutes later Moser came up the trail alone . . . " He trailed off and I tried to kiss away the haggard look on his face.

"I'll tell you about it after I've done something for your arm. It needs to be wrapped up."

"Melissa, there's nothing you can do! And I'm not about to let you out of my sight to go look for that backpack. I'll be all right. I applied pressure to the wound the best I could."

"It still needs to be wrapped up! You'll be too weak to walk if we don't do something!"

"What about you?" he countered. "Your hands and face are cut and your clothes look like—"

I saw the anguish in his eyes and answered quickly, "I'm all right, darling. I took a tumble, that's all. Moser never touched me." I thought of the bloody porcupine and said softly, "The forest has a way of looking out for 'guardian spirits.'"

Jesse's hand reached out to touch my face and the pallor of his own was frightening.

"There's got to be something I can do!" I said, looking down at my filthy jacket and t-shirt and torn Levis. "What I need is a nice white petticoat!"

He managed a smile. "Too bad they're not the fashion."

I straightened up suddenly and kissed his cheek. "I know!"

"You know what?"

"First, let's get off the trail and into the trees." I stood up and gave him my shoulder to lean on, then pointed to a cluster of pines. "Right over there."

When Jesse was sitting more or less comfortably against the trunk of a lodgepole, I moved behind him and took off my jacket. I pulled my t-shirt up, slipped my arms out of the sleeves, then unfastened my bra.

Jesse glanced over his shoulder and color rushed into his wan face. "Are you trying to give me first-aid or a heart attack?"

"Jesse, turn around!"

"I am!"

"The other way!"

He relented with a sigh and a grin. "I don't know what you have in mind, but I feel better already!"

I laughed and took off the bra, then slipped my arms back into the t-shirt and pulled it down. Only minutes ago, I never expected to laugh again.

"Do you still have your knife?" I asked him.

"Yeah, it's hooked on to my belt. Here."

I cut the straps off first, then, as the bra fastened in the front, I cut through the elasticised fabric in the back, dividing it in two.

Jesse watched the process with an interested smile on his bearded face. "I'm impressed!"

"You know what they say about necessity being the mother of invention," I told him and laid the cut pieces of soft tricot carefully aside. "Now, can you help me take your jacket off? I'll try to be careful."

We managed the sleeve of his good arm first, then slid the blood-stained fabric off his injured arm. His shirt-sleeve was soaked with blood and I winced the entire time I cut it off. Then, biting down hard on my lower lip, I looked at the torn flesh. As he said, the bullet had passed straight through the fleshy part of his upper arm and the exit hole was much larger than the spot where the bullet had entered. Gingerly, I placed a soft cup of tricot on either hole, then tied them securely with the straps.

Jesse stared determinedly at the pine boughs above him the entire time I dressed his arm, flinching only once, when I tied the straps. I unfastened one of his shirt buttons and lifted his hand carefully inside the shirt to act as a crude sling.

184

"Does it—feel all right?" I asked anxiously.

His face was pale but he gave me a smile and said, "It feels fine! Really, it's much better. What size am I wearing, by the way?"

I smiled and shook my head, then bent down carefully to kiss him. His good arm came around my waist, drawing me closer, and we sat for a long moment with not so much as the call of a bird to break the silence. Then I put my cheek next to his and asked, "What are we going to do? They've got Doug."

Jesse answered me with a frustrated sigh. "The only thing we can do is walk out and get help." He glanced up at the sky where evening's deep blue was powdered with pink and gray clouds. "There's still time to put a few miles behind us before dark. Then we can sleep till the moon comes up."

"How many miles is it back to Trail's End?"

He gave me a close look. "Around thirteen or fourteen."

I seriously wondered if I would be able to walk at all, but I didn't want him to know that. I got to my feet and said briskly, "Well, we'd better get going then."

Jesse stood up with a grimace of pain, put his good arm around my shoulders, and together we walked down the dusky forest trail.

Chapter 17

I'm gonne build me a cabin
Up on the mountain so high
That the blackbird can't find me,
Nor hear my sad cry . . ."
Old Mountain Song

Our progress was painfully slow. Frequent stops were necessary for both of us and in an hour's time we had covered less than two miles. We trudged on through the dim light for another ten minutes, then dropped down on the trail to rest.

"How much farther do you think we can get before dark?" I asked, wishing he would say we were going to stop here and spend the night. To our left, thick brush sloped down to the stream and beyond was a broad strip of marshy meadow bordered by a forested ridge of black pines. To our right, the pine forest met the edge of the narrow trail. All I needed was a soft, dry spot under a tree, any tree, and I would be asleep in less than a minute.

"I'd hoped to get as far as the wilderness sign-in box," Jesse said, carefully shifting position to favor his injured arm, "but we're not going to make it. In a half hour, maybe less, it'll be too dark."

I looked up at the sky and said, "Do you remember, years ago, when you told me about the two different kinds of nights in the Uintas? The first kind, with a full moon is almost as bright as day and you can see well enough to hunt; the other kind, with clouds and no moon, is so black you can't see the hand in front of your face."

Jesse nodded. "I remember . . . I also remember walking a certain little girl back to the guest cabin every night because she was afraid of the dark!"

We shared a smile and a memory, then I reached into my jacket. "I've got some jerky and apricot leather if you're hungry. Which would you like?"

"Some jerky'll be fine."

I broke off a piece and handed it to him. We sat, chewing the salty beef and saying nothing as darkness deepened under the pines and blurred the movement of the stream below us. The quiet was a sound in itself.

Then, out of the stillness, I heard shuffling footsteps and the plodding gait of a four-footed animal. I tensed, listening, when a gruff voice barked out: "One of these days, you'll push me too far, Mrs. Green, and I'm gonna blister yer rump with a willow switch!"

Jesse and I exchanged puzzled smiles and stared into the fuzzy gray dusk behind us where two moving shapes assembled themselves into an old man leading a dun-colored mare. The man wasn't more than medium height and his wiry frame was spare almost to the point of gauntness. A flannel shirt clothed his bony shoulders, faded denim trousers were held up by a pair of thick suspenders and a weathered cowboy hat covered hair that was grayer than the dusk. The little mare had the same wiry build as her master and carried a dilapidated pack frame on her back.

I was so surprised to see someone, I didn't stop to think that the sight of Jesse and me, dirty and ragged, sitting beside the trail, would be equally surprising to anyone who saw us. The old man stopped with a jerk, stuck out his grizzled chin and peered at us through the fading light.

Jesse stood up and a smile creased his features. "Ezra, is that you? It's been a long time, old man!"

"I don't keep track of the time, Jesse Chisholm!" came the gruff reply. "You oughta know that by now!"

187

The mare whinnied and gave her master's back an impatient nudge, but the old man shoved her head aside and drew closer, giving Jesse and me a sharp-eyed glance.

"You in some kind of trouble, boy?" he asked in a softer tone.

Jesse nodded. "Bad trouble, but it'll take a while to explain."

"Well, this ain't the time or place to stand around gabbin'! Maybe you ain't noticed, but it's gettin' dark out here! Where's your horse and gear?"

"My horse was shot and killed this evening," Jesse answered quietly, "and I had to leave my gear behind."

The old man stared at Jesse, then rubbed his chin. "Maybe you'd like to do some of that explainin' with a roof over yer heads. My cabin ain't too far from here."

"We'd like that very much," Jesse said, putting a hand on the man's bony shoulder. Then he turned to me. "Melissa, this is Ezra. He's been living and trapping in these mountains longer than I can remember!" He smiled at the old man and said, "You know—you've never told me your last name."

"Don't matter none. Ezra'll do."

I forced my uncooperative legs to stand and mumbled a tired, "Hello."

The old man touched his hat, but I wasn't sure if the slight twitch passing over his wizened features could be interpreted as a smile or not.

"We'd better git movin' along," Ezra said, giving the mare's rope a tug. "It's gunna be blacker'n the devil before we git there."

"It's nearly dark now," I said with some apprehension. "How will we find your cabin?"

"Don't you worry none about that. Mrs. Green here knows the way," Ezra assured me. "Don't make no difference to her whether it's light or dark. I'll just give her her head and she'll take us home. It's all her fault I'm out this late, anyhow. The fool animal nearly got me killed!"

"What happened?" Jesse asked as we followed him down the trail.

"Oh, this dang mustang hates mooses! If'n I don't hold on to her and there's a moose nearby, she'll take off after it every time! I was busy checkin' my traps and Mrs. Green here, startled a bull calf in the meadow a couple of miles back. The next thing I knew, old Momma was chargin' after us, and I spent the last hour and a half up a tree!"

I smiled at the image of the wiry old man scrambling up a scratchy pine tree, and also at his whistling account of the incident. Several of Ezra's teeth were missing and the gaps made his speech a unique tonal combination of gravel and tin.

"I'm sorry you had such a close call," Jesse said, "but it's sure a lucky thing for us that you happened along."

"That's so. That's so," Ezra agreed and looked over his shoulder at the mustang mare. "Mrs. Green, yer forgiven—this time!"

We had been walking for perhaps ten minutes when Ezra stopped and took a rope off the horse's pack. He tied one end of the rope to the pack frame; the other, he tossed to Jesse with the gruff instruction, "Loop this around yer belt good an' tight! The goin'll be a mite rough through the trees. I don't need to tell you to hang on to yer lady!"

He left the trail then and started climbing up slope near a small stream. From that point on, the sound of rushing water became our constant companion as we followed Ezra up the wooded hillside.

Tonight wasn't one of those 'black' Uinta nights, but it was still very dark. I could distinguish the sky from the feathery columns of pines, but the ground itself was blurry and out of focus. I had no depth perception at all and trying to keep my balance involved an almost total reliance on touch and sound. Jesse's firm grip on my hand kept me from falling whenever I tripped and stumbled over rocks and bushes, but our jerky progress must have been terribly painful for him. Finally, the steep slope leveled out and the rushing voice of water was all around us.

"We're nearly there!" Ezra's voice called from up ahead. "The stream forks here and we need to cross it, so you might git yer feet wet."

There was no choosing which rock to step on, or which part

of the stream was most shallow. When you can't see, you just tramp straight through. The water was icy and swift, and in some places, it splashed well over the tops of my boots. Once, I slipped on a mossy rock and went down on my knees before Jesse could break my fall. I gasped and scrambled to my feet as the rope pulled us forward once more.

We felt our way onto the bank and some distance past the stream, I noticed a sweet, grassy fragrance in the air. Peering through the darkness, I began to realize the trees had given way to a small meadow near the top of the ridge. My eyes could barely make out the squat, sturdy shape of a log cabin crouched against the forest's edge.

The little mare's excited whinnies rang through the black night air and Ezra's voice echoed strangely as he called to her.

"Slow down, Mrs. Green! I know yer glad to be home, but slow down!"

There was a sudden tension on the rope as the horse pulled us eagerly forward. It was getting harder and harder to lift one foot after the other and that last little spurt nearly did me in. I sagged against Jesse's side and he let go of my hand to grasp my waist instead.

Moments later, the rope went slack and Ezra's voice was announcing, "We're here, folks. Now you jest stay put while I git Mrs. Green inside the stable and light the lantern."

I could hear his shuffling movements and the mare's contented nickers. There was the creak and scrape of a wooden gate, then more shuffling footsteps and another creaking sound.

The mellow light of an oil lantern suddenly warmed the blackness and outlined Ezra's wiry frame against the doorway of the small cabin. I blinked and put a hand to my eyes as he motioned for us to enter. Jesse ducked his head, and as we stepped inside I felt as if we had passed through a time portal to another century.

The cabin had a dirt floor, no fireplace and one small window. I glanced at the rough furnishings revealed in the lantern's dusky yellow light. There was a table and bench of rough pine; functional at best, but still looking more like part of the forest than pieces of furniture. Nearby, was a chair fashioned of knobby pine and rawhide thongs. Against one wall I saw a single bed. The four posts were slim lodgepole trunks and the frame was laced with tough rawhide. On top of this, a sleeping bag had been neatly rolled up. Overhead, traps swung on metal chains from the log ceiling, their jagged, iron jaws making bizarre shadows in the dusky light. A variety of dried plants, tied in neat bunches, also hung from the ceiling. The pungent odors of yarrow, mint, salsify and others, mingled with the musky scent of animal pelts in various stages of drying and curing to give the room an atmosphere that was primitive and earthy.

Ezra set the lamp on the table and motioned for Jesse to sit on the bench. To me he said brusquely, "Sit yourself down in the chair, Miss."

I sat down and my body gave up. "The End" was written on every muscle, every bone. It even hurt to think. I put a hand to my head and watched as Ezra bent down by the bed and pulled out a small propane stove.

"I jest keep this on hand for emergencies," the old man explained, as if he were embarrassed for us to see him using such a modern convenience. "'Course it does come in handy sometimes, when it's rainin' and I don't feel like buildin' a fire outside," he admitted.

"How long have you been living here?" Jesse asked. "The last time I saw you, you were living in that old cabin complex near Bull Park."

"This is my third summer here. Don't like stayin' too long in one place. Besides, a wolverine got into the other cabin during the winter and tore everything apart. I didn't like the idea of sharin' the place with him so I moved out."

"A wolverine?" I said in surprise. "I didn't think there were any left in the Uintas."

"Oh, they're still up here. Ain't too many of 'em though, thank the Lord! Them's the ugliest lookin' devils—and mean! There ain't nothin' more cussed and ornery!"

Jesse glanced up at the glossy pelts and paraphernalia hanging from the ceiling. "Was the roof still on this cabin or did you have to build a new one?"

191

Ezra got out a chipped enamel coffee pot and a small saucepan, poured fresh water from a metal jug into each, then placed the pans on the stove's two burners. "There were a few logs caved in, but it didn't take much to get it in shape. Put fresh sod on 'er this spring." He reached up and selected two bunches of dried leaves. One could have been yarrow, the other some variety of mint. The mint leaves went into the coffee pot, while the others he crushed with his palms and put into the saucepan.

"While we're waitin' for this here water to boil, you might as well start some of that 'long explainin' you told me about," he said.

Jesse gave a tired nod and began.

I leaned back in the chair and stared at the ceiling as he told Ezra about finding the wrecked plane and its cargo of drugs. I really didn't want to listen. My mind automatically tried to block out the terror of the day's events by turning to the past. I blinked and watched the pattern of wavering shadow and smoky gold light on the burnished pelts of muskrats and weasels. Looking at the old cabin, it was easy to imagine some long ago mountain man sitting under this very roof on a black Uinta night. I could almost see his buckskin clothing, heavy with fringe and beads. But when I tried to picture his face, all I could see was Jesse's. My eyelids fluttered and closed.

Some time later, I felt a hand shaking my shoulder.

"Drink this, honey. It'll help."

Something hot and wet touched my lips but I couldn't open my eyes. The darkness was thick and heavy. It was almost like drowning in a well of blackness.

"Melissa—Ezra made this tea especially for you."

The hot liquid teased my lips again and a small amount trickled down my throat. I swallowed and coughed, then mumbled with closed yes, "I'm too tired."

"I know, honey, and you can go right back to sleep as soon as you drink your tea. Come on now. Have some more."

My eyes struggled open and I saw Jesse kneeling beside my chair with a tin cup in his hand. Ezra was standing just behind him, hatless now, with eyes as gray as his hair peering anxiously at me.

Jesse put the tin cup to my lips again and I drank deeply this time. The tea was mint-flavored and strong. It didn't taste particularly good, but it felt wonderful going down. I finished the cup and Ezra moved beside me to refill it.

"Oh, no thank you. This is fine."

"Have some more, Miss. It'll do you good."

He poured the steaming liquid without waiting for my answer, so I thanked him and said, "It's very good. Jesse, you should have some."

"I have. Three cups," he told me. "How are you feeling now?"

"Mmmm. Better. What about you? Your arm—" I sat up straighter in the chair, noticing the starkness of a clean white bandage against the tanned flesh of his upper arm. A sling had been fashioned out of what must have been Ezra's spare flannel shirt.

"It feels fine. Ezra washed me up and changed the bandage. I hated to part with yours," he added with a grin, "but it couldn't be helped. By the way, Ezra thinks your bandaging technique is quite unique."

I blushed and looked down into my cup, finishing the last bit of tea. "Thank you for the tea, Ezra. It was wonderful."

The old man took the cup from me and his gray eyes lingered on mine a moment longer than was necessary. I thought I noticed a painful gleam of remembrance in their depths, but I couldn't be sure.

"Ezra's made up the bed for us," Jesse told me, "so you can climb in and sleep as long as you want."

I started to rise, then stared at Jesse. "What do you mean—as long as I want? We've got to get out and tell them about Doug and Travis!"

Jesse took my hand and helped me to my feet. "While you were sleeping, Ezra and I made a few plans. As soon as the moon is high enough overhead, he's going to ride out for help. He'll make a lot faster time than we ever could."

I turned grateful eyes to the old man who was sitting on the bench. When I tried to thank him, the words suddenly caught in my throat. I swallowed hard and said to Jesse, "Do you think the police can get there in time?"

Jesse didn't answer right away. Then he put a hand to my cheek and said gently, "I don't know. That's why I'm going back to the lake."

My knees went weak and I grabbed the edge of the table for support. "Jesse—you can't! You're hurt—"

"I don't know any other way to say this, honey, but you know as well as I do, once Doug shows them where the plane is, he's a dead man. If I can get back to their camp before dawn, there's a chance I might be able to get him and Travis out of there."

I blinked rapidly and bit down on my lower lip to stop my chin from quivering.

"Honey, don't look like that! I've got to try!"

I looked down at the table's rough surface and whispered brokenly, "But—but what can you do? They've all got guns!"

Jesse pulled me against his chest with his good arm. "Hey, don't cry! It's going to be all right. Thanks to Ezra, I won't be walking in emptyhanded. He's loaning me his deer rifle and that'll help the odds. Besides, they all think I'm dead. They won't be expecting any trouble, especially from me."

He lifted my chin and said, "I know it's risky, but I've got to do something! Tell me you understand."

My throat was too choked with tears to answer, but I nodded and he held me close.

Ezra stood up and said gruffly, "You two better git some sleep. I'll wake you up before I go."

I sniffed and wiped my eyes on the backs of my hands. "But where will you sleep?"

"I don't plan on doin' much sleepin'. The chair'll suit me fine."

I sighed and looked at the small bed next to the log wall. Ezra had placed a foam rubber pad over the rawhide frame and the sleeping bag over this. I turned my gaze from the bed to Jesse's big frame standing beside me and said, "Do you think we'll both fit?"

He grinned and rubbed his beard with the back of his hand. "I don't know, but it should be a lot of fun trying."

I gave him a tired smile as Ezra cleared his throat loudly and said from the chair, "Jest so you know, I don't approve of you two sharin' the same bed—but under the circumstances, there ain't nothin' else to do. But no shenanigans, you hear?"

My cheeks were hot with embarrassed color as I bent to unzip the sleeping bag and Jesse said with a low chuckle, "Aren't you going to take off your jacket and your boots?"

"Hmmm? Oh! Of course I am!" I sat down on the bed and began untying the laces. Jesse eased himself down beside me and said, "When you're done, would you mind giving me a hand with mine? These boots are hard to get off with just one hand."

I smiled and nodded, then set my hiking boots beside the bed with my outer pair of stockings tucked inside them.

Across the small room, Ezra was perched in the log chair, watching us like a grizzled old owl.

I pulled off one of Jesse's boots and whispered, "Is he going to keep that lamp on all night?"

"I don't know. Why don't you ask him?"

"Why don't *you* ask him!" I countered.

"I may be gettin' on in years, but there ain't nothin' wrong with my hearing!" Ezra grumbled. "And I'll turn out the lamp when I'm good an' ready!"

Jesse and I exchanged amused glances as I unlaced his second boot and pulled it off, along with his outer pair of stockings.

Ezra continued to stare at me. "You've got Alice's eyes," he said softly.

I gave the old man an inquiring look. "Alice?"

"She was just about your size, too, with the same small hands and feet. Her hair was dark, though."

"Was Alice your wife?"

The gray head moved almost imperceptively from side to side. "She married my brother. I couldn't take seein' 'em together—the way she looked at him—so I went away to the mountains. It was easier that way."

I took off my jacket and laid it across the end of the bed. "Did you ever see her again?"

195

"Nope. Never did. But somehow, seein' you makes her feel real close. Real close."

He looked so lonely and withered, sitting there in the shadows, I had to go to him. I bent to kiss his leathery old cheek and whispered, "Goodnight, Ezra—and thank you, for everything!"

He looked away quickly to stare at the wall. "You'd best git to bed, Miss." His voice was as gruff as ever, but I saw the sudden quiver of his chin.

I left him alone with his dreams of Alice and returned to Jesse who was trying to ease his way out of his shirt and having very little success.

"Let me help you with that—but won't you be too cold?"

"No, I'll be fine. And I hate to get blood stains all over Ezra's sleeping bag."

I slipped his injured arm gently out of the sling and Jesse held it while I removed the blood-stained shirt. I laid it on the bench next to the table as Jesse stood up and said, "Why don't you get in first? That way my bad arm will be on the outside."

I climbed into the bed and Ezra blew out the lantern with a small huff. Thick blackness closed around us. I scooted over to the far side of the little bed to make room for Jesse, and in the darkness, the sound of my every movement seemed to be amplified at least ten times. The bed groaned even louder under Jesse's weight as he eased himself down beside me.

I pulled the sleeping bag over us both and he whispered, "This isn't exactly the way I pictured our first night together. We always seem to have a chaperone."

I started to smile when I saw my brother's laughing face at the lake earlier today. Pain sliced through my heart. Where was Doug now? What was happening to him? Then I thought of Jesse going back to Hicks' and Moser's camp and cold dread clenched itself around me.

"Don't think about tomorrow," Jesse said. "Worrying won't help."

My voice was tight and thin. "How do you know what I'm thinking?"

196

"I know you," he answered softly. "Your thoughts . . . your pain . . . it's always been that way."

"Then you must know how frightened I am for you!" I whispered, staring into the blackness above our heads. "Jesse, if anything happens to you—"

"Shhh! Come here."

"But your arm—I might hurt it."

"It hurts a lot more having you scrunched way over there on the edge of the bed when I want you next to me."

"Jesse! Ezra will hear you!"

"He's sound asleep. Aren't you, Ezra?"

"Just like a baby," came the gravelly voice.

I smiled in spite of myself.

"Come here, Melissa."

I put my head on his chest and relaxed against him. His good arm came around me, pulling me closer still. Under my palm I felt the strong, steady beat of his heart. Fatigue and fear melted away until the only reality was the warmth and feel of his body next to mine.

"You're sure I'm not hurting your arm?" I asked breathlessly.

He sighed deeply. "Honey, that is the last thing on my mind right now."

Our lips met in the darkness and his mouth made a warm exploration of mine. I rubbed a hand over his chest and murmured, "Maybe I just didn't notice before, but I never remember you being quite so—so—"

"Hairy?" he supplied with a quiet chuckle.

I laughed and nuzzled his beard.

"Funny, I was just thinking that you've changed in a few ways yourself," he said.

Our lips met in another lingering kiss and I molded myself even closer to him, feeling a deep, spreading warmth inside.

Suddenly, Jesse called into the darkness. "Ezra—you still awake?"

"I'd like to know how I'm supposed to sleep with all this racket goin' on!"

197

"Well, as long as you're awake, there's something I was wondering about."

"What's that?"

"Have you ever been a ship's captain?"

I smiled and traced the firm line of Jesse's mouth with my fingertip.

"What in the—?"

"Or maybe a minister?"

"Hell, no!"

"I didn't think so."

There were a few seconds of silence in the cabin, then Ezra demanded in his gruff bark, "Well, now that you've woke me up and got me all curious, ain't you gonna tell me what all them questions was for?"

Jesse sighed and murmured against my hair, "Never mind. I was just checking."

The old man harumphed and the chair creaked as he settled back.

Jesse brushed my forehead with his lips and whispered in a resigned voice, "Goodnight, Tidbit."

I caught the frustration behind his light words and my love for him at that moment was a physical pain throbbing inside me. With a quick little breath, I turned out of his arms and sat up.

Jesse asked in a surprised whisper, "What's the matter?"

It took a moment to answer. "Nothing—nothing. I'm just trying to get comfortable. Is your arm asleep?"

"Which one?"

"The one I was lying on."

"No, it's fine. Now why are you squirming around?"

"These stupid mosquito bites! I must have got bitten when I was hiding down by the stream. And don't tell me not to scratch them, because I'll go crazy if I don't!"

Jesse chuckled and I felt his long fingers on my back. "Tell me where to scratch."

"Right between the shoulder blades. Mmmm—there."

When his fingers ceased their rubbing and began a gentle

caressing, the mosquito bites were quickly forgotten. My only thought and desire was to be closer to him.

"Is that better?" he asked in a husky voice.

I smiled into the darkness. "Almost . . ."

A moment later, I lay back down against him and felt his sudden, indrawn breath. "Oh, Melissa—"

"Shhh! Don't say anything—just hold me," I whispered, trembling from the engulfing sensations of being close to him at last. His arm tightened around me and I said on a sigh, "I know we can't have everything—but at least we can be close."

*   *   *

I slept deeply and dreamlessly in his arms until Ezra's gruff whisper pierced the darkness.

"I'll be leavin' now, Jesse. The moon is barely over the ridgeline, but I kin make my way."

Jesse carefully lifted his right arm from behind my head and sat up with a muffled groan of pain. He covered my shoulders with the sleeping bag, then stood up, whispering, "You take care, old man! Be sure and tell my father that Melissa's all right and will be waiting here at the cabin."

I had been drifting on the edges of sleep, but Jesse's words brought me fully awake. There was the scrape of a match as Ezra lit the oil lamp. I kept my eyes closed against its yellow glare and listened.

"You watch out fer yer own hide!" Ezra whispered back. "My rifle's on the table and there's enough bullets to clean out that whole pack of vermin!"

"Thanks, but I hope I won't need it."

"Is there anything else you need before I go?"

"No, I don't think so. Well, I guess there is. Could you give me a hand with my shirt and boots? I hate to wake up Melissa."

"Sure thing, son."

My eyes opened just a slit and I saw Jesse sitting on the pine bench. Then I shut them again as Ezra came over to the bed for Jesse's boots.

199

"You ought to be on yer way in a half hour or so," Ezra instructed in a low tone. "Follow the stream downhill and it'll take you straight to the trail."

"I will, and thanks."

I risked another peek to see Ezra tying the laces on the boots and Jesse trying to button his shirt with one hand.

"Are you clear on the plane's location?" he asked the old man.

"'Course I am! You think I don't know these mountains or somethin'!"

Ezra stood up then and shuffled to the door. "Anything else you want me to tell them rangers?"

"No. Just make sure they understand it's a hostage situation. You know the rest."

Ezra nodded and turned to go, then added in a tone that was sadly mellow. "Take good care of yer lady. She's a purty little thing." He opened the door and mumbled, "Almost as purty as Alice."

I lay very still after the old man had gone, with my heart pounding like a wild thing and my throat dry with excitement and fear. Jesse wouldn't like it, but there was no way I was going to stay behind and let him go back to Red Castle without me. No matter what happened up there, it couldn't be worse than the agony of waiting here alone—waiting and worrying, hour after hour. The problem was, how to convince Jesse to take me along.

I opened my eyes and saw him standing beside the table watching me. His brown head brushed against the glossy skins and pelts hanging from the ceiling and shadows glanced off his bearded face. He could easily have belonged to another century, but time had been kind. Jesse belonged to me.

I brushed the hair away from my face and said quietly, "Do you have to leave now?"

He nodded and picked up the rifle, inserting some bullets into the magazine and stuffing the rest in his jacket pocket.

Silence hung around us.

He moved to blow out the wick and I said quickly, "Would

200

you mind leaving the lamp burning? I—I'd rather not wait in the dark."

Jesse glanced up from the smoky gold flame and his blue eyes were burning with a light of their own. "This isn't going to be good-by," he said in a low voice. "You have to believe that."

I knew then exactly what I was going to do. I gave him a small nod and whispered, "I love you, Jesse!"

In one swift movement he was beside me, kissing me with a violence and desperation that should have been terrifying. It wasn't. I met his turbulant emotions with a storm of my own, then suddenly, he was gone and I was left shivering in the cold air.

I waited for a long moment, listening to the muted sounds of his departure before throwing back the sleeping bag and reaching for my things. It took less than two minutes to dress and blow out the lantern. Then, with a murmured prayer and a pounding heart, I slipped out of the cabin and into the moonlit night.

Chapter 18

"And we are here as on a darkling plain
Swept with confused alarms of struggle and flight."
Matthew Arnold

The moon was two nights past the full, but large and bright enough to illuminate the mountainside with its clear, white light. Black columns of pines stood crisply against the sky and the meadow wore a milky glow. I could see my own shadow as I ran across the open area past the cabin and approached the stream. Moonlight made my crossing much easier, and soon I was into the trees, following the stream's downhill course. I couldn't see Jesse as yet and I was much too worried about masking the sound of my own footsteps to listen for his. I purposely avoided trying to identify the various rustlings in the forest. It was much easier not to know what might be prowling through the undergrowth nearby.

The trail was clearly defined in the moonlight and I breathed a shaky sigh of relief when my feet touched its smooth surface. A dry rustling stirred the underbrush somewhere nearby, and I tensed immediately. The sound was not repeated and except for a slight breeze moaning through the higher branches of the pines, the night was completely still. I shoved my fears aside, put my hands in my jacket pockets and strode forward at a determined pace. I hadn't gone ten feet when something big and black leaped out from behind a pine tree and onto the trail in front of me.

I let out a scream that would have curdled the blood of a banshee. A hand shot out and grabbed my arm before I had a chance to run, then a man's voice said, "Just where do you think you're going!"

"Jesse! You nearly gave me a heart attack!"

"Me—give you—? How do you think I felt when I heard someone crashing through the brush on the hillside behind me?"

"I—I tried to be quiet. You didn't have to jump out at me like that."

"Why are you following me?" His voice was as cold as the night air.

I shivered and looked up at his rugged frame outlined by moonlight. "Jesse, don't be angry! I couldn't stand waiting there alone—not knowing what was happening . . ." He remained silent and I finished quietly, "I knew you wouldn't take me along, so I—I decided to follow you."

He sighed and released my arm. "So now what am I supposed to do with you?"

"You—you don't have to do anything."

Reaction and the cold sent shudders quaking through me. "Melissa—"

Behind the gruffness was a familiar note. I moved closer to him and wrapped my arms about his waist. He stiffened at first, then I felt his body yielding against mine and his hand in my hair.

"You're shaking all over," he said, not so angrily now.

"I'm all right. You just startled me."

After a moment, he released me and reached for Ezra's rifle which rested against the trunk of a nearby pine.

"You'd better go back now," he said.

"Jesse—"

"Honey, I don't know what's going to happen up there, but I do know I don't want you anywhere near those creeps!"

"I'm not going back to the cabin! I'm going with you."

He sighed and looked down at me. "How am I supposed to be angry when you look at me like that?"

I smiled and said, "Do you want me to carry the rifle?"

203

Jesse stood immoveable in the center of the trail. "Melissa, we're not heading for a picnic."

"I know that, but Doug's up there and I—I have to be with you." My voice cracked and I said again, very low, "I have to!"

We faced each other on the moonlit trail, then without a word Jesse began walking and I took my place beside him.

We traveled in silence most of the time, moving through the black forest, past meadows and the area I had named the "avenue of streams," on our hike up. The air was cold enough to chase away thoughts of sleep and provided a chilling incentive to keep a brisk pace. Several times we heard the movements of animals and once a startled doe leaped directly across our path. I stayed close to Jesse, trying to match my stride to his and grateful that his injured arm kept him from walking faster than I could follow. We took a five-minute rest at the bridge where I had had my first view of Red Castle, then moved on through the trees toward the switchback trail. I didn't remember the switchback as being nearly so long or steep, but watching Jesse's labored, painful progress up the trail, my own discomfort and fatigue seemed a small thing.

Finally, we reached the top of the ridge and took the trail into the meadows. Red Castle loomed before us, a massive black outline against the starry sky. Overhead, Taurus and the Seven Sisters watched our dogged progress with glittering eyes. The moon was much lower in the sky now, moving sleepily toward the western horizon. We stopped for another rest at the bridge above the waterfall.

"We've made pretty good time," Jesse told me. "We should be back at the lower lake in less than an hour."

I heard the pain edging his voice and asked, "How's your arm?"

"Stiff."

"I'll carry the rifle for a while."

"Thanks, honey."

"Jesse?"

"Hmmm?"

"What are you going to do when we get there?"

"Find out where they're holding Doug and Travis, first of all."

"And then—?"

I saw the shake of his head in the moonlight. "I don't know."

Night's deep blue was fading as we took the trail around the lake's west side. Red Castle wore a shroud of gray cloud and above her head, a single star was winking its crystalline light. Our footsteps made little sound as we trod the soft path. The silence was deeper than the waters of the lake.

Jesse made a cautious inspection of our old camp site before giving me the go ahead to join him. Everything was untouched from the night before. Doug's backpack and mine were resting against a log beside the fallen tents, and a few feet away, I saw Saskatoon's pack frame on the ground. My throat tightened up and I felt a sick twinge inside as I thought of the creamy buckskin mare lying dead near a line of trees.

Jesse laid Ezra's rifle next to our backpacks and picked up a canteen. "Want a drink?"

"I'd love one." I gulped the cold water, then passed it to Jesse.

After a long drink he said, "I think we ought to grab some food while we're here. If I'm able to get Doug and Travis, we're going to have to keep out of sight until help comes."

If . . . I refused to dwell on the implications of the word and helped Jesse go through the food bags. We packed what we could in our pockets and he gave me the rest to carry in a plastic bag. We took the time to eat a candy bar and some fruit, then Jesse kissed me and picked up the rifle.

"Why don't you rest here while I go around the lake and have a look."

"I'm not tired," I lied cheerfully. "I'll come with you."

"We've been through all this before," Jesse said. "You'll be a lot safer right here and it won't take me long to find out if Doug and Travis are in their camp, and if they're being guarded."

"But—but how will you help Doug and carry the rifle at the same time?"

"Travis can help."

"But what if Travis is hurt, too?"

"I'll manage," he said firmly.

I took his arm and said, "Jesse, I don't want to argue, but—"

"But what?"

"I'm coming with you." He started to protest and I added a quick compromise. "—Only as far as the other side of the lake. Please! I won't go near their camp—I promise!"

"I don't want you to go," he said and let out a long sigh. "But I can't stop you."

Dawn stars were fading and the breeze was moist and chill against our faces as Jesse and I made our way around the lake. We ran quickly through the open, grassy area edging the far bank and headed for a thick cover of willows where a stream emptied into the lake. Beyond the willows was another open area and a steep fall of boulders lying at the rocky base of Red Castle. Past the boulders, a dark line of trees hid Hicks' and Moser's camp from our view.

As we negotiated the stream and pushed our way through the willows, Jesse said, "This is as far as you go, Tidbit. I'm going to make for those boulders and come in behind their camp. If I'm not back in say, half an hour, you head back to our old camp—but stay in the trees. Whatever happens, don't come looking for me!"

I looked up at his face, gray and tense in the half-light and nodded. "I'll wait here. Be careful!"

He bent down and kissed me hard on the lips, then ran for the boulders. I watched until his figure was no longer discernible against the landscape, then settled down to wait.

I was tired. Almost too tired for sleep. And cold. The predawn temperatures were bone-chilling at such high altitudes, and I huddled close to the willows, avoiding the breeze as much as possible.

Minutes passed and I watched the lake's dark surface take on a silver-like sheen. Overhead, the sky had paled to a soft, dove-gray. There was the thin piping of a bird, then another.

Soon the dawn chorus would begin. A mosquito whined around my head and I shook it away.

How long had Jesse been gone? And how on earth was I supposed to know when a half hour was up? I sat down on a dry, lichen-covered stone near the fringe of willows and rubbed my palms together.

The rocks and trees along the shoreline were coming into clearer focus now and every point along Red Castle's jagged horizon grew sharper against the brightening sky. My gaze lowered to the mass of boulders where I had last seen Jesse. Nothing. No sound. No movement. If he were in trouble, surely I would have heard something. Sounds carried so far up here. The chirp of a robin on the opposite shore came singing across the water to me. Then the soft neighing of horses, somewhere closer by.

My eyes left the boulders and glanced toward the nearby shore where two men on horseback were making their way around the lake. I took in Bushman's burly figure and Moser's insolent posture with a dazed sort of horror. My first thought was they were coming after me, but as the shock waves began to subside, I realized they couldn't have seen me yet. My position near the willows provided an effective screen of cover—but only momentarily. In a minute or two, their present course would take them directly past where I was sitting.

Slowly, with my back hunched over, I edged my way further into the willows. My hiking boots made soft, sucking sounds in the moist earth that seemed enormously loud to my ears. The men's voices carried clearly through the morning stillness. I could even hear the creaking of their saddles. I held my breath and stepped quietly back to crouch behind a bush. One of the horses nickered softly and I knew the men must be only a few yards away. Any moment now, they would pass by my hiding place. I backed up one more step and stumbled into something. Glancing down, I saw a tawny head lying face down in the grass and mud. I stared at the sticky, brownish-red stains on his shirt, the twisted position of his body, and my heart gave a sickening lurch. Nothing could have prevented the scream that tore from my throat.

"Travis? Travis—! Dear God, don't let him be dead! Please don't let him be dead!"

Futile pleas were repeated in hoarse, muttered phrases as I dropped down beside his body. His shoulder was cold and rigid to the touch. I spoke his name again on a choking sob and stroked the tawny hair.

Rough hands suddenly grabbed me from behind, pulling me to my feet and jerking me around. I stared into Moser's pale eyes and my scream was smothered by his thick fingers.

"Not one word!" he hissed. "Not one—or you'll be lying in the mud next to your friend!"

I jerked my head back and bit down hard. Moser gave an angry yelp of pain and I twisted out of his grasp. I turned and ran headlong into Bushman's fleshy bulk. The big man seized both my arms and I gave his shins a vicious kick, struggling like a wild animal caught in a trap. Bushman's bulk was immovable and his puffy eyes held an ugly gleam as he grunted and said, "You ain't goin' nowhere, little girl, so calm down!"

"No! Let me go! Jesse—!"

Bushman's hand delivered a heavy slap across my mouth that would have sent me staggering if his other hand hadn't held me. Then Moser yanked my head back and the sudden, stinging pain left me gasping. While Bushman held my arms, Moser gagged my mouth with his handkerchief.

"What're we gonna do with her?" Bushman asked.

"Take her back to camp," Moser told him. "Hicks ought to be in a better mood when he sees the little surprise we've brought back for him." Moser reached for his horse's reins that were tied to a willow branch and quickly mounted. "Give her to me!"

As the big man shoved me toward the brown gelding, my brain was a frenzy of fear but my body responded with pure survival instincts. I fought, kicked and twisted, but those big hands never loosened their grip. Moser reached down and pulled me onto the horse so I was sitting across his lap. My struggles spooked the animal and it side-stepped into the willows with a nervous snort. Moser pulled in hard on the reins and Bushman grabbed the bridle in an attempt to control the animal.

"Toss me that rope in your saddle bag!" Moser yelled at the big man and yanked my body closer to his. "Hurry up, dammit!"

I fought harder and the horse reared with a frightened whinny. Moser's grip loosened as he grabbed the reins to keep from falling. I slid out of his grasp and down to the ground, rolling away from the animal's hooves. I stumbled to my feet and tried to run. Bushman's hands were reaching out for me and suddenly, it was as if someone had flicked a switch on a movie camera and the film was going in slow motion. I took one, slogging step before Bushman's fist lurched out towards my face. I felt a heavy, bruising pain—and that was all.

As consciousness returned, I became aware of low voices and soft, moaning cries. The voices sounded far away and pulsed with the throbbing vibrato of an echo. The soft moans, I gradually came to realize, were my own. Something cold and wet touched the side of my face and my body jerked involuntarily.

My eyes opened and I saw my brother bending over me.

"Missy? Are you all right? Missy?"

"Doug—"

His arms came around me and we held each other in a fierce grip.

"Oh, Doug . . ."

It hurt to talk. I put a hand to my face and felt the tender swelling on my jaw. Doug placed the cold cloth against it once more as I asked him, "What happened? Did I find you or did you find me?"

"Neither one," he answered soberly. "Moser and Bushman brought you into camp a few minutes ago. Don't you remember?"

I tensed and sat up. Four men were standing a few feet away, watching us closely. I stared dully at their faces. Hicks' florid complexion and the Chicano's weasel-black eyes. Bushman's bearded jowls and Moser's thick, curling smile. I closed my eyes and opened them a few seconds later. The faces were still there. Memory returned and with it, the horror and grief of my discovery. I turned to Doug and whispered brokenly, "They killed Travis! I—I found him, lying in the willows."

Doug nodded and his voice was raw with emotion as he handed me a canteen. "Drink this, Sis."

A sharp pain shot along the side of my face when I tried to swallow. I choked on the water and tears sprang to my eyes.

Doug grimaced at my discomfort and threw the canteen on the ground in anger and frustration. "Filthy bunch of sadists!" he spat out.

Hicks smiled and said calmly, "If your sister is stupid enough to struggle, it's her own fault if she gets hurt. Bushman, bring the horses around. Since the girl's feeling better now, we'll be on our way."

I stared, uncomprehending, and Hicks went on to explain with an ingratiating smile. "Your brother has been kind enough to offer to show us where the plane is. Last night, he couldn't remember the crash site, but this morning—after my men brought you into camp—his memory improved quite remarkably." Hicks took an automatic out of his sheepskin jacket and smiled once more. "Just in case either one of you should have another lapse of memory," he explained. "Of course, it isn't always necessary to get—physical. Not when you understand your choices."

"What kind of choice did you give Travis?" Doug said bitterly.

Hicks shrugged. "Your friend tried to make a run for it once he realized we weren't undercover agents. Naturally, we had no choice but to stop him."

Bushman returned then, leading three horses. "We ain't got enough for all of us to ride," he said to Hicks. "Who's gonna walk?"

"You ought to know the answer to that question, since *your* horse is in no condition to be ridden!" Hicks snapped.

"I'll take the girl with me," Moser said smoothly and Hicks gave an assenting nod.

"Sanchez, you stay behind and break camp," Hicks ordered. "I want everything packed and ready to go by the time we get back with the stuff."

The Chicano wasn't at all pleased with his assignment, but he gave a grudging nod and lowered his eyes before Hicks could see the flash of black anger burning there. It seemed no one argued with Mr. Hicks.

Doug helped me to my feet as Hicks motioned to Bushman. "Put the brother on Sanchez's horse."

The big man grabbed Doug by the arm and shoved him toward the animal as Moser approached me. His pale eyes moved slowly over my body, then he caught me up in his arms and swung me onto the gelding's broad back. With a possessive hand on my knee, Moser turned to Doug. "In case you get any cute ideas about making a run for it—you just remember, your sister's gonna be riding with me!"

Sunlight was painting the tips of the pines with gold as we made our way around the lake. Some fifty yards down the shoreline, two fishermen were testing their skill. As I watched them cast their lines into the calm water, Moser nudged my cheek with his lips and said in a low tone, "All you have to do is cry out and you'll get a lot of nice people killed. And that goes for anybody we meet on the trail. One word, doll, and I'll kill them. Understand?"

I twisted my head away and stared straight ahead, trying to control the shuddering revulsion I felt at his touch.

"Now that the sun's up, you don't need that heavy jacket," he continued in a silky tone. "Why don't you take it off."

"No! No, I'd rather keep it on. The breeze is still cool," I added hastily.

Moser grabbed the front of my jacket and yanked the zipper down. I shoved his hand away and he gave a low chuckle, pulling the jacket off despite my struggles.

"Now, isn't that more comfortable?" he said with a leering grin and tossed the jacket into some bushes beside the trail.

I stiffened in his arms and stared unseeing at the surrounding forest. My instincts were to scratch and fight but somehow, I sensed this was exactly what he wanted me to do. For a man like Moser, there was as much sick pleasure in the struggle as the taking.

"I plan on having you," he said in my ear. "No matter what

Hicks or anybody else says. So you just plan on that, little lady!" To prove his point, Moser pulled my head back with one hand and covered my mouth with a bruising kiss. Pain exploded along my jawline, but his lips kept up the grinding pressure despite my moans. Then he let the reins go slack to reach a hand under my t-shirt. In a panic, I grabbed the reins and gave him a stinging rawhide slap across the neck. Moser released me with an angry curse, but before he could deliver any recriminations, Hicks was riding back to us with a black look on his face.

"Have you got a problem, Moser?" he asked in deadly, even tones.

"Nothing I can't handle!"

"That's where you're wrong," Hicks stated with tightly-controlled anger. "You're going to have a hell of a lot more than you can handle if you don't stop messing around with that girl!"

Moser relaxed his hold on me and gave Hicks a nonchalant grin. "All right. I can wait."

"See that you do!"

The air was much warmer and birds were singing in the topmost branches of the towering old firs and spruces as we took the forest trail to the big lake. Doug led the way with Hicks riding a close second. Moser and I followed, while Bushman puffed along at the rear. Looking at my brother's dejected figure ahead of us, I remembered Jesse's words: ". . . once Doug shows them where the plane is, he's a dead man."

Jesse! I had to bite my lip to keep from shouting his name out loud. He must have seen Bushman and Moser bring me back to camp, but there wouldn't have been anything he could do under the circumstances. I glanced quickly into the sunlit trees. He might be following us even now! My breathing quickened and for the first time, a glimmer of hope made its way into my heart. I couldn't give up! Even if Jesse weren't following, there was always the chance that help might be on the way. How many hours would it take the authorities to get here after receiving Ezra's message? Two? Three? Somehow, I had to delay our arrival at the crash site. It wouldn't be easy. Especially if Hicks or Moser realized I was stalling for time. I glanced around, wishing I could remember how close we were to the plane's location. I didn't have the vaguest idea.

"What are you looking for?" Moser demanded suspiciously.

"Oh, nothing. I was just trying to remember the place where we turned into the trees." I ignored Moser's scowl and called up to my brother. "Weren't we supposed to turn right at that big rock back there?"

Doug glanced over his shoulder with a puzzled frown. "No. We have to get up to that marshy place and those potholes before we leave the trail."

"Are you sure?" I asked him. "You know what a *lousy* sense of direction you have. I'm positive we just passed the place!"

Doug's expression didn't change one whit. He shrugged and turned his horse's head, saying to Hicks, "She's probably right. I always have had a lousy sense of direction."

We must have spent a good half hour diligently searching the wrong side of the trail. It almost became a game. Doug and I purposely chose the steepest routes and rockiest areas to examine. Bushman's breathing was harsh and labored as he struggled to keep up, and his shirt was dark with sweat. Hicks managed to conceal his irritation for the most part, but finally insisted that we return to the main trail.

"I thought you said you knew the location of the plane," he said, scowling at Doug.

"I thought so, too," Doug told him apologetically. "But this is only the second time I've been up here, and we were coming down from the other direction before."

Moser frowned. "I think the kid's stalling for time."

Doug met his suspicious stare with a frank look. "Why would I do that?"

Hicks took another look around with his binoculars and said, "I think we should try looking on the *left* side of the trail. Didn't you mention a marshy area with some pot holes a while back?"

Doug shrugged and gave him a blank look. "I don't know. Did I?"

Hicks put the binoculars to his eyes and said, "I see a place

213

like that not too far ahead—on the *left* side of the trail," he added with cold emphasis.

Barely fifteen minutes later, Hicks spotted a flash of sunlight on the plane's wings as we were searching the trees. I slumped visibly at his exultant cry. The game was over.

Hicks' bland expression grew more animated as we approached the plane, and he ordered Moser to check the contents in a tone that could almost be called excited.

Moser's hand stroked my throat and he said, "Looks like this is the end of the ride, doll." Then he released me and I slid off the gelding's muscular withers. Moser dismounted, handed Hicks the reins and approached the wrecked fuselage. Bushman was right on his heels. The two men peered inside and Moser shouted, "It's here!" holding up a cellophane bag in each hand.

Hicks uttered a satisfied sigh, then looked at Doug. "You—off the horse."

My heart began to pound with thick, heavy beats as Doug dismounted and faced Hicks' thin-lipped expression. I could see he was having trouble standing on his bad ankle and hurried to his side. Doug gave me an encouraging smile, but the hand that came around my shoulders was trembling.

Hicks took the reins of both horses along with his own, and said as calmly as if he were giving the time of day, "Moser, start loading the drugs into the saddlebags. Bushman—take the girl and her brother off and kill them."

Chapter 19

"The forests had done it. There they stood,
We caught for a moment the powers at play.
They had mingled us so, for once and good,
Their work was done—we might go or stay.
They relapsed to their ancient mood."
Robert Browning

Bushman took a large caliber revolver from his shoulder holster and checked the bullets. He was still breathing hard from the hike and my nostrils caught the rank odor of his body as he walked toward us. Before the big man could raise the gun, Moser left his task of unloading the drugs and confronted Hicks.

"Hold it, man! What's the big rush? We've got the stuff, so—"

"Yeah, and we've got to get out of here!" Hicks interrupted tersely.

"What's a couple of minutes? Bushman can knock 'em off after I've had the girl."

"You're forgetting something," Hicks said coldly. "I give the orders, and I don't need you or anybody else interfering!"

"Who's tryin' to interfere? All I want is some time with the chick. What's it matter if Bushman shoots them now or in ten minutes?"

Moser's smile and tone were meant to placate the older man but the very lightness of it terrified me. Doug's arm tightened around my shoulders as Hicks faced Moser with a smile that was equally engaging. "Like I said before, Moser, I believe in giving people choices." He took out his automatic and pointed the barrel against Moser's chest. "If you're so anxious to be with the girl, Bushman and I can carry out the stuff by ourselves. You want the girl?" he taunted. "Go on over there—you can all die together!" Moser's hands were balled up in tightly-clenched fists, and his stance was arrogant despite the older man's threat. "It's your decision, Moser," Hicks continued. "You're not indispensible, you know. None of us are."

Bushman was grinning broadly at the blond's discomfort and added with a wave of his revolver, "If you wanna join 'em, it's all right with me, Moser. I'd kinda like to see what a .357 slug could do to your hide."

Moser threw me one last look, then stalked back to the plane in angry silence.

"Excellent choice, Moser," Hicks said with a smile, then motioned to Bushman once more. "Get rid of them! Over there!"

Bushman pointed the revolver in the direction of a grassy area behind the plane and grunted, "Get movin!"

Doug and I walked slowly away as Red Castle stood in watchful silence. The sky above its rugged stone turrets was a fragile, aching blue. I glanced around the peaceful forest, feeling totally numb.

"That's far enough!" Bushman said. "Now move apart!"

Doug held me even closer to his side and shook his head.

Bushman shrugged and extended both arms in front of him. I turned my face into Doug's shoulder and waited with closed eyes and pent-up breath.

Doug whispered a clumsy, broken, "I love you, Sis," over my head, then the air exploded around us.

There was no pain. Doug's arms still held me and I could feel the frantic racing of his heart as well as my own. Then his voice, hoarse and unbelieving, came to my ears. "Dear God in Heaven!"

I opened my eyes. Where Bushman had been standing there was no one at all. I blinked and stared in total confusion. Then I saw what was left of him lying several feet away. His chest was gone. My stomach heaved at the sight of the bloody, gaping

216

hole as Doug cried, "The shot came from over there! Near those trees!"

He was pointing to a massive stand of spruces grouped near Red Castle's rocky base. For no more than an instant, my eyes caught the sudden flash of sunlight on metal, and realization forced its way through the numbness.

"Jesse!"

Even as his name left my lips, Doug was yelling, "Make a run for it! Now!"

I watched my brother dive for the trees, limping and crawling over the ground. I wanted to follow him. I tried to, but my body couldn't seem to understand my mind's directions. Shock and fear held me rigid and my legs refused to move.

Doug reached the safety of a giant spruce and slithered behind its trunk as another shot ripped the air. I glanced toward the plane and saw Moser crouched behind the wrecked fuselage, revolver in hand. He fired again and Hicks struggled to control the frightened horses. Jesse returned Moser's fire and the animals broke loose, scattering into the trees. Then Hicks made a dive for the plane and fired several shots from his automatic.

I backed away from the stream of bullets on trembling legs. There was no way to reach Doug. I turned and stared at the marshy meadow behind me. I would have no cover at all, but if I hurried, I might be able to work my way around to Jesse. I staggered out of the trees and heard a loud throbbing above me in the air. Out of nowhere, a helicopter suddenly skimmed the trees beyond the meadow and rushed straight toward me. Confused and afraid, I backed away. More gunshots came from behind. I glanced over my shoulder to see Hicks firing another volley of shots and Moser—I gasped as his tall form broke from the cover of the plane to come lunging after me.

Adrenalin finally freed my limbs, but Moser tackled me from behind before I had covered five feet. I went down hard with him on top of me and my vision was suddenly obscured by his heavy mane of hair. I shoved away the lank strands and saw the helicopter landing in the meadow, only fifty yards away.

Seconds later, several men, carrying rifles, ducked under the spinning roters.

"The police—!"

Moser grabbed my arms and pulled me against his body with an angry curse. His harsh breathing filled my ears as he muttered, "You're comin' with me, doll!" and dragged me into the trees.

When Hicks saw us he immediately ceased firing, and except for the breathy throb of the rotors, there was silence in the forest. Then Moser's rasping voice called out, "I've got the girl! You hear me? I've got the girl! If anybody makes one move to help her, or follow us—I'll kill her!"

He made a quick gesture to Hicks who was frantically stuffing his pockets with plastic bags. "We gotta get out of here! A helicopter just landed in the meadow!"

Hicks paled and his mouth went slack. "But—the horses are gone! Which way do we go?"

"Keep to the trees!" Moser said and pulled me after him.

Moser ran headlong through the sunlit forest, never easing his savage grip on my hand. Even if I had been able to break away from him, my flight would have met a swift and certain end as Hicks was racing right behind.

My lungs felt like they were bursting and my chest was a tight band of pain, long before we reached the lower lake. Moser slowed his pace to a swift walk as we came onto the trail. Gasping and dizzy, I staggered along at his side. We were still under cover of the trees, but sunlight and open meadow could be seen ahead, glinting through the slim trunks.

Somewhere below us, I heard laughter and voices and Moser stopped with a jerk. Hicks reached for his automatic. The blond pulled me close to his side and put an arm around my waist. Beads of sweat were dripping down his surly face. "You better remember what I said, doll!"

I swallowed and managed a slight nod.

Around the curve of trees, four backpackers, all young, with stubbled faces and eager steps, approached us on the dusty red path. Moser stood aside to let them pass and Hicks offered a mumbling, "Morning," as they walked by. I kept my head low, afraid that if one of the young men chanced to see my face, he would know immediately that something was wrong.

A slim man with ruddy hair and a sunburned face gave us a friendly smile and asked, "You been up to the big lake?"

Moser shook his head and urged me down the trail as Hicks answered them with a brief, "No. Not that far."

Hicks kept a close watch on the trail after that, but we saw no one else. Soon, the forest opened up and the sheen of blue water became visible through the trees.

Moser slowed the pace as we approached the meadow and glanced cautiously around.

"We're not being followed," Hicks assured him. "Let's get back to our camp. Maybe the horses are there."

A loud whirring buzzed over our heads and a second helicopter came into view, making for the open meadow just ahead of us.

"We're cut off!" Moser spat out and Hicks' smooth control dissolved in a puddle of fear. "We've gotta get out of here, Moser! There's gotta be a way out of here!"

Moser smiled at the older man's visible panic. "Calm down, Mr. Hicks. We're gonna make it, O.K. And this little girl is our ticket out!"

"The police will have all the trails blocked," I told him in a dry voice. "You'll never make it."

"Then we won't take the trails!" Moser pointed to the forested ridge along the lake's northwest side and said to Hicks, "They won't be able to spot us if we keep in the trees. I remember seeing that ridgeline on the map. It leads right back to the East Fork of the Smith's Fork."

His grip on my arm eased a fraction and I let myself go limp, feigning total exhaustion as he and Hicks discussed possible escape routes. Then, acting on a desperate mental signal, I twisted away from him and started to run. My freedom was short-lived. Moser's hands were like grasping claws. One grabbed my waist and the other seized my jaw, jerking my head around. I cried out from the pain as his fingers tightened cruelly.

"That wasn't very smart, little lady! One more trick like

that and you're gonna get a bullet in that soft body of yours!"

"Tie her hands!" Hicks ordered, resuming command once again.

Moser lifted up my t-shirt and unbuckled my belt. I gasped and struggled and he gave a hard laugh. "Relax, doll! There isn't time for that now!" He took the belt and bound my wrists in front of me, then, jerking the leather tight, he held on to one end and gave the order, "Get movin'!"

Climbing the ridge was a tortuous trek. I have never felt such limb-shaking weakness or nauseous exhaustion. My one satisfaction lay in the fact that my condition slowed their progress considerably. Moser avoided the open area near the top of the ridge and kept to the tree-lined slopes along its side. Once or twice, I saw the sparkle of blue-green water far below, but then the lake was lost to view as we followed the curve of the heavily wooded hillside.

It was impossible to measure time or distance. The sun was climbing higher in the sky and the longer we walked, the more uncertain I became about our direction. Lodgepole pines grew in dense, dizzying columns on every side, some so close together we had to edge our way sideways through them. The deadfall was especially thick. I heard an uneasy creaking above our heads and glanced up where a dead pine tree was leaning lightly on its living neighbor. Jesse had given me numerous warnings about areas of the forest where deadfall was heavy. Sometimes, no more than a slight breath of wind was enough to send a tree crashing to the ground. I cringed and held my breath as Moser plunged heedlessly through the timber, pulling me roughly along behind him.

Hicks was having a definite struggle matching the younger man's pace. "I think we should rest for a few minutes," he panted, dragging his sheepskin jacket carelessly behind him. "Nobody could follow us through this stuff. We'd hear them coming a mile away.!"

Moser reluctantly agreed and Hicks leaned against one of the tall trunks to mop his florid face. A deerfly buzzed around my head and I shook it away.

Somewhere behind us, there was a sudden snap, then

silence. A few seconds later, the brittle crack came again and my heart jumped. Jesse!

Moser tensed and his hand automatically reached for the revolver in his shoulder holster.

The older man tossed a frightened look over his shoulder. "What was that?"

"Probably just an animal," I said, trying to keep my voice light and unconcerned. "There are deer and elk all through this area."

The noise stopped, but the strength of Jesse's presence came pouring into my soul, pushing out fear and the hopelessness of my situation.

Moser listened a moment longer, then gave my belt a vicious yank and pulled me after him through the trees. I don't know if he suspected we were being followed, or whether he was just exerting extra caution, but from then on the pace quickened to a killing speed. Moser snaked his way through the deadfall, never pausing, while Hicks staggered along behind, grasping at trunks and branches. My own endurance had gone far beyond its normal limits, but the thought of Jesse, following somewhere behind us kept me going.

Moser and I were climbing over a jumbled pile of logs when we heard the groan of rotten timber, then a heavy crash mingled with a high-pitched scream. I knew what it was even before he jerked me around and we saw Hicks' body pinned by a fallen lodgepole. The heavy trunk had crushed his back, but he was still alive and groaning with pain.

"Help me! Moser—help me," he got out before a deep, gurgling spasm robbed him of breath.

Moser observed the older man's agony with pale, expressionless eyes. He started to turn away but I pulled back on the belt.

"You can't just leave him! We might be able to roll the log if we try!"

"You're crazy!"

Blood was trickling from Hicks' mouth now and his breathing was barely audible.

I looked up at Moser, searching the surly face for some sign of compassion. "You've got to help him—you've got to!"

Moser shrugged and let go of my belt to bend down beside Hicks. I watched in unbelieving horror as he retrieved two packets of drugs and shoved them in his shirt pocket. "You're not indispensible," he said, smiling into the man's pain-filled eyes. "None of us are—remember?"

Moser stood up and I whispered hoarsely, "What kind of animal are you? Don't you care about anyone?"

"Why should I? No one's ever cared about me!" he flung back and struck out through the forest once more.

Gradually, the deadfall thinned and the forest began to spread itself out, giving the trees more sunlight and space. We crossed a fast-moving stream and I longed to stop for a drink of its icy water, but Moser's pace never faltered. Downslope, our view was expanding and I recognized the broad, flower-starred meadows above the switchback. Throughout our march, I kept straining to catch the sound of footsteps or the crack of a twig, but the only sound in the forest was the crashing of our own feet. I began to wonder if that sound in the deadfall had only been an animal, after all.

Jesse had told me once how to distinguish a noise made by an animal from one made by a man. A crash, silence, then more crashing usually meant that a person was nearby, while a sudden crashing followed by silence would indicate the presence of an animal. Or was it the other way around? My tired brain couldn't remember. As my hopes began to sag, so did my body.

I dropped to my knees and panted, "Please—I've got to rest . . ."

Moser's brows narrowed and he gave me a heavy-lidded look, then leaned accommodatingly against the trunk of a tree.

I avoided his eyes and stared at the pine-needled ground, trying to catch my breath. The sun was warm and I could feel a narrow stream of perspiration trickling between my breasts. Their rise and fall was accentuated even more by the clinging t-shirt.

"You're lookin' pretty beat, doll," Moser drawled. "Maybe

222

you should lie down for a few minutes. I think we've got time now."

As he stepped toward me, the heavy soles of his boots crushed a slender stalk of lupine. The horror of what was to come, shot through me with greater force than any bullet. I couldn't just let it happen—I couldn't! My wrists fought uselessly against the leather belt as Moser knelt beside me. I shuddered as his pale eyes came closer and he breathed, "Go ahead and fight, little girl! Fight all you want."

Above the sigh of the breeze, a faint throbbing came to my ears, gradually building in volume until the air around us was pulsing with the sound. Moser yanked me to my feet with an angry curse and I glanced up to see a helicopter flying almost directly overhead. Before I could cry out, Moser's hand covered my mouth and he shoved me under the spreading branches of a tall pine.

The chopper slowly searched the ridgeline and finally moved toward the open meadows below us. Tears slipped down my cheeks, wetting Moser's hand, but he didn't seem to notice. When the sound of the rotors was only a faint whir, he grabbed the belt and moved on.

It was becoming more difficult for him to find thick cover. I could look down now and see the red trail cutting through the meadow, and the flashing white foam of the waterfall. Just beyond, was the signpost and fork in the trail.

Moser stopped near the edge of the trees and I could read frustration and indecision on his face. He shoved back a handful of yellow mane and stared at the two trails.

"All the trails will be blocked," I said flatly. "You'll never make it."

"Where does the left fork go?" he demanded. "You were heading along that trail last night when we caught up with you." He grabbed my shoulders and ground out in rising anger, "Where does it go?"

"I don't know—I've never been on it before!"

"You're lying!" He shook me and I cried out, "I'm not lying! It wouldn't matter if I were. They'll find us no matter which trail we take."

Moser gave the belt a vicious yank and chose the left fork, keeping to the thin line of trees where the two trails came together. Glancing around, I suddenly realized we were nearing the place where Jesse had been shot.

Straight ahead, I heard a frantic commotion in the pines. The birds were screaming—not scolding or screeching—but screaming. Their cries, high-pitched and shrill, seemed tinged with—fear? I stared at the pines and felt a chill of fear myself, then faint surprise. I had already experienced more terror in the past twenty-four hours than I ever imagined possible. What more could there be?

Moser's pale eyes were shifting nervously from side to side. He, too, sensed something was wrong.

Then, lying in the grass not far from the trail, I saw a familiar tan shape. Saskatoon. The screaming in the trees grew louder as we approached the mare's bloody carcass. I had the strongest impression that we should turn back, but Moser seemed fascinated by something he saw near the horse. Bloody fangs and a dark, bear-like face lifted from the side of the mare and my breath rose in a sharp gasp.

The animal stood on its haunches and snarled a warning, but Moser moved closer until we were barely five yards away.

"What is it? he asked in a low voice. "A badger?"

I stared at the ugly black face, the massive front claws and shook my head. "No—it's a wolverine! We've got to get out of here!"

"What're you so scared of? I've got a gun!" Moser reached for his revolver and pulled me forward, but I held back.

"No! Don't go any closer!"

The stink of the carcass and the sight of those yellow fangs filled me with a fighting desperation. I struggled to get away and Moser yanked me around, giving my face a hard slap. I heard a snarling growl and screamed as the dark, humped body sprang toward us.

Moser let go of me and fired, but the shot went wild. Before he could fire again, the animal was on him. I backed away in open-mouthed horror as the wolverine's fangs came down on

224

Moser's leg in a bone-crushing bite. Moser went down with a scream of agony and put his arms up to protect his face.

The air was drenched with blood and screams as slashing claws and tearing fangs ripped into the man's body. The attack surpassed the horror of any nightmare. It was as if the animal's sole purpose was to mutilate and destroy. When the fang's found Moser's throat, I swayed back a step and shut my eyes. My face felt hot and my lips were tingling strangely, but faintness refused to come. Even after the screams had stopped, the snarling and tearing went on. I heard a faint gurgling and covered my face with my bound hands.

Finally, the snarling ceased. The silence forced me to look. Moser's bloody, torn body lay still and those glittering black eyes turned in my direction with vicious intent. Even as he sprang at me, there was a thunderous report and the "devil beast" was hurled backwards on top of Moser's lifeless body.

The silence that followed was more deafening than the screams had been. My ears rang with it until I thought they would burst.

Into the silence came the innocuous chirp of a bird. Then a squirrel chattered in the pines above my head.

I heard a light rustling in the trees behind me and turned to see Jesse's tall form emerge from the pines, rifle in hand. My lips formed his name before I dropped to the ground.

*   *   *

"It's over, honey. It's all right now. Everything's all right." His arms and the sound of his voice did more to reassure me than the words themselves.

I was too weak to stand. Jesse held me in his arms beside the trail and gradually, his low murmured words began to reach my consciousness. It *was* over . . .

I felt the warmth of the sun on my face and arms. The breeze was laden with the spicy scent of pine and wildflowers. Over . . . As the fear and tension left my body, I began to shudder. Hard, bone-shaking tremors shook me again and again. For a long, horror-filled moment, my mind went back through the morning, flashing scenes and images like a wildly-spinning kaleidoscope. I saw Bushman's puffy face and sunlight glinting off the cold steel of his revolver . . . then endless columns of pines, creaking deadfall, and Hicks' flattened body. Moser's yellow mane and pale eyes mingled with the grisly vision of pointed fangs and blood-drenched flesh. My body pushed away the horror with one final shudder. It was over.

Jesse held me tightly against him until the tremors stopped, kissing my face and murmuring broken phrases of endearment. Finally, when I lay still in his arms, he asked quietly, "Do you think you can walk?"

"I'll try."

Leaning on each other, we took the trail back to the fork. We passed the waterfall and followed the red path into the meadows just as a helicopter came over the ridge. Jesse waved and soon it was circling the meadow, hovering over the wildflowers like a giant dragonfly. Moments after it touched down, two men ducked under the spinning rotors and came running to meet us. One of them was limping and shouting my name.

Chapter 20

*"This day two trails converge. Two paths
unite and flow together into one."*
Glennys Sabuco

Three days later, Jesse and
I sat around the big wooden table at Trail's End with his family,
my brother and Barbara's husband David. A platter of fried
trout occupied the center of the table and alongside, a Pyrex
bowl was heaped high with hash-brown potatoes. I stared at the
tray of hot scones being passed around and felt a slight shiver
creep along my flesh.

So much was the same. And so much had changed. Only
seven days ago we had arrived at Trail's End. Travis was sitting next to me then, with his tawny head and flashing jungle
eyes. Only seven days . . . In some ways, it seemed like seven
lifetimes. I set my fork down, only half listening as Doug
related some of the details of our experience to Barbara's
husband.

After our rescue, we had flown to Salt Lake City with
members of the S.W.A.T. team and had spent two days there,
answering questions, signing statements and filling out endless
forms. Numerous agencies were involved in the case, from local
sheriffs and the highway patrol to the F.A.A. and Federal Narcotics Bureau. Almost all the cocaine had been recovered, including those packets found on the body of Vernon Hicks, a
former city councilman and prominent real estate broker.

Members of the sheriff's posse had also found Jesse's backpack, and both my camera and film were now state's evidence. Doug and I stood as witnesses that Jesse's shooting of Clyde Bushman had been justifiable homicide and Tony Sanchez freely confessed that Bushman had killed Travis. The Chicano had also given pertinent information about their drug dealings in return for plea bargaining.

Jesse made most of his initial statements from a hospital bed which he insisted on leaving after that first night, despite the doctor's advice. We telephoned my parents the next day and their first impulse had been to drive immediately to Salt Lake. Jesse and I finally convinced them there was nothing they could do and arranged to meet them at the cabin instead.

A car drove up as we were finishing dinner and Barbara, glancing out the window, said, "It's Aunt Beth and Uncle Will!"

I looked nervously at Jesse who gave my cold fingers a firm squeeze.

"I think I should talk to your folks alone first. Would you mind waiting upstairs for a few minutes, honey?"

"If that's what you want."

"I think it would be best."

"The rest of us'll wait out here before bargin' in on you," Uncle Chuck said and Milly gave an assenting nod.

"Just play it cool," my brother called as we left the kitchen.

I climbed the narrow pine steps and entered the small dormer room, leaving the door ajar.

Moments later, I heard my parents' voices. Worry and concern was woven into the greeting they gave Jesse.

"Where's Doug—and Missy? How are they? It's so terrible about Travis! Jesse, how's your arm?"

Jesse answered all their questions in turn and I peeked out the crack in the door to see him lead my parents over to the couch.

Dad glanced around and asked, "Where are your folks?" and Mom said fearfully, "Missy is all right, isn't she?"

"She's just fine. But before we join the rest of the family, there's something I need to tell you."

228

There was a lengthy pause and I put a hand to my pounding heart.

"I—uh, thought you'd like to know that I—that I decided to get married," Jesse said.

"Why, Jesse, that's wonderful!" Mom put her arms around his neck in a fond hug. "I'm sure your folks are thrilled to death! Isn't it wonderful, Will?"

The beginnings of a smile turned the corners of my father's mouth, while Mom went on in a quieter tone, "Does Missy know yet?"

I smiled as Jesse answered, "Yes, she does. You see—"

"How is she taking it?" Mom interrupted, not giving him a chance to finish.

Jesse cleared his throat and I could hear the suppressed laughter in his voice. "She's taking it very well."

Mom's relief came out in an audible sigh. "Thank heavens for that! I'm sure I don't need to tell you that Missy's had quite a crush on you all these years. Of course, I always knew she would get over it someday, but I hate to see her get hurt."

Jesse looked at my parents and said quietly, "I don't want her to be hurt either. I promise you—I'll make her happy."

Mother stared up at him and her face paled. Dad's pleased chuckle filled the uncomfortable silence as he stepped forward to give Jesse's hand an enthusiastic pumping.

"Welcome to the family, son!"

I could see the relief on Jesse's face, but my mother's expression was still dazed and unbelieving.

"Jesse, you don't mean to tell me—You and Missy—? You're not—?"

Jesse smiled and put an arm around her slender shoulders. "Aunt Beth, I think it's time you met my wife."

I left the bedroom and walked out on the landing with a nervous smile. "Hi, Mom and Dad!"

Mom didn't move. Her gray eyes gave me a hurt, "How could you!" look as my father came forward to meet me at the bottom of the stairs. He took my hand and smiled at the thick gold band on my ring finger.

229

"So this is the new Mrs. Chisholm," he said and I went into his arms.

Jesse glanced at my mother's pale face and rigid expression. "I know it's kind of sudden, but neither one of us wanted to wait. I hope you're not too shocked or—disappointed."

"About as shocked as I am to see the sun come up in the morning," Dad answered when Mom remained silent. He gave Jesse an awkward smile and took Mom's arm. "Come sit over here, Beth."

Mom's eyes were bright with unshed tears as she silently sat down in the recliner. Looking at her face, I felt a hard, tight knot inside my chest. Jesse and I moved to the couch and for a long moment, the only sound in the room was the loud ticking of the clock on the bookshelf.

"Well now, when and where did the big event take place?" Dad asked a shade too brightly.

Jesse cleared his throat. "Yesterday afternoon—in Evanston."

Mother sat up straighter in the chair and repeated incredulously, "You were married in Evanston, Wyoming? Where on earth do people get married in *Evanston*?"

I was glad to see a little life come back into her face. At least she was talking now. That was always a good sign. With my mother, there is nothing worse than the silent treatment.

"We were going to be married in Salt Lake," I told her. "We got the blood tests taken care of while Jesse was in the hospital, but then we found out there was a three-day waiting period, so we stopped in Evanston on the way back to Trail's End."

"But—but—who married you?" she stammered.

"I have a good friend there who's a Mormon bishop," Jesse answered and I filled in with a little smile, "Doug and Uncle Chuck were the witnesses."

"A Mormon—a Mormon bishop?" Mom looked at Dad with a dubious frown. "Is that legal?"

Dad nodded and choked back a laugh.

"Married in Evanston by a Mormon bishop," she murmured. Her tone implied a ceremony performed on Mars by the presiding alien. "I'll bet you didn't even have a dress to wear."

"Yes, I did. Jesse bought me a lovely white dress while we were in Salt Lake," I said, glancing up at my husband with a smile.

There was another silence, then Mom looked at me and that hurt expression was still in her eyes. "I'm sorry if I don't seem very happy or—excited, but—you're my only daughter, and I—" She stopped and blew her nose vehemently. "All these years I've dreamed about your wedding . . . how beautiful it would be—"

"We can still have a reception or an open house," I said gently. "We can do whatever you like."

"And Mom wants to talk to you about planning something for our family and friends in Logan," Jesse put in. "I have about four hundred aunts and uncles and cousins who never believed I'd get married again. I know they'll be anxious to meet Melissa."

Mother sighed. "I'm sure that will be very nice—but it isn't the same! I still don't understand why you couldn't have waited!"

"I don't blame you for feeling disappointed," I said quietly, "and I want you to know that I wouldn't hurt you and Dad for the world, but—" I paused, searching for the words and felt Jesse's hand close around mine. "Jesse and I have been waiting such a long time for each other . . . If we'd planned a wedding down in Scottsdale, I would have had to leave him again—and I can't do that! Don't you see?"

Mom looked at me and sighed again. Then she smiled. "I'm beginning to see a lot of things. In fact, I don't know why I was so surprised! I had a feeling something like this might happen the first time I saw you two walk into this cabin hand in hand."

Jesse's blue gaze was intent on her face. "Are you sorry it did?"

Mom got up from her chair to kiss Jesse's cheek and hold us both. "Of course, I'm not sorry! I just need a little time to get used to the idea." She sniffed and wrinkled her nose. "I think it'll take me a lot longer to get used to that beard!"

"Sorry about that, Mom!" Jesse laughed and gave her a big bear hug. Then, winking at me, he added, "Melissa likes it!"

231

The evening was like so many we had spent over the years. The log walls were deep in shadow and a fire crackled in the old stone fireplace. From my place on the couch, I could hear Mom and Milly chatting in the kitchen, catching up on gossip and comparing notes as new grandmothers. Mom's voice was more than a trifle smug as she announced the fact that Mark and Julie's new son weighed three entire ounces more than little David had at birth. Barbara sat in the rocking chair, contently nursing her son and totally oblivious to the discussion going on in the kitchen. Dad and Uncle Chuck were in fierce concentration over a chess board as Doug and David finished the last few kernals of what had once been a mountainous bowl of popcorn.

I leaned back on the couch and stared into the fire, feeling the warmth of family ties and years of friendship as keenly as the heat from the burning pine logs. Trail's End had always been more than just a retreat or vacation spot. Now, it was my home.

The cabin door opened then and my husband walked in. Our smiles met across the room. His long stride quickly spanned the distance between us, and leaning over the back of the couch he said softly, "You still haven't seen the inside of the tipi. How would you like to spend tonight there?"

"I'd love to!"

Jesse's glance was warm and lingering. "I've got a fire going and everything's ready. Do you want to go now—or wait a while?" He looked at the clock ticking away on the bookcase and said with a boyish grin, "It's only nine-thirty. Do you think it would be too obvious if we left?"

I smiled and reached up a hand to touch his beard. "I'm not feeling very subtle right now, anyway. Let's go!"

His touch, as he took my hand, was familiar and excitingly new at the same time. We said goodnight to both families and left the cabin.

Memories hovered around us in the dusk as we walked slowly down the road toward the meadow. In my mind, I saw pictures of our past: a scrappy little tomboy hiking along forest trails with a tall young man . . . fishing together in companionable silence beside a sunlit stream . . . or skipping stones across the blue expanse of a mountain lake. Then, the under-developed body of an adolescent sitting on a hilltop, finding acceptance and strength in the quiet words and steady blue eyes of a friend . . .

Beside the road, a clump of mountain bluebells nodded in the fading light. Their fragile blue shade suddenly reminded me of wild flax and bending down, I picked a stalk drooping with blossoms. I twisted it gently between my fingers as we left the road and walked through cool meadow grass toward the tipi.

Jesse lifted the flap over the doorway and together, we stepped inside.

The interior was warm and spacious. Firelight illuminated the simple furnishings and I glanced to my right, where a large sleeping bag lay on a cushiony mattress of pine boughs. To the left, I saw two willow-rod backrests and a glossy fur robe. A small fire pit had been dug in the center, ringed with smooth, rounded stones. Burning alderwood and birch filled the air with a sharp, sweet fragrance and a thin veil of smoke curled upwards some fifteen feet to the open smoke hole.

"It's beautiful," I said.

"According to tipi etiquette, men generally sat on the north side and women on the south," Jesse told me, "but I think we can forget about that."

"I think it will be much cosier if we do."

Jesse smiled. "And if you have to cross between a person and the fire, it's proper to say, 'excuse me, brother,' or 'excuse me, my father.'"

"I'll try to remember."

"There's a lot more I want to do with the inside," he said, pointing to the canvas lining or dew cloth which stretched around the tipi's entire circumference. "The Indians used to paint their war records and personal experiences on the inside lining. I've been thinking, it might be nice to write our history on the walls."

I smiled and reached up to untie the bear-claw necklace encircling his muscular neck. "Not in too much detail, I hope!"

Jesse grinned and kissed me, then I helped him unbutton his shirt. After laying it on one of the willow-rod backrests, I crossed between him and the fire, saying with a teasing smile, "Excuse me, my husband!"

His eyes followed my movements as I knelt beside the sleeping bag and laid the stalk of blue flowers on his pillow. Past years seemed very close as our eyes met in the silence of the Uinta night, but I no longer had any desire to cling to childish memories or the way things used to be.

As Jesse closed the flap to the entrance and tied it securely, I began to undress. He stood motionless, watching me, and I could hear his rapid breathing in the stillness and see the rise and fall of his chest.

The past was gone and so was the child "Missy," as I stood before him in the firelight.

A long while later, we lay close together, looking up into the night sky where a few stars peeped through the smoke hole. Like the campfire, the heat of our passion was spent and our bodies were filled with a deep, glowing warmth.

My gaze left the sky to seek out the light in my husband's eyes. "I hope it won't be too long before the birth date of your son is written on these walls," I said.

Jesse smiled and answered softly, "I'd be just as happy to write 'little Missy's' birthdate."

Coming from his lips, the nickname I had despised and hated for so long, held the promise of something infinitely precious and beloved.